BEAUTIFUL LIAR

CIN MEDLEY

MED'S PUB

BEAUTIFUL
Liar

CIN MEDLEY

The characters in this book are not real people. They have been made up. They are by no means related to or pertain to anyone.
This material is copyrighted. No portion of this book can be used without written permission from the publisher.

Published by Med's Pub Publishing
Copyright © 2017 Cin Medley
All Rights Reserved
ISBN-13: 978-0-9989748-1-1
ISBN-10: 0998974811
Cover Artwork Used with permission from Bigstock ©
Cover Design by: Amanda Walker P.A. and Design Services
Edited by: Kendra's Editing and Book Services- Kendra Gaither
Formatted by: Med's Pub Publishing

To my husband, who never fails in his encouraging words and undeniable support.

To my beautiful daughter, Miss B, your patience and love make my world a brighter place to be. I love you.

Veronica, thank you again and again for all of your support and for believing that I get better with each book. I love you. And for guessing the ending of this one.

Amanda, words cannot do what you do for me justice. You are incredibly talented, and I adore you. Thank you.

Kendra, as always you fix my words to make my stories beautiful. Love you to the moon and beyond, my sister by another mother.

PROLOGUE

There comes a time in a person's life when you find yourself with your back against a wall. To the left is danger, to the right is danger, and right down the middle is sure death. So many times, your brain actually struggles with which direction to go. Or do you just stand there, watch the train wreck happen in front of you, and hope to God you don't become a casualty?

Me, well, I am most certainly not the type of person who would just stand there and let something bad happen. I couldn't do a damn thing to stop the train that tore the other half of me completely in two, but I can do something about the fucking train that barreled through the peaceful and beautiful life of one of the most beautiful souls I've ever known.

I go by many names, depending on which day of the week it is, which city I am living in, and what needs to be accomplished. I have many who help me along the way, but no one is responsible for me, except me.

I am the only one who can stop the train. Many have tried, and they have all failed. I will not fail.

There is only one place where I truly find peace: a place of complete innocence, a place where I am everything, a place that owns my heart. I promised, no, I vowed to stop the train, and then made sure there was no way the train would win when it hit the brick wall of me. As farfetched as this is, it's my story.

CHAPTER ONE

VICTORIA

"Cassie, can you grab three of the specials and get them over to table six?" Jerry yelled at me.

I smiled and nodded to him, but what I really wanted to do was stab the fucker a few hundred times in the chest and watch his face while I did it. I swear, if he accidently touched my ass one more time, I would break his arm. Walking into the kitchen, I saw the right hand of Andy Marciano standing by the door. I knew that bastard was in the building. I just didn't know who he was. No one had been able to get a picture of him in the ten years he'd been a player, so he was basically a ghost. It took everything in me not to bend over and grab the knife strapped to my ankle and slice that fucker's throat wide open. Johnny McDonald—fucking asshole, rapist, and murderer.

Sal handed me three of the specials. "Thanks." I turned to head out to table six.

As I passed Jenny walking to the bar, she shot me a look, her eyes full of fear. I knew Jerry forced her and a few other girls to fuck some of his customers. He asked me once; I told him no fucking way. I quit that day. I could still remember him chasing me out the kitchen door.

"Come on, Cassie. I just thought you might want to make some extra

money. I mean, with a body like yours, my customers are always asking." I wanted to gut the fucker then.

"I am not a fucking whore!" I shouted at him.

"You're the best god damn waitress I have. I promise I won't ask again. Come on, I'll even give you a raise," he shouted as I rounded the back end of my beat-up Chevy, causing me to stop.

"How much?" I asked.

"Another five an hour. You're good for business with that tight ass of yours." He smiled.

"You're a disgusting pig, Jerry. You make my skin crawl."

"So, you'll stay? I swear, I will keep you safe."

I chuckled to myself, thinking, I don't need you to fucking keep me safe. "I'll do it, but don't you dare think for one minute that I am going to fuck anyone."

His smile touched his eyes. "I promise."

He waited for me to walk toward him. I knew he was sweet on me, and I believed the fucking prick might even have thought he had a chance with me. Never would have happened. "If I'm your best waitress, then why do you keep hiring the bimbos?"

"Because they fuck the customers." He chuckled.

"You do know that running a whore house is illegal, right?"

"It's only illegal if you get caught. Besides, the guys are the guys. They can get a piece of ass wherever they want. No one says no to them."

"I just did. So, what, should I watch my back now?"

"No, you are safe."

"Why? Why am I safe, Jerry, and the rest of the girls aren't? What makes me immune?" I stopped walking. I needed to keep this job. I needed to find that bastard Marciano. I needed to end him and all his fucking buddies.

He chuckled. "Because when I asked you, you had balls enough to tell me to fuck off. I have to respect that. Those other bitches just buckled and did it. Now, I own them."

I shook my head. "You're a disgusting pig, Jerry. You know that, right?"

He laughed. "I do. But come on, don't quit. You bring a bit of class to the joint."

"Fine, whatever. But if you ever try to sell me again, I might not stop with just walking out the door."

"See, you aren't afraid of me. I like that."

"What are you, some kind of sick masochist? You get off on a strong-willed woman? Please don't tell me you like to be tied up and whipped." I had to actually swallow the bile that rose up in my throat.

"Fuck no. You remind me of my mother."

"Great, thanks a fucking lot."

"No, not like that. She was a proud woman. She didn't let life beat her down, no matter how hard it was for us. She squared her shoulders and faced life head on. You're like that. No matter how bad it gets, you hold your head up and stand proud. I respect that."

I think he just paid me a compliment. "Thank you?"

"Come on, you still have three hours on your shift. I'll even be nice and not dock you the twenty minutes we've been out here."

I walked back into the kitchen to grab another order. Fucking Johnny was still standing at the back door. I heard him say to Jerry as I walked by, "Hey, I like her. How much is she?"

Jerry laughed. "That one, I'm afraid, is not for sale. She has the bite of a cobra, trust me."

"Aww, Jerry, everyone has a price." He looked at me as I walked out.

"Not that one, and if I were you, I'd watch your balls. You may end up with them in your hand."

I looked up at him and smiled. The look I got back was one of pure evil. "Ah, little girl, the things I could teach you about obedience," he said laughing.

Shaking my head, I ignored him. He would end up in the morgue just like the rest of them. He would be number fifteen. I often wondered what Mr. Marciano thought of his men disappearing. Apparently, not much, because new ones just appeared to take their place.

After finishing my shift, I headed back to the rat hole I had taken as a residence for this job. I hated this place, but I needed to make sure I wasn't followed. I followed my nightly routine to a T. Making it look like I was getting ready for bed, I turned on the shower and pretended to use it. After, I walked around in front of the windows, changing my clothes in full view, then turned off the lights and left through the back door of the building. There, a car waited by the curb to take me to the luxury apartment downtown for my day job. It was tiring, but I was so close to the end of this two-year fucking nightmare.

Walking in, I dropped the short black wig in the drawer, stripped off the sweats, and hit a real shower, one with white walls and no mold or bugs crawling all over the place. I turned the water to the hottest temperature my body could stand but still couldn't scrub myself hard enough to make all the grime of the other place go away. But I had to do this. I needed to end this.

After I ran the hot water out, I wrapped myself in one of my luxurious white towels and made my way to the bed, the only place I could take my heart out and make myself feel warm inside. Reaching for the nightstand, I pulled the phone from its secret compartment underneath it and turned it on. This was the best part of my day. As it came to life, message after message arrived. My smile widened and my heart sped up.

Opening the first one, I could feel the tears stinging my eyes.

~I miss you~

~When are you coming home~

~We made chocolate chip cookies. Ruth put some in the freezer for you~

~I have to go to bed now, I love you~

My heart hurt as the tears rolled down my face. It was like this every night. Every day, as I moved through the motions, setting up each piece of the puzzle, I knew the reward. It made each day one step closer to the awaiting peace. I typed back a few responses.

~I miss you too~

~Soon, my love. Soon, I will be home~

~Thank you for saving me some. I hope it's enough for you to share them with me. Tell Ruth thank you~

~I am going to bed now as well. I love you more than the flowers love the sun~

6

Pulling the phone to my chest, I cried silently, wishing none of this had happened. Wanting my life to be my life again. My happy, stupid, carefree life. I missed Steven. I looked at my hand where my wedding band used to sit, the memory of leaving him still so fresh in my mind.

He came home from work shortly after I got the news. He walked in to me throwing the dishes out of the sink and onto the kitchen floor, screaming.

"What's wrong?" he asked. I looked up at him. "Whatever it is, beautiful, we can get through it."

I shook my head. "No, we can't. I can't. It's just too much. This isn't going to work. I need to go."

I went to walk out of the room, and he grabbed my arm. "Where are you going?"

"I'm leaving. I'm done. I don't want to be married to you. I can't be married to you anymore. I feel like I'm going to suffocate." I stormed out of the kitchen and out the front door, tears falling from my eyes. He was the love of my life, the greatest man I'd ever known, but he couldn't know. He must never know the truth.

"I love you," I whispered to the air. "I miss you each and every day."

That was two years, eleven months, and twenty-five days ago. That's how long I'd been working to end this.

Turning off the phone, I slipped it back into its compartment and took my day phone out of the drawer, turning it on and setting it down while I put on my shorts and t-shirt. Crawling back into bed, I picked up the phone to see eleven missed calls and a few texts. Turning off the light and getting comfortable, I went through the texts. Nothing important, just Kelly from my day job wanting to get together this weekend for drinks. I turned on my alarm and went to sleep. Well, I tried to sleep. I didn't do much of that anymore.

The ringing of the phone startled me. It was as if I was standing by the front door watching, but not participating. The me in my dream, she ran down the stairs, down the hall, and into the kitchen. I was drawn to this other version of me, with her hair long and red instead of how it was now, still red but short enough to hide under whichever wigs I needed. As she disappeared through the doorway, the ringing stopped.

"Hello," I heard myself say, sounding out of breath. "Yes, this is she. Wait, who are you?" I laughed. "Steven, is this a joke?"

I watched on as the smile slowly left my other face. Tears welled up, and I could actually feel my body shaking. Other me dropped the phone and barely turned to the sink in time to vomit. I wanted to rush over and hold myself, but I stood riveted to the spot by the doorway. After she, or I, rinsed my mouth, I picked up the phone again.

"Yes, I understand. I'll be there tonight. Thank you." My voice sounded robotic, clear of any emotion or life.

I could feel every emotion: fear, sadness, anger. Watching myself look around the kitchen, I knew. I knew it was over. This life, my life. After eight years of marriage to the perfect man, my life was over. Victoria Holmes was gone. I watched as the anger came out. Screaming, throwing things. It didn't make me feel any better, but I was mad, pissed. I was terrified. I could feel it, like it was real, like it had happened yesterday.

When the front door opened, I turned to see Steven, and my heart hurt knowing I would only ever see him again in my dreams. I loved him completely and he would no longer be in my life.

I woke in a panic, my heart slamming in my chest, and sat straight up in my bed. I ran into my closet, pulling up the carpet in the back corner. Picking up my wedding band, I slipped it on my finger and grabbed the picture that laid upside down. My hands shaking and my eyes blurred from the tears, I traced his face. "I love you so much. I'm so sorry."

When I finished with my pity party, I slipped my ring off my finger and put the only two pieces of my love back under the carpet for safe keeping. I wasn't going to get any more sleep, so I just stayed up and got ready for my day job. It was time again to become Sue Costello.

CHAPTER TWO

VICTORIA

Walking into the accounting firm that Andy Marciano used to launder his money from prostitution, drugs, sex trade, gun running, and everything else the bastard was into made me feel dirty all over again. I was so far into this fucking monster's world that I felt the need to shower every minute of every day. At least, tonight, I didn't have to work for fucking Jerry. It was my two nights off from the diner, which would allow me to spend a bit of extra time here to see what I could learn.

As I walked through the office, I was greeted by my colleagues. "Morning, Sue," I heard. With my fake smile plastered on my face, I greeted them in return. I'd been here for the past six months. It wasn't easy getting a job here; these people were lifers. Once they were in and privy to the numbers, their fate was sealed.

I smiled, thinking about the process of getting the privilege to actually do accounts. I had to literally sign my life away. The document was a legally binding confidentiality agreement, including a paper that said I couldn't work for another accounting firm for eighteen months if I chose to quit. But you didn't quit a job like this; you were removed and then your body was found a few days or weeks later. Since I'd been here, three people had been found dead—died of things like a heart attack or were hit by a bus. So, yeah, I signed the paperwork. I had no intention of going anywhere until I found the paper trail to that fucker.

Sitting at my desk, I turned on my computer. My assistant, Sherry, who was actually my second assistant in six months—I had no clue what happened to the first one—came in. "I have a few messages for you, and the boss man wants you in a meeting at ten." She handed me my messages.

"Thanks, Sherry. Please let Mr. Simon know that I will be there."

She nodded as she walked out, pulling my door closed behind her. I returned the calls and got to work on an account for a business on the lower East side, a little place called Dragon Cleaners. It was confusing to me why such a small company would need an accounting firm as big as Simon & Simon. Definitely a red flag. Putting the name in my mental bank for later, I continued to work. At nine-forty-five, I headed to the conference room for the meeting with my boss, but the room was empty. Walking back to my office, I saw Sherry talking to one of the office girls.

"Excuse me, Sherry, but did Mr. Simon say where the meeting is?"

She looked at me like I was talking Spanish. "In his office, didn't I say that?"

Shaking my head, I told her, "No, you didn't." I turned and headed to his office. I was a little skeptical about this meeting. I'd never been to his office before.

Walking up to his secretary, I smiled at her. "Miss Costello, please go right in. Mr. Simon is waiting for you."

I wasn't aware anyone knew who I was, so I actually felt a bit uncomfortable as I knocked and then walked into the office. The first things that caught my attention were the floor to ceiling windows surrounding the room, then the four men standing in different places. Sitting in a chair in front of Mr. Simon's desk was another man.

Mr. Simon looked up and smiled at me. "Miss Costello, please come in and have a seat." He stood and motioned to the seat next to the man sitting with his back to me.

Nodding, I walked across the room and took my seat, not looking at the man sitting next to me. Mr. Simon sat back down. "Miss Costello, I'd like you to meet my brother and partner, Paul. Paul, Miss Costello."

Smiling, I turned my head, but my breath caught in my throat when he turned to face me. I was stunned, and I mean stunned. The man was drool-worthy stunning. His eyes were turquoise, like the most beautiful ocean imaginable. His smile reached his eyes when he looked at me.

"Miss Costello," he greeted me in a deep baritone voice, gentle, not harsh. He reached his hand out to shake mine, and like an idiot, I just sat there with my mouth open more than it should have been. I was speechless. My hand just automatically came up of its own accord. When I put it in his, a charge of electricity zapped my entire body. Apparently, he felt it, as well. He just sat there holding my hand, looking into the depths of my soul.

I had to force myself to pull my hand away. "Mr. Simon," I started, not sure if it was my voice coming out. Turning my head, I looked at the first Mr. Simon. I had to snap out of it. "Is everything all right with my work?" I needed to know if I was going to get fired.

"Yes. In fact, you're here because of the stellar job you are doing. I wanted to give you a few more accounts. My brother here has reviewed your efficiency on the accounts you do have."

"Your attention to detail is very admirable," the second Mr. Simon said in his baritone voice. "You seem to have a knack for numbers."

I smiled. "Thank you, but it's just my job. It's what I do."

"Well, I will have the accounts brought over to you. Thank you, Miss Costello." Mr. Simon stood at that statement, my cue to leave. I nodded my head and walked out of the office, unable to breathe until I was back behind my desk.

Holy shit. What the fuck was that? Oh my god! I sat there for a few minutes trying to get my head straight. I got back to work, trying not to think about that man's eyes or his voice that made me wet.

Sherry knocked on my door. "I'm going to lunch. Do you need anything?"

"No, I'm just going to grab a sandwich and eat it here. Thanks anyway."

She nodded and walked away. I shut down my computer, which was a rule in the office, then grabbed my purse and headed out. When I opened my door, I stopped in my tracks when I nearly collided with a wall of nothing but solid muscle.

"Miss Costello," the baritone voice said.

I tilted my head to meet his gaze. "Mr. Simon, can I help you?"

"I was wondering if you would have lunch with me?"

Anger like nothing before shot through my body. Shaking my head and not removing my eyes from his, I said as calmly as I could manage, "No, thank you, Mr. Simon. I work for you. You are my boss, and I don't think it would be proper."

He chuckled. "Let me rephrase that. Miss Costello, I would like to have lunch with you."

"Mr. Simon, I am not going to get involved with you. If you want someone to play with, try one of the secretaries. I am not for rent, lease, or sale. Now, if you'll excuse me, I need to go. I have work to do."

I moved to walk around him, and he placed his hand out, landing it on my stomach. "Clearly, you don't understand," he said as he leaned into me.

God, he smelt heavenly. I closed my eyes, removing his hand from my body. "Don't ever think it is acceptable to touch me. I am not going to lunch, dinner, or breakfast with you, and I'm pretty sure we aren't going to have coffee either. If my job is on the line by refusing you," I made sure he saw my face, "then shove it up your ass. I quit!"

Shoving my way past him and into the outer office, I saw the four men from earlier standing at various places around the room. I shook my head and kept on walking to the elevator. A hand grabbed my arm, spinning me around as I waited for the doors to open. It was a natural instinct to shove him back. "Don't fucking touch me!" I screamed as the elevator pinged and its doors opened. Stepping backwards into the elevator just as the doors close, I slammed my finger on the button and the car jerked into motion.

When they opened at the ground floor, one of his men was standing in front of the door, blocking my exit. "Mr. Simon wishes to talk to you."

I laughed. "Tell Mr. Simon to go fuck himself." I moved to walk out, and he put his hand on me.

Swinging my clenched fist, I hit him in the throat. When he bent and clutched at his throat, I brought my knee up, slamming his face into it, then kicked him in the balls before pushing him to the floor. "Don't fucking touch me." I ran out into the street and jumped into a cab.

I fought the bile rising slowly in my throat. When I got out of the cab, I ran into my building. I couldn't get into my apartment fast enough. Stripping on my way to the shower, I turned the water on as hot as it would go and then let the tears fall. Sliding down the wall, I cried and screamed.

No one was allowed to touch me. "I love you," I whispered between my sobs.

When the water ran cold, I got out and moved to my bed, crawling in, crying myself to sleep. No matter how hard I had become, no matter what I had done, the thought of another man touching me made me madder than all of this. He was my love, the only man who I ever allowed to have me. I loved him, and I would love him beyond this life.

When I woke, it was dark in my room, which meant I slept the day away. I managed to get up and put on some yoga pants and an old t-shirt then made my way to the kitchen to get something to eat. There was some leftover Chinese food, so I reheated it and went to sit on the couch. My mood warranted some Netflix.

Halfway through the food, my phone started ringing. Pulling it out of my bag, I saw it was Mr. Simon, my boss. "Hello," I snapped.

"Miss Costello, is everything all right? You didn't come back after lunch. I had my secretary call you several times."

"Didn't your brother tell you? I quit."

"No, he didn't. What happened?" He sounded a bit sincerer than I was expecting.

I chuckled. "He came on to me. He touched me, grabbed my arm. I won't work for someone who thinks he has some kind of power over me. Thank you for the opportunity to work for you, but I won't be coming back."

"Miss Costello, I am sincerely sorry for that. Paul had mentioned that he found you captivating. I didn't think he would actually act on it."

"It's irrelevant, Mr. Simon. I'm not coming back. I will abide by the agreements I signed, but I quit. If he tried it once, he will try it again. I know how men like him work. Again, thank you, but no thank you. Goodbye, Mr. Simon." I hung up before he had the chance to say anything.

CHAPTER THREE

PAUL

"Son of a bitch!" John yelled through the phone.

"Hello, little brother. What can I do for you?" I smart-mouthed, knowing he was obviously pissed.

"What the fuck did you do to Miss Costello?"

I chuckled. "I asked her out for lunch. She beat the shit out of Denny. The girl is a spitfire for sure. I could utilize that spirit."

"Are you fucking kidding me? She quit. She is good at what she does, asshole. We've waited for someone like her to take over the books and make them right."

"Just offer her more money." I glanced at the clock on the wall.

"You don't get it, do you? You can't go around thinking that every pretty girl belongs to you. What, are you on some kind of power trip? You need to make this right. Get her back here!"

"John, I don't beg anyone for anything, and besides, she made me fucking hard, harder than I've ever been. I just wanted to taste her, maybe fuck her for a bit. I'm not doing anything of the sort."

"Yes, Paul, you will," he countered. "I don't give a shit how you do it, but you better swallow your goddamn ego. Apologize to her and get her back here. If you don't, then I'm out."

"Why, brother, do you have a thing for this girl?"

"Fuck you, Paul. You know damn well I don't swing that way. She is that fucking good at her job. We need her. Now do it."

I sighed, already ready to be done with this conversation. "Fine, give me her number and I'll call her and apologize."

John calmed some. "She really took Denny down?"

I laughed. "Yeah, I found him lying on the floor in the lobby holding his balls. He said she fucking slammed him in the throat then kneed him in the face."

John chuckled. "She weighs like a buck ten if that."

"I know. The guys have been giving him shit all day. Listen, give me her number and I'll call her and make nice. But I want to make it clear; she turns me on big time. I don't know what it is about her, but man, I walked out of that building with the hardest cock. I had to fuck some poor girl at the club for like an hour before I was content enough to go home."

"Really, I don't need to know this. You and that club."

"You should come out, John. We've got guy on guy shit happening. You never know, you might enjoy yourself."

"No, thank you. I'm not into deviant sex."

"Ouch, that hurt. There is nothing wrong with tying up a beautiful woman and fucking her raw."

"Stay away from my accountants. Get it done, Paul."

John hung up, and I shook my head. She might be a damn good accountant, but they were a dime a dozen if you knew where to look. I really just wanted to spend an evening fucking her, but I'd play it his way for now.

Victoria

I must have fallen asleep on the couch, because my phone ringing woke me up. I didn't even look at the caller ID. "What?" I was in no mood to talk. No one really called me on this phone, just work shit.

"Well, hello to you, too, Miss Costello. This is Paul Simon." The baritone voice on the other end, even on the phone, caused a reaction in me. I hung up the phone turned it off.

"No fucking way, asshole," I said to the phone as I tossed it on the table. Getting up, I cleaned my small mess and made my way to bed. I needed to get up and find a new job the next morning. I was sure, when I checked the paper, something would be there.

My alarm went off at six, and I was ready for a new day. After fixing my hair, I put on my tan suit with my nude pumps and headed out. I was going to treat myself to a coffee and a Danish while I looked through the paper. When I opened my door to leave, my way was blocked by a huge vase of roses. Shaking my head, I plucked the card from the bouquet.

Please accept my apology, Miss Costello
I was rude and I shouldn't have been.
Paul Simon

"Asshole," I said loudly, just in case one of his henchmen was lurking about. Picking up the flowers, I walked across the hall to Mrs. Jones's door and set them down. Dropping the card in my purse, I headed out.

Stopping at the newspaper stand, I smiled at the kid working it. "Good morning, Miss Costello."

"Good morning, Jimmy." I handed him money for the paper then headed to the coffee shop on the corner. There was a booth open in the back, so I made my way there. I ordered my coffee and a cheese Danish and got to work looking for a new job.

As I scanned the want ads, I saw what I was looking for. Apparently, I had a meeting this afternoon at The Bean. Not what I wanted but I could work it in. I'd go to the Art Museum when I was done. I found a few prospects for jobs. I needed to make a stop at the library and print off a few resumes. With coffee in hand, I slipped the paper into my bag and headed out.

I loved walking the streets of this city, but my heart belonged in England. *Soon, baby. Soon, I can come home.* I'd been saying that for the past two years. I had been home two times in between jobs. Maybe I could go home for a bit. I'd have to think about it.

As I headed toward The Bean, my phone rang in my purse. Not paying attention to what I was doing, I stepped off the curb right into an oncoming car. The driver laid on the horn, slamming on his breaks. He scared the shit out of me, and I spilled my coffee all over the front of my suit. Turning my head, I slammed my fist on the hood of the car, screaming, "Fucking asshole."

Slamming the car into park, the guy got out. He was fucking huge, wearing a suit I was sure cost five grand. He rushed up to me, looking at his car. Grabbing my arm, he said, "You're going to pay for that, you little bitch."

"What about my suit, asshole?" I screamed at him. "I think the cost is about the same."

"That's a seventy-five-thousand-dollar car."

"This is an eight-hundred-dollar suit. We're even." I ripped my arm out of his grip and started walking.

He grabbed my arm, spinning me around. "Where do you think…"

That's all he got out of his mouth before I slammed my fist in his throat, screaming, "Don't fucking touch me!" As I was turning to walk away, the back door of the car opened. The man getting out of it was slightly bent over, but as he came to his full height and turned, I nearly fainted.

"Miss Costello, we meet again," Paul Simon said, smiling at me.

"Are you fucking kidding me?" I turned and walked away, continuing across the street.

I heard footsteps coming up behind me. I felt him before I saw him take up stride next to me. "Miss Costello, that would be the second man in my employ you have managed to disable."

I stopped walking and looked at him. "Don't touch me, Mr. Simon, or you will be number three."

He chuckled, putting his hands up in the air. "I wouldn't dream of it. Please, let's sit and talk. I really would like to ask you to come back to work." He made a gesture toward the bench along the walkway.

Rolling my eyes, I walked over and sat down. "I have no desire, Mr. Simon, to work for a man who thinks he has privileges to my body just because he signs my paycheck. I am not for sale."

"Technically, I do pay you for your services, so you are indeed for sale." I opened my mouth to scream at him, but he put his hand up. "I get that you are not for sale, Miss Costello, and again, I am sorry for being so forthcoming with my desire to see you outside of the workplace. You are a very beautiful woman. Although, I'm not really a part of the overall business part of our company, I didn't see a problem with asking you to share a meal. I realize now that I was wrong. My brother would really like it if you would come back to work."

I sat there looking at him. "Are you for real? Trust me, you don't strike me as a man who would waste his time with an underling such as myself."

He let out a hardy laugh. "You would be correct in your assumption, Miss Costello. I did view you as a quick fuck, but I can see that you are not that kind of woman, so please accept my apology of ignorance. I will make sure to never make that assumption again where you are concerned. Respect is all you will get from me."

I wasn't sure if I should believe this man or not. He was some kind of arrogant, that was for sure. He was playing me, pacifying me for some reason. "Why does it matter? I'm sure you can find another accountant. I'm pretty sure we are a dime a dozen."

"Well, as it would seem, my brother has taken a liking to you. He told me, either I apologize to you and make it right or he's quitting. So, here I am."

Fire blew through me. I stood and turned on him. He stood to face me. "So, let me get this straight. The only reason you are here is because your brother threatened to quit if you didn't say you were sorry?" He nodded. "Well, you know what, Mr. Simon? Go to hell. If you can't see that what you did to me, what your fucking goons did to me, was way out of line and beyond disrespectful, then I've got nothing for you. Nowhere in this world is it acceptable to treat a woman with such disdain. I wasn't put on this planet for you or anyone else to use and abuse as you see fit." I leaned into him. *God, he smelled fantastic.* "Fuck you." I turned and walked away from him.

I smiled, knowing this was all recorded. I couldn't wait to see the footage. Fucking asshole. I didn't bother turning around to see if he was still standing there. I just kept on walking.

Paul

I must admit that I had never wanted to tie someone up and whip her ass with a riding crop more than I did in that moment. Watching her walk away with that perfect fucking ass of hers had my cock fucking straining against my pants.

I didn't know if I should be pissed or impressed. Of course, she had no idea of my true identity, but let me say this. She would. My body seemed to react to her like no other woman I'd met before. I needed to make this right for John. Hell, for me.

Turning on my heels, I started back to where I got out of the car. My guys were standing here and there. By the time I reached the street, my car was waiting for me. I climbed in. "Take me to my brother's."

"I'm sorry, sir. Do you know that woman? I didn't mean to manhandle her like that."

I laughed. "I think it was the other way around, don't you?"

"She is a tough broad."

Smiling, I said, "Well, Mr. Hinkle, I can assure you she is no broad. That, my dear fellow, is a first-class spitfire. I am going to enjoy her immensely."

He nodded and we headed to my brother's.

Walking into John's office, I had to chuckle. The man looked like he had been to hell and back. "John, don't look so frustrated."

"Fuck you, Paul. What the hell are we going to do? We need her."

"She can't be that good. Though, I've now seen her take down two of my men. The woman knows her self-defense, that's for sure."

"What are you talking about?"

"Max nearly ran her over on the street. Spilled coffee all over her beautiful suit. She turned around and dented the hood of my car when she punched it." Laughing, I continued, "He got a little rough with her, and she took him down in the middle of the street. I followed her and we had a conversation on a bench."

"Is she coming back?"

"Not sure, I don't think she thought my apology was sincere enough."

I watched as John picked up a file and tossed it onto his desk in front of me. Picking it up, I opened it, scanning the contents.

"Jesus, she did this?" The report was stellar, and that was being modest.

"Yes, she did. Do you see what I mean? She can do this. I had her vetted before she came to work here. The woman has high honors in accounting. She has a natural ability with numbers. We need her. Paul, you need to make this right."

"John, I have never apologized for anything I have done. I am who I am. I am not about to beg or bow down to a woman, even if she is an angel sent from God himself."

"Yes, I am well aware of your ideals as to what a woman is good for, but this one is different. She is special, and you need to swallow that fucking holier-than-thou ego of yours and bend down and kiss her fucking feet. I don't care what you have to do, you need to get her back here."

I sat there looking at my brother for a long time before I spoke. "I'll be damned if I am going to allow a woman to bring me to my knees."

"What's the matter, Paul? What are you afraid of, the fact that you want her so desperately that you're willing to fuck this up, or that you want her so desperately it's scaring the shit out of you?"

I laughed. "Both, brother. Both. She sparked something in me, something I haven't..."

"Felt since Sylvia?"

I admitted, "Yeah. I never thought I would feel like this again. Especially after all these years."

"So, the giant that you are is in fact bending at the knees. Don't fuck this up, Paul. Don't try to fuck her. Just do this and leave her alone."

"See, brother, that's the problem. I'm not sure I can. I only have to think about her and I'm fucking hard. Hell, I've got a raging hard-on right now just talking about her. Not since... well, it's been a long time."

John's voice softened. "I know, brother. I was there with you. I know all of this is to spite your anger. You've never really grieved for her. You've never let yourself feel the loss. You just blocked it all out and became this man."

"Yes, perhaps. But this man has made us both billionaires."

"Maybe so, but it has left you a shell of a man. You're not living your life the way you should. A different woman every night hasn't helped you. Hell, I'm pretty sure it hasn't touched how you feel."

Leaning forward, resting my arms on my knees, I looked my brother in the eye. "I'm terrified, John. She could be the one who makes me want a decent life, a life like I had with Sylvia."

"Then get her back here. If you check your fucking ego at the door, maybe she can get us out of this and you can win her heart and be happy. I love you, but I loved you better before all this shit."

I looked at him for a very long time. "I'll do my best."

He nodded and I stood. As I walked to the door, I turned. "What size do you think she wears? I think I'd like to buy her a new suit. I'm pretty sure that coffee isn't coming out of the one she was wearing earlier."

John laughed. "I haven't a clue. I know nothing of women and their sizes. I can tell what size just about every man I meet wears. Why don't you talk to one of your many girls at the club? I'm sure one of them can tell you."

"John, I'm scared," I whispered. "I'm terrified. I think that's why I'm acting the way I am concerning her. I want to fuck her so hard. I think she is the only woman who could appease me."

"Brother, I'm sorry to tell you this, but she isn't the fucking kind. She has a huge wound imbedded in her heart. You are going to be lucky if you can get near her. Someone hurt her, and they hurt her deeply."

"You think?"

"I know emotions, and Miss Costello has been destroyed beyond repair."

I smiled. "So was I but meeting her has made me realize that there is life after pain like that. Maybe I'm the same for her. I mean, she hates me, but maybe she is just as attracted to me as I am her."

"Good luck. Just get her back here. It's time to end this. Time to fix it all. May I suggest, if you want a chance in hell with her, that you get rid of that club. I can guarantee you she will not understand."

"I was going to anyway. It's just not fun anymore." Turning, I walked out of my brother's office and headed to meet my lawyer. Time to start the process. I needed to clean up my act if I were to stand a chance in hell of having Miss Costello.

Victoria

I was so pissed as I walked to Millennial Park. When I approached the person I was supposed to be meeting, I smiled and kept on walking down the street to the Art Museum. I bought my ticket and made my way inside, keeping myself invisible just to make sure one of Mr. Simon's goons didn't follow me. I spied my contact walking in, but I waited another five minutes to make sure. When I felt comfortable, I gradually made my way to my favorite place, to my favorite artist. Monet. The bench in front of his "The Customs House at Varengeville" was where I spent my time on most weekends. It reminded me of home.

Walking up, I saw him sitting, waiting for me so I sat down. "What's happening?" he asked softly.

"Fucking men, that's what's happening. No offense. Listen, I need you to check out Paul Simon. Something about him doesn't add up. The man has too many bodyguards around him."

"Is that who approached you in the street?"

"Yep."

"So, you kicked his guard's ass?"

I smiled. "Not just one, but two, and Mr. Simon nearly found himself on the floor. No one man handles me. Oh, and I quit, so I need some prospects for a new job."

"Victoria, we need you in that office."

"My name is Sue, Sue Costello. Don't worry about it. I'm going back; I just need to make sure Mr. Simon knows he isn't going to touch me again."

He chuckled. "Have you discovered anything new?"

"Mr. Simon, the one I work for, wanted me to start a few new accounts for his brother, the Mr. Simon from the street. That was when he thought it acceptable to touch me. I can feel it. Something is not right with this guy."

"All right."

"Oh, and I would like the feed from my encounters with Paul Simon please."

"I'll have them to you by the time you get home. Same place?" I nodded.

I sat there for a good hour looking at the painting, my mind at home. I could almost smell the sweet jasmine scent. My heart hurt for the love nearly eight thousand miles away. It wasn't fair that I had to be here. I needed to do this to make it safe for us, to make life worth living, because if I didn't finish this and we were discovered, we'd be dead. At least, this way, if I wound up dead like the other half of me, life would go on.

With a sad and heavy heart, my eyes burning with unshed tears, I made my way back home. I stopped and got my mail, dropping the card Mr. Simon gave me in the mailbox. Making my way up to my apartment, I stopped in my tracks when I saw yet another vase full of flowers. Walking over, I picked them up and set them in front of my neighbor's door, pulling the card from them.

You are correct in your observation, Miss Costello.
I do not apologize for anything I do.
But I am a man of my word, and I was wrong.
Please reconsider
Paul Simon
Shaking my head, I opened my door and went inside.

CHAPTER FOUR

VICTORIA

I needed to go to the library and get some resumes copied. Grabbing the paper, I headed to the coffee shop. My usual booth was empty, so I made my way there. After ordering my coffee and Danish, I opened up the Classifieds section. Three jobs appeared where there wasn't any the day before. I smiled a little smile, guessing they had something to do with fucking Marciano. I wish someone had a fucking picture of this guy. For two years, I'd been chasing a ghost.

Sometimes, I wondered if he was even a real person and not just made-up. Hmm, I wondered if that angle had been approached. We'd been moving on the pretense that he was a flesh and bone person, but what if he, or the name, was like a dummy corporation? I would have to present this. As I took the last bite of my Danish, I felt him. I looked up and found both Mr. Simons walking up to my table.

"Miss Costello, may we join you?" my boss asked.

I looked at his brother. Shaking my head, I put my hand out, indicating they could sit. They both ordered coffee, and I ordered another.

"Miss Costello, I want to apologize for my brother. I'm here on his behalf. I would really like for you to come back to work." He looked at the paper and the ads I had circled. "Please."

"Miss Costello," Paul began. "I am regretful in my actions and would really appreciate it if you would consider my brother's offer. We are willing to increase your pay by fifteen percent."

I laughed, looking him right in the face. "I cannot be bought, Mr. Simon. The salary you pay me now is more than sufficient. Please, stop sending me flowers."

"You don't like flowers?" He smiled.

"I like flowers just fine. What I don't like is your arrogance in believing you can buy me." I smiled at him. "I'm sure my neighbor, Mrs. Jones, is appreciating your flowers, though."

I watched as he reined in his temper, his eyes closing just a second longer than a blink. "I will not send you anymore flowers."

Our waitress brought over our coffees, and my boss started talking. "So, you will consider coming back?"

"I will consider it, but I want a guarantee that I am not going to be harassed or man handled."

Paul laughed. "Trust me, my men are a bit afraid of you."

Shaking my head, I continued with my boss. "Do I have your promise?"

He nodded. "You have my word. Why don't you take the rest of the week off and we can begin on Monday?"

"I appreciate that, Mr. Simon, but I'll be there in the morning. I really don't have anything to do, and I'm not the type of person who can just sit and do nothing." *That was a lie. I could not wait until I didn't have to do a fucking thing but wake up and love.*

"Thank you, Miss Costello." He stood. "We will leave you to your coffee. See you in the morning." He looked at his brother.

When I turned my head to look at Paul, his eyes had a softened look to them. Smiling a gentle smile, one that didn't feel forced, he said, "It was good to see you again, Miss Costello. Again, I apologize for my behavior."

I watched him gracefully lift himself out of the booth. I didn't intend to scan his body, but I did, my eyes landing on his lower section. I could see his cock was hard and rather large. I didn't mean to lick my lips, but I did.

I looked up to see him looking at me, and he nodded his head. "Have a lovely day, Miss Costello." He turned and walked away.

What the fuck was that, Victoria? Jesus, you love Steven. This man is a fucking asshole, a pig. No way can you even think about this shit. Your life is in grave danger, and there is no way you can drag someone into this shit.

Shaking my head, I got up and left the coffee shop, heading back home. I needed to grab my suit and get it to the cleaners.

Paul

Sitting in the car, John looked over at me. "You promised me you would stay away from her."

"Brother, there is something that draws me to that woman. I can't promise I will stay away. But I can promise to try. I went to see my attorney, and I am selling the club. I'm getting out."

I watched John smile. "Well, good luck. But don't fuck this up for us. Let her do her job so we can end it right. If you want to walk away, then stay away."

"Yeah, I know you're right, but I just don't know if I can."

I dropped my brother off and headed to Saks to buy Miss Costello a new suit. I knew this was something that would bite me in the ass later, but for some reason, I wanted to get her riled up again.

I explained to the saleswoman what I was looking for and what size. She showed me a few to choose from, so I took them both and two blouses to go with them. I wanted to buy her some sexy lingerie, but for that, I was pretty sure she would hand me my balls. I asked them to deliver the clothes to her home by the end of the day.

Victoria

When I got back from the cleaners, I grabbed my mail. I could see I needed to visit the museum again, so instead of heading upstairs, I headed over. When I got my ticket, a lovely older gentleman handed me a head piece, telling me there was a lovely tutorial on Monet today. I smiled and thanked him. Taking my headset, I sat in front of Monet's "Water Lilies." So peaceful. I finally put my headset on.

Good Afternoon, Victoria,

Seems you've hit the big time with this job of yours. Not only does Simon and Simon hold the accounts for Mr. Marciano, but it would seem that Mr. Paul Simon has taken up doing a background check on you.

What the fuck.

We have done extensive research into Mr. Simon's life, and yes, the red flags have been flying. You were correct in your observation that perhaps he is more than what he seems. I know this isn't part of what you signed up for, but we think it might be the better of two evils if you got closer to Mr. Simon.

I shook my head. "No fucking way," I whispered.

We are going to need for you to quit the job as the waitress and put all of your efforts on this job and Mr. Simon. If you need a face to face, just go to the curator's office. I will be there for another fifteen minutes.

The headset went dead. I pulled it off my head and slowly got up. As I turned to look around the room, there was only one other person sitting on a bench. It didn't feel right to me. The last time I was here, there was only one other person in this room. I made my way through the museum, to the curator's office. Once inside, I was taken through a back door and down a few flights of stairs to the basement, then to the other side and into a room where my contacts were waiting for me.

"I am not going to fuck that man. I want nothing to do with him. I did not sign up for this shit. I am here to find that bastard and end him. Not bring him in to stand trial but to fucking end him. I walked away from everything to do this. I am not up for sale. I volunteered for this. You don't own me."

"Victoria, things don't line up with this guy. He could be more than your boss. Your instincts are good; you are the best we have. You have gotten closer than anyone. You can do this. No one said you had to sleep with him. We just want you to get closer."

"Are you fucking kidding me? That man wants me. I've seen his fucking hard cock. I cannot get close without leading him to believe there might be something more. I'm not doing this."

"Do you want Andy Marciano? Do you want to end him? I'm telling you, this guy isn't who he says he is, and from what I've seen, you can handle him. Remember, the sooner you get this done, the sooner you can go back to England."

I looked at him. "I don't think you remember who I am. I can go back to England today if I want. You don't own me. I am not on contract. That bastard took my other half from me and left me with nothing. I am here only because I choose to be, not because you hold anything over me."

"Victoria, that fire you hold is exactly how you can handle Simon. You've already shown him. We viewed the tape from the bench yesterday. The man is interested, very interested in you. Just see where it goes while we investigate him."

"I need a dinner date tomorrow so I can have a report. If he is interested in me, it may not be safe for these meetings. I want someone who is fucking gorgeous to look at, who doesn't look like a fucking cop. He must have manners. He can pick me up at six-thirty tomorrow night."

I turned and walked out the door. *Is this day ever going to stop?* I made it home and into my apartment, sliding down the door. I wanted to go home. This was becoming a lifelong search. I wanted my husband. I wanted Steven. I needed to know if he re-married. I just walked out of his life.

I got up and ran into my bedroom, getting my secret phone out of its secret compartment. Sitting on the floor next to my bed, I turned it on. Text after text loaded.

~I miss you~
~I fell today at the park with Ruth and hurt my knee~
~The cookies we made were horrible so we threw them away~
Ruth promised we could make more for you~

~My birthday is coming soon~

~Will you be home for my birthday~

With shaking hands and tears starting to cloud my vision, I typed back responses.

~I miss you so much, my love~

~I'm sorry you hurt your knee. I hope it wasn't too bad~

~It's fine about the cookies. We can make more when I get home~

~I know your birthday is coming, but I'm afraid I will have to miss it. But I got you something wonderful~

~You are my heart~

Kissing the phone, I turned it off and slipped it back in its secret compartment. We needed to be safe. I had to finish this. I climbed on my bed, and I must have fallen asleep, because knocking on the door woke me. By the time I got there, the knocking stopped. I looked out, but there was nothing.

After eating, I peeled off the long blond wig and took a shower. Looking at myself in the mirror, I missed my hair. It was now short and spikey, not me at all. Shaking my head, I took myself to bed.

When the alarm went off, I was grateful for no dreams. I actually slept all night long. I went through my morning ritual, and when I was finished, there was no sign of Victoria Holmes. I was looking in the mirror at Sue Costello, shaking my head at myself in disgust. I turned and headed toward the door. When I opened it, there was a box sitting in front of my door with a big bow on it. Picking up the box, I carried it into the apartment to the table. Opening it, there was a card on top of the tissue paper. I picked it up.

Miss Costello,

I cannot tell you how sorry I am for Mr. Hinkle's behavior and for ruining your lovely suit. I hope these can replace the one that was ruined.

I wasn't sure of your size, so I asked one of the sales ladies to help me out. If they don't fit, please feel free to exchange them.

Inside were two of the loveliest tan suits I have ever laid eyes on. "What the hell?" I said to the room, looking at the card.

I hope to make amends by this gesture, and I hope you might recon-sider perhaps sharing a meal with me.

Paul Simon

I put the lid back on the box, picked it up, and walked out the door. I grabbed a cab and headed to the office. Once there, I walked into Mr. Simon's office and sat the box on his desk. "Please tell your brother that I am not interested in being bought." Turning, I walked out and headed to my office.

"Good morning, Miss Costello," my secretary said.

"Good morning, Sherry. I'm going to be busy this morning, so if you could hold my calls until after lunch, that would be great. Also, could you make dinner reservations for two at Acadia for seven."

"Miss Costello," she said as I walked into my office. Low and behold, Mr. Simon was sitting in a chair in front of my desk. "You have someone waiting in your office," I heard as I walked away.

"Why are you here?"

He stood, buttoning his jacket as he turned. "I was hoping to talk to you."

"Make an appointment. I have a busy day, Mr. Simon. Please don't waste my time." I stood by the door, waiting for him to leave.

He just stood there smiling at me. "Miss Costello, I have apolo-gized time and time again, more times than I have ever apologized to anyone." His tone was sharp.

I stood there looking at him. *Did he just threaten me?* "Am I supposed to feel something here?"

"Yes." He chuckled.

"Oh, well then, what exactly should I feel?" I couldn't wait to hear his explanation.

"You have dinner plans this evening? Do you have a boyfriend?"

"None of that is any of your business. What do you want?"

I saw Sherry move, and I turned to look at her. Her mouth was hanging open. I closed my eyes, shaking my head. I felt him before I smelt him. When I opened my eyes, he was standing right in front of me. "You are very beautiful, Miss Costello," he whispered. His hand moved to touch my face, and I stepped back.

"Don't touch me. What do you want?"

He smiled. "You, of course."

I think I actually saw a bit of softness in his eyes. There was no way this was happening. This man wanted me. Al was fucking crazy if he thought I would get close to this man. "I am not for sale, Mr. Simon, nor am I available to you. Please, just leave. I have work to do."

"I was hoping perhaps you would change your mind and have dinner with me."

"I already have plans this evening."

"Well, perhaps tomorrow. It is, after all, Friday. Maybe we could go to my lake house and spend some time getting to know one another. I am really not a horrible person."

I actually had to stifle a giggle. "Mr. Simon, I will not be going anywhere with you, especially to your lake house, for any amount of time." I looked him right in the eyes, just so he would know I wasn't kidding. I even leaned in for effect. "I am not available to you. Not tonight, not tomorrow, not ever." What I didn't expect was his response.

He grabbed my face and kissed me. My God did he kiss me. I was in shock. The power of his touch sent me careening off a preverbal cliff. I was so stunned it took me a minute to get my brain to function. I bit his lip, hard. When he pulled back, I slapped him across his face as hard as I could and ran out. I didn't stop moving. I didn't wait for the elevator; I hit the stairs. When I came running out of the stairwell, I must have looked like something terrible happened. People stopped to look at me.

Two security guards came running up to me. "Miss Costello, are you all right? Has something happened?"

I couldn't say anything, so I just nodded and then shook my head. Pushing past them, I ran out the door and right into his driver. He put his hands on me to steady me or stop me. I don't know which. I didn't care. I shoved at him, but his grip felt like my arms were clamped down with steel bands. I reacted and slammed the heel of my shoe into his foot. He let go, and then I kicked him in the balls and took off. I found a cab about a block away and got in it.

"Please take me to Oak Street Beach," I told him. Twenty minutes later, I found myself sitting on the beach. No man except for Steven had ever kissed me.

Paul

I was so turned on; I had to do it. I just wasn't prepared to feel what I felt when I did. Nor was I prepared for the aftermath. "Fuck!" I yelled.

Her secretary came running in. "Oh my God, Mr. Simon, are you all right?" She looked out the door, watching her run away.

"I'm fine, Sherry. Did you see where she went?" I started out the door. Fuck, my jaw hurt. I had never before been slapped by a woman in my life. I would love to show her who was boss.

"She headed down the stairs."

"Thank you," I said as I pulled out my phone. "Max, Miss Costello is headed down via the stairwell. Would you please stop her from leaving? I would like to talk to her."

I headed to the elevator. When I walked out, I saw Max lying on the ground. I couldn't help but smile; she'd kicked his ass again. When I got outside, he was getting up. "I should hire her to drive me, perhaps make her my bodyguard. What did she do this time?"

"Fucking slammed her high heel into my foot then fucking kicked me in the balls. The fucking bitch is crazy. I swear, I'm going to hurt her when I find her."

I laughed. "No, Max, you're not." I looked around. "Did you happen to see where she ran off to?"

"Ahm, lying on the ground in pain. No, sir, I didn't."

"All right, if she comes back, call me. I need to go talk to my brother." I turned and walked away, rubbing my jaw. Damn, she hits hard.

Walking into my brother's office, I sat in the chair, not saying a word. He walked over and laid a box in front of me. "What are you doing, brother?"

"Fucking your life up. Not intentionally. What's this?"

"Miss Costello brought it in. She told me to tell you that she wasn't interested in being bought."

"Fuck," I said, dropping my head into my hands.

"What the hell has gotten into you? I asked you to stay away from her, and what the hell happened to your face?"

"Miss Sue Costello happened. John, I stopped by her office to ask her to reconsider having a meal with me, and to see how she liked the suits. One thing led to another, and I kissed her. She didn't take kindly to that, and she fucking jacked me and ran out. I tried to get Max to stop her so I could talk to her and apologize to her, but she beat the shit out of him again."

John laughed. "You should get a tougher driver and bodyguard."

"I know, right? That's what I said to him. John..." I took a deep breath. "Something happened when I kissed her. I can't explain it, but fuck if she isn't in me. I don't know what to do."

"How about you leave her alone so I can end this? How about you stop apologizing to her and stop bothering her?"

"I don't think I can. Do you know I haven't been with anyone since I met her? I don't want anyone but her."

He chuckled. "Out of all those beautiful women in your club..."

I put my hand up. "Not my club anymore."

"You can't find one woman to fuck?"

"Oh, I can find many, but... Aww, fuck it. I've got work to do. Can you have your secretary return those for me?"

John slapped me on the back as I walked past him. "It'll get better, Paul."

I felt beaten down. I had a business to run. I didn't know who this woman was or why she was under my skin. I looked at John. "She has gotten under my skin, John. I'm going to need your help with this. It's been so long. I'm so used to taking what I want."

He looked at me. "Paul, she isn't the taking kind. She's like Sylvia; you need to earn her respect. You'll figure it out."

"Thank you, brother." I walked out of his office feeling a bit better about it. I would have to work at gaining her trust and respect after that kiss. But fuck me if she didn't set me on fire. She kissed me back for a few seconds. I reached up to touch my jaw. The smile was auto-matic. When I got in the car, I called my secretary and had her make reservations at Acadia for seven thirty. I needed to see if Kathy, my VP, would have dinner with me. I could take her under the pretense of a business meeting. Miss Costello didn't need to know otherwise.

Victoria

I sat on the beach for a few hours, then made my way back to the office. I spent the day locked in my office working. I needed to end this. That man wasn't going to derail me. I wanted to go home, to put this behind me.

Sherry buzzed me. "Miss Costello, I'm heading home now. It's six, and you have dinner plans at seven."

"Thank you, Sherry."

I shut down my computer and headed home. At six-forty-five, a knock drew me out of my lovely daydream. I could not wait to go home. I just needed to be very careful. Being sidetracked could mean a death sentence. When I opened the door, I was taken aback by the sight of the man standing there.

"Miss Costello." He smiled. "I'm Jacob Miles."

"Sue, and come on in."

"We are going to be late, so perhaps we should head out."

I nodded, agreeing, and we left. We both knew we couldn't talk until we were out of the cab. On our way into the restaurant, he handed me my earpiece and said, "We have a great deal to discuss."

I smiled and nodded, slipping it into my ear. The oh-so-familiar voice that usually whispered in my ear was there to greet me.

"Good evening, Victoria. There is much to tell you. Your Mr. Simon is a very powerful man, one of the richest in the country. His hand is in many pots. Over the course of the next hour, you are going to learn a great deal, and perhaps you will understand the necessity of you getting closer to him."

I smiled at Jacob as we were shown to our very private table. He ordered a lovely and expensive bottle of red. "I'm sure the voice has given you the rundown so far?"

I always loved how everyone referred to him as 'the voice'. I couldn't stop the giggle. "This spy shit is ridiculous." I knew he could hear me.

"Yes, but it is necessary, Victoria," the voice in my ear said gently.

The waiter returned with our wine, and we went through the process of tasting it. I smiled and went along. When he left, Jacob looked at me. "I would assume that this was set up as a date for a reason." He reached out and took my hand. "For the sake of eyes upon us, you should move a bit closer to me."

I looked at him. "What eyes?" I immediately scanned the room. Yep. Mr. Simon's eyes were definitely on me. I could clearly see at least two of his men in the restaurant. "Are you fucking kidding me?" I whispered as I moved over a bit in our booth.

"Victoria, the man has been running check after check on you," the voice said. *"Having a background developed was probably the best thing you did before we started this. At least, you know the background you developed. Because, from my experience, you are going to be questioned."*

Jacob smiled at me and picked up my hand, kissing my fingers. "Play this right, Victoria. We are supposed to be dating."

I leaned in. "You kiss me and they will need to pick you up off the floor."

He laughed. "I'm not a stupid man. I reviewed the tapes. I know what you are capable of."

Our waiter came over, and Jacob ordered for us. I had no idea what he ordered, because I was listening to the voice in my ear.

"Victoria, our research has indicated that Paul Simon could very well be Andy Marciano. You might be right in thinking the name was fake."

"Why would you think that?" I whispered.

Jacob leaned in like he was going to kiss my neck. "Your Mr. Simon just pulled up out front," he said softly.

I brought my hand up and curled it around his neck. "I suppose then that we need to make this look good."

"Victoria, you are playing a dangerous game with this man. Jealousy is

not something a decent man could handle. He is, or was up until a few days ago, the owner of one of the biggest BSDM clubs in the city."

I whispered in Jacob's ear, "Are you telling me he likes to tie women up and beat them?" My eyes shifted toward the door as he walked in. I watched him scan the room, his eyes coming in contact with mine as I slowly closed them, kissing Jacob's neck. "It's a go."

He pulled back, his hand coming to my neck, his thumb brushing my cheek. "Please don't kick my ass," he whispered while looking deep into my eyes. I think he saw the anger boiling in them.

I smelt him before I heard him clear his throat. Jacob slowly leaned in and kissed me sweetly on the lips. I grabbed his thigh, squeezing it hard. He chuckled and released me.

"Miss Costello," Paul said rather angrily. I could feel the rage pouring off his body.

I looked up at him. "Mr. Simon, what can I do for you?"

Jacob's hand found mine, and he entwined our fingers. Picking up his glass, he took a sip of his wine. As he set it down, he lifted his head in a confrontational way. "Yes, Mr. Simon, what can we do for you?"

If he could kill Jacob with a look, he would have. His eyes shifted back to me. "Could I have a word please?"

Jacob answered, "I'm sorry, Mr. Simon, but we are having dinner. If you need to talk to Sue, you can do so during regular business hours. Now, if you'll excuse us."

The voice in my ear said, *"Rein him in Victoria. He is going to get himself killed."*

"Jacob, I'm sure it's fine. I'll be back in a minute," I said softly.

He turned, bringing my hand up to his lips and kissing it gently. "I'll be right here if you need me."

"I'll be fine."

"Be careful, Victoria. From what I can see, Simon is on the cusp of exploding."

I walked away from our table. "What do you want?" I was so rude.

He was obviously struggling. "I want to say I am sorry for what took place in your office. I had no idea you were in a relationship."

"Mr. Simon..."

The voice interrupted me. *"Victoria, be careful."*

"My personal life, hell, my life is not your concern. I work for you and your brother. My time in the office is your time. You pay for it. But anything beyond that is my life. You don't own me; you don't decide for me."

"I'd like the opportunity," he said so softly I almost didn't hear him.

"This is your chance," the voice said.

I just stood there looking at him. A range of emotions moved through his eyes. "I don't know what you want from me," I said softly, my eyes never leaving his. Either he was telling the truth, or he was the greatest liar on the planet.

"I would just like the opportunity," he said.

"Be ready. Jacob is moving into place. This is your chance."

Jacob walked up to us. "Excuse me." He wrapped his arm around my waist, pulling me to him. "I think you've had enough time with my girlfriend."

Rage boiled in Paul's eyes when Jacob pulled me up against him. I put my hand on Jacob's chest. "I'm fine. Please, give us one more minute."

"No, you are here with me. I don't get enough time with you as it is," he said as he tried to pull me away.

"Jacob," I said rather sternly. "You need to stop. We talked about this." Lowering my voice, I told him, "You don't own me."

Paul reached over, grabbing his arm. "The lady asked you nicely. Let her go."

I put my hand on Paul's chest, pushing on him gently. "Please." Turning to Jacob, I put myself between them with a huge smile on my face. I put both of my hands on his chest. "I'm fine. Would you please give me a minute? I'll make it up to you later."

"Victoria, please be careful."

Jacob smiled. His hands coming to my hips, he pulled me flush with his body. "You have one minute." Turning, I watched him walk away. I had to wipe the smile off my face before I turned around to face Paul.

Paul

Every fucking nerve in my body was on hyper-aware mode. To see him touching her, I felt rage like I had never known. When she gently placed her hand on my chest, I wanted nothing more than to take her in my arms and kiss her.

When she turned around to face me, I watched that fucker walk away, and she said softly, "Mr. Simon…"

I interrupted her, "Paul."

Smiling, she said, "Paul, I cannot be an option for you. I am an employee, and my contract strictly forbids fraternization between colleagues. I'm pretty sure that includes my boss. I have a relationship with Jacob."

I chuckled. "He's a tool. I would just like the opportunity to get to know you better. Nothing more."

She giggled. I suppose that was a good thing; at least, she wasn't hitting me. "Ah, but Paul, you and I both know that there is something more, and I'm afraid that I am unavailable for something more."

"Does your date know that?" I spat out.

"Be careful, Paul. Your fangs are out. Yes, he knows and is accepting of it. This is all redundant. It isn't going to happen."

I felt my resolve slipping. I felt like I was drowning. "At least have dinner with me and then you can decide. I'm really a nice guy." *God, why am I doing this?* Standing here looking at her in that fucking dress, my eyes traced every goddamn curve, the swell of her magnificent breasts. I would have gotten on my fucking knees. I was trying with all that I am not to scan her beautiful body.

She just stood there looking at me. Tilting her head, she whispered, "Fine."

My heart jumped. "Tomorrow night?"

She turned her head to look at her date before turning her attention back to me. "I have plans. But I'm free on Saturday."

I smiled. I wanted to end that fucker sitting there looking so smug. "Great, do you have a time?"

"Why don't I meet you at Oak Street Beach around noon. We can see where it goes from there." Smiling, she said, "Goodnight, Paul."

I watched her turn and walk back to her table. *Fuck me!* She had the perfect heart-shaped ass. I'd never seen an ass so perfect. I nodded to her date as I made my way back to my table. I couldn't tell you what the hell I ate or what I talked about. She had clouded my brain. I didn't want that fucking man to touch her, and he was constantly touching her.

I listened to them laugh and giggle. When they got up to leave, I had to physically force myself to stay in my seat. When they walked out, I texted Max and had him send a guy to her house. I wanted to know if he stayed over.

~

Victoria

"*Victoria,*" the voice in my ear said. "*You did good. I'm rather impressed that you set the ground rules.*"

"I told you; no one touches me. If you want me to do this, I do it on my terms. I am not for sale."

"*All right, you get some sleep. Keep the earpiece for Saturday.*"

Laughing, I said, "I don't think so. My terms. I do not want you in my ear."

Jacob walked me to my apartment. He came in for a minute while I gave him the earpiece. "You going to be all right?" he asked.

"I'm fine. Thank you for doing this."

He smiled a weird smile. "It was my pleasure. I look forward to future dates."

"If this plan works, there won't be any more dates. Goodnight, Jacob."

He put his hand on the handle and paused. "Victoria," he whispered.

"Sue, my name is Sue, and you would be wise to remember that. If you accidently blow my cover, I'll kill you myself. I want this done. I want my life back. Do you get that?"

"Sorry, yes, I got it."

He opened the door and turned around to say something. "Good-night, Jacob," I said as I was closing the door.

"Goodnight, Sue."

CHAPTER FIVE

VICTORIA

Friday came and went with no interruptions from Paul. I was given the new accounts and couldn't help but notice things weren't right. I filed them into my brain for my report. The day blew by. It usually did when I was into the job. Before I knew it, it was seven at night. Mr. Simon, my boss, was the only one still in the office when I was leaving. I noted that as well.

My night was dreamless, but I woke feeling a bit panicked. I took a shower and became Sue Costello then put my hair back in a ponytail. I loved the wigs; they were made of real hair and you couldn't even tell they were fake. After dressing in a pair of jeans with a peach tank top and tennis shoes, I grabbed my jacket and my smaller purse, which I crossed over my body, and headed out to the beach.

Taking off my shoes, I headed toward the water. For a beautiful Saturday afternoon, it wasn't crowded yet. I found a place to sit and wait. I didn't really like having idle time on my hands. My mind wandered too much, wandered back to the life I had before the train wreck took my life away. If this man was the reason, I was going find the greatest of joy slitting his fucking throat.

My phone buzzed in my purse. I pulled it out. The text had one word: *Contact.* I quickly erased it and stood up, putting my hands in my pocket. I felt him as he walked up, which bothered me. I only ever felt Steven like that; our bodies were so in tune with each other. I didn't want this man to affect me like this. I wanted him to be the horrible monster I knew him to be.

Paul

When I woke up, I felt different. I felt alive. I was going to make this woman want to spend time with me. I showered and shaved. As I was in my closet, I had to laugh. What the hell would I wear? I'd never been this nervous about a date before.

Opening my drawers, I found a pair of jeans and a t-shirt. As I got dressed, it dawned on me. I hadn't worn clothes like this in probably twenty years. I felt like a teenager. I found an old pair of tennis shoes, grabbed my jacket, and headed out.

"Mr. Simon," Max said as he opened the car door.

"Max, take the day off. I'm taking a cab." I smiled at him.

"But, sir."

"I'll be fine. Go enjoy some deserved time off." I turned and walked down the street, grabbing a cab, and headed to the beach. As I walked onto the sand, I bent and took off my shoes and socks. I saw her sitting on the sand and headed toward her. She stood, her hands going to her front pockets, pulling her jeans even tighter across her ass. The gap between her legs bought my cock to an instant erection. I was happy that I'd put on a longer t-shirt to cover myself.

Walking up to her, I had to put my hand in my pocket to stop myself from touching her. "Good afternoon, Miss Costello."

She laughed. "My name is Sue, and good afternoon."

"Is it Sue or Susan?"

"It's actually Suzanne, but no one calls me that."

Looking at her, I said, "Would you mind if I called you Suzanne? It's a very beautiful name, and I really don't want to be like everyone else."

44

"That's fine. Would you like to walk?" She turned around. "What, no goons?"

I laughed. "They are all terrified you are going to beat their asses."

She giggled. God did it sound like music to me. "As they should be."

"No, but in all seriousness, I'm just Paul today. No goons, no car, no suit. Just me."

"Hmmm, why would you try and be someone you're not?" she said as she started walking down the beach.

"All those things are not me. This is me, or as close to me as I can get, or that my life will allow me to be. Is this you?" My hand motioned up and down her body.

Smiling, she said, "Not really. I'm more a countryside girl. I love working in the garden and just enjoying a laid-back lifestyle. I suppose I got that from my parents. My mom was always in the garden. I find it very calming. It's such a contrast from the city."

She was sharing part of her life with me. I should do the same. "My mother loved her garden, but I am thinking hers was more on a grandiose scale."

She raised her eyebrows. "Please, don't tell me you were born with a silver spoon in your mouth."

I laughed. "My parents worked hard for what they had. Not a silver spoon, but a comfortable life. One that afforded my mother to stay home and raise us." I spied a little food truck. "Would you like something to eat?"

She turned her head. Looking at the truck, her face lit up. "I would love a hotdog."

"Then, let's have hotdogs." I hadn't had a hotdog in a very long time, but hey, this was her day. She needed to see the real me, and once upon a time, I loved hotdogs. I'd grown into a very shallow, very selfish, very arrogant man, and that was not the kind of man she wanted. It felt good stepping outside of the world I had built. I was being reminded every minute I spent with her that life is so much more than what I had made it. Sylvia had a similar effect on me.

Looking at Suzanne, I could very much imagine a life outside of this city with her. No work, just enjoying her company.

We got our hotdogs and lemonade and found a place on the beach to sit and eat them. We chatted a bit more about our parents and how our lives were a bit similar. When we finished, as we were walking to the garbage, I couldn't resist. "Would you be interested in going to Navy Pier?"

She turned to look at me, her eyes wide and full of life, her smile touching her eyes. "Are you kidding me? I would love it. But only if you ride the rides with me."

I laughed. "Deal." We grabbed a cab and headed that way. She was so beautiful when relaxed. I couldn't help but wonder if this was the real woman she was. Her head turned, our eyes locking.

"You're staring at me," she whispered.

"I'm sorry," I said softly. "You're very beautiful."

"Don't ruin this, Paul. It's supposed to be us getting to know one another. Please, I already told you, I am unavailable to you. You are my boss. The only reason I am here is because I love my job, and I think it would be easier to do it if I didn't hate you. If you didn't disgust me. You want one thing from me, and I cannot be bought or owned. Either we are friends, or we are nothing."

She could have ripped my heart out, but she was right. That was the reason we were together today. I couldn't take this someplace else. Not yet anyway. "We are friends. I am accepting what you are offering me. I asked for the opportunity to get to know you and for you to get to know me, and you have been gracious enough to give it to me. So, friends." The cab stopped, and I wiggled my eyebrows at her. "We're here. You ready for this?"

Her smile took my breath away. "So ready." She jumped out of the cab while I paid the driver. This was one of those times when you held your girlfriend's hand. I so wanted to touch her, to share this with her on a level beyond friends. But I couldn't. I had to do this slowly, not my alter ego asshole persona. The more time I spent with her, the more time I wanted to spend with her. She was so beautiful, and her smile was so warm, so real.

Victoria

Being with him wasn't awkward like I thought it would be. I found myself relaxing after a while. My laughter wasn't forced with him. He was genuinely funny and charming, but the glint of desire never quite left his eyes. Still, he had made no attempt to touch me. When I caught him looking at me, I saw only warmth in his eyes. I felt my body react to him.

Riding the rides was fun; we shared some serious laughter. We played some games in the arcade, and he won me a little stuffed penguin. We had snow cones and walked along the pier. All in all, we had a lovely day. More than once, I felt myself drawn to him, which confused me and pissed me off all at the same time. As we got ready to leave, I could tell he was feeling off.

"Suzanne, I had a lovely day."

I smiled at him, because I was feeling good. "It was a wonderful day. Thank you, Paul, for being real. At least, I hope you were being real."

He laughed. "I don't think I've been this real in a very long time, so I need to thank you for making me see how much of an arrogant asshole I really am in this life. I was wondering if you wanted to get dinner? I know a place that you wouldn't expect me to know that has great burgers."

I could see in his eyes that he was being sincere. "I would love to have a burger with you."

"Yeah?"

"Yeah."

We walked out to the street and grabbed a cab. As we drove, I realized where we were going and started to panic. I needed to not go here. *Shit!* I hit the glass between us and told the driver, "Please pull over." I needed to get the hell out of here.

"What's the matter?" Paul asked.

The driver pulled over, and I shook my head, telling him, "I need to go." Opening the door, I jumped out and took off running in the opposite direction. There was no way I could go to the restaurant. Jerry would recognize me, and my cover would be blown. I just kept running. I couldn't do this. I couldn't allow this man to get close to me. He could be Andy Marciano. Just the fact that he knew the bar was implication enough. I got too comfortable around him. I couldn't have feelings for him. I loved Steven. I saw a cab and jumped in it. Giving him my address, I sank down in the seat, trying to calm myself down. I needed a good cover story for the way I just acted.

Pulling out my phone, I sent a message. *~Help~*

As I walked into my building, I saw Jacob standing by the elevators. I let out the breath I was holding, and my nerves relaxed. When Jacob turned and walked away, I felt him.

"Suzanne," he whispered.

He was inches from me. I closed my eyes. "I can't."

"Please turn around and look at me. What happened?" he asked softly.

"Paul, I... I can't. I just can't. It's too much."

"What's too much?"

I didn't mean to do it, and I can't explain why I did, but I was freaking out. I had no back story for my actions, but my hand slowly moved behind me. Gently, I touched his fingers, and he closed his hand around mine. The current that flowed through my fingers and up my arm freaked me out. "I can't," I whispered and stepped forward, away from him. He didn't pull me back. As our hands lost contact, so did the feeling. I kept walking, the elevator doors opened, and I walked in.

When I turned to push the button to my floor, I looked up. He was just standing there looking at his hand. Slowly, he raised his head to look at me. His face looked as stunned as I felt. The door closed, and I fell back against the wall.

This was bad. This was way bad. I couldn't do this. He could be... Hell, who was I fucking kidding? *He very well may be Andy Marciano. Why, of all the places in this city, did he have to take me there? Did he know who I was? Was this his way of calling me out?* The doors opened, and

Jacob was standing at the end of the hall. He saw me walk out of the elevator and met me at my door.

Once inside, he handed me my earpiece. "Thank you. Please excuse me." I opened the door so he could leave.

I put the earpiece in my ear and headed to the bathroom, turning on the shower. "I need help."

"Tell me what happened."

I filled the voice in on what took place. "This doesn't make any sense. Why, of all the dive joints in this fucking city, did he take me to that one? Could he know who I am? Is he Marciano? Tell me what you know."

After an hour-long conversation, I was convinced he didn't know who I was. But I sure did have more information on him than I cared to have.

"I need time. I'll get in touch with you when I figure this out. Thank you for your help," I said to the voice. I took the earpiece out and went to the door. When I opened it, Jacob was standing there. He came in, and I gave him the earpiece.

"Are you all right?" he asked.

"I will be. Thank you for coming."

"Sue, we are getting closer to the end."

"Not close enough. Listen, Jacob, I need some time to myself, so if you'll excuse me…"

"Sure." He turned and opened the door. My head was down. I was feeling more than a little overwhelmed. "What the hell are you doing here?" he snapped.

"I'm here to see Suzanne." He looked at me as I picked my head up. "Are you all right?"

I nodded and then shook my head. "Jacob, it's fine. Please, I just need some time."

He played his part well. Turning, he said to me in a very soft voice, "Sue, I want this between us. Believe me."

I nodded and watched as he turned and walked out. I gave him a longing look. Paul ate it up.

"What happened today?" he asked softly.

I just shook my head. "I can't do this."

He stepped forward, bringing his hand up to my face, wrapping his fingers around my neck. "I know I promised, but I can't stop myself."

His mouth slowly and gently covered mine. I was terrified, but I couldn't stop myself. Steven never kissed me like this. His tongue gently swiped over mine. When he realized I wasn't pulling away and I wasn't going to hit him, his other hand gently landed on my hip as he moved closer, deepening the kiss.

Slowly, he ended the kiss. "Jesus," he whispered on my lips.

"Please, Paul. I can't do this," I said as I stepped back from him. He let me go.

"Suzanne."

I shook my head. "Please, I just need to be alone."

He nodded and reached for the door. "Thank you for a beautiful day. Thank you for reminding me that life is good." He smiled at me and walked out the door.

My hand came up to my lips, and the tears fell.

Paul

I just stood there in her hallway. My mind was numb; I think I was in shock. *What the hell was that?* I looked at her door. "Jesus," I whispered. Even with my wife, I'd never felt like that. It took me a few minutes to get my bearings. As I slowly moved down the hall to the elevator, I couldn't calm down.

I felt like I was walking on air. *What the fuck is happening?* I made it to my car. Max asked if I was all right. Shaking my head, I simply said, "No, and I don't think I am ever going to be all right again. Take me home."

Victoria

I couldn't stop them. *How could I feel like this?* The man could be a murderer. I knew for a fact that he was shady and had his hand in many pots, many illegal pots. *What was happening to me?*

My phone buzzing in my purse brought my mind back. Without opening my eyes, I reached in, grabbing it. I didn't even look at the caller ID. "Hello." My voice came out as just a whisper. I don't think I could get my voice to go any higher.

His deep baritone voice sounded through the line. "I... ah... I just wanted to make sure you were all right."

"I'm not sure," I whispered.

"I know what you mean. I've been sitting in this chair since I got home."

"I've been lying on the floor since you left," I whispered.

"Suzanne," he said breathlessly.

"I know."

"Can I see you again?"

"Is that really a good idea?" I wasn't sure I could handle seeing him again.

"I'm not sure."

"Maybe we should just not... I don't know." The tears were building again. I loved Steven, so I couldn't possibly have feelings for this man.

"Please don't cry," he whispered. *How did he know I was crying?* The silence was long while I tried to rein in my tears. "Hey," he said softly. "We didn't get to have dinner. Do you like Chinese?"

"Yes," I said as steadily as I could manage.

"How about I pick some up and come over? We can talk about this... whatever this is," he said cautiously.

I wanted to say no, but my head was nodding yes. I needed to say no. He was dangerous. "Okay," I whispered.

"Is there anything you'd like?" I could hear him moving around.

"No, whatever you choose will be fine," I managed.

"All right, I'll be there soon. Suzanne?"

"Yeah," I whispered.

"It'll be all right."

"Okay."

"I'll see you in a bit."

I nodded and he disconnected the call. I dropped my phone on the floor. Rolling onto my side, I was doing what Al wanted me to do. I'd done so much already, so what the fuck difference did it make? He wanted me to get close to him, so I was only doing what needed to be done. I was a professional, so what fucking difference did any of this make?

I closed my eyes, trying to pull the pain back. Trying to get control. I must have fallen asleep, because a gentle knock on the door woke me. Once I got up and opened the door, his face said more than I wanted to know. He stepped in, setting the bags on the floor, and he pulled me into his arms and held me. I wanted to pull away, but it felt so damn good to be held, and he smelled so fucking good.

"I'm so sorry for doing that. I know what you said about not touching you. Please, don't cry."

I shook my head. He thought this was because of him. Well, it was, but it wasn't. I pulled away. "I don't know what's the matter with me. I'm going to go and wash my face. Come in." I walked down the hall to my bedroom and right into the bathroom. Those two rooms were the only rooms that weren't wired for sound or with cameras. I washed my face and made sure my wig was on the right way.

Looking at myself, I decided I was presentable. Taking off my jacket, I tossed it on the bed on my way out into the living room. He had all the bags unpacked with everything on the coffee table.

"I got just about everything on the menu," he said softly as he stood up. A perfect gentleman. Not the deviate, murderous, drug pushing, gun running bastard I believed him to be.

"Thank you." I sat down.

He handed me a pair of chopsticks. "Dig in." He picked up a container.

"Maybe we should address the elephant in the room first," I said softly.

Setting his container down, he said, "You need to eat. You are obviously upset, and if memory serves me right, women tend to not eat when they are upset."

I chuckled and nodded. We ate the majority of what he brought over. When we finished, he turned to me, looking me in the eyes.

"You want me to go first?" I nodded. He took a deep breath. "For the past five years, I haven't led a nice life. My brother would call it deviant, and in a way, I suppose it was. I viewed it as the only way I could survive what happened. I was married, and my wife was murdered right in front of me. I'm afraid I didn't handle it very well. I went off the deep end, bound and determined to find the bastard, but somewhere I got lost, and until four days ago, I was walking through life feared, respected, and oblivious to those around me. I took what I wanted, when I wanted, and I didn't give a shit about anyone or anything."

I just sat there in shock, looking at him. I could see the pain flash in his eyes when he said his wife was murdered. "Paul, what happened with your wife?" I was holding my breath, terrified at what he would say, hoping it was the truth. We were being watched and recorded. Whatever he said to me would be investigated. I needed to be very careful here.

He chuckled, but it was a humorless chuckle. "She was in the wrong place at the wrong time, I suppose. I had gotten involved with some people that I probably shouldn't have been involved with." He saw my eyes go wide, so shaking his head, he said, "I am no longer associated with them. But I was threatened, and because of who I was, they knew they couldn't touch me, not physically anyway. So, I believe they waited for the moment to destroy me the only way they could. We were out celebrating Sylvia finally getting pregnant." I felt myself take a deep breath at the same moment his eyes changed. I saw his pain. "I left her standing in front of the restaurant while I went to get the car. She thought it was silly to wait for me, so she started walking toward where we'd parked. It was all so... I don't know, surreal. A man stepped out from the shadows, grabbed her by the hair, and slid a knife across her throat."

I watched as a tear fell from his eye. I wanted to touch him, but I couldn't bring myself to do it.

"Just as fast as he appeared, he disappeared. I thought, at first, it was just a mugging gone wrong. But as I sat in a state of shock for weeks after, I realized, when he did it, he was looking right at me. It was done on purpose, to send me a message. I heard it loud and clear. I changed in that moment of realization, becoming this hard, unfeeling, callous, take what I want man. I used to be proud of who I was. But in the past five years, I've come nowhere near finding the bastard who did this."

He dropped his head. I knew he was crying, and I could only imagine how difficult that was for him to relive, to tell me. I figured it was my turn.

"Two years, eleven months, and twenty-eight days ago, I woke up to a phone call. My other half had been murdered. Everything I had was gone. There is nothing left for me. I've been floating through this life trying to find something to ground me to it. I don't want to be touched because he was the only one who ever touched me. It physically makes me sick." I lowered my voice. "Today, when you kissed me, I felt it," I whispered, "so much so, that it can't ever happen again. I love him. I will always love him. He is the only man that I've ever been with." The tears came and I couldn't stop them.

"I know just how you feel. All the women I've been with have been about self-gratification. I haven't kissed a woman since my wife. You are the first, and I don't even know why, but I couldn't not do it. It changed me. I know it's not what you want to hear..."

I shook my head. "It changed me, too. I think that's why I am in so much turmoil right now, because I never thought or believed that I could feel like this again."

"I know what you mean. I feel like life matters again. Suzanne, I'm changing my life. I'm going to do the right thing. If anything, this has taught me that life can be good again. No matter what happens, I wanted to tell you that and to thank you."

We just sat there, not saying anything.

With tears falling silently from my eyes, I asked, "Does it get any easier?"

"Yes. I should go. I just needed to tell you. Thank you for listening."

I nodded and stood up, moving toward the door. I felt his fingers on my arm, and I stopped moving. He walked around in front of me. "Suzanne," he whispered. Picking my head up, he kissed me. It took my breath away. "Thank you." He turned around and walked out the door, leaving me standing there.

Paul

I leaned against her door when it closed behind me. I didn't want to leave. I don't think I ever wanted to leave her. But she wasn't ready; she didn't want this. Not yet anyway. I had a lot to do still to clean up my life. Just knowing she was here and didn't hate me was enough for now.

CHAPTER SIX

VICTORIA

Somehow, I made my way to my room and curled up in a ball on my bed. I couldn't figure out why he made me feel, or how he made me feel like this. My mind, body, and soul would always belong only to Steven. I wanted to know if he was happy. I needed to know. Picking up my phone, I texted the word *Art* and then erased it. I was going to get some answers. I needed to know.

Could the same person who killed his wife be the same person who killed my other half? I needed some answers. Sleep came too easily for me. When I woke, I was ready to go. I showered, dressed, and headed to the Art Museum. I didn't bother with Monet. I went straight to the curator's office. I was led to the room in the basement.

When I walked in, there were five men in the room. Two I knew—Jacob and Al—but the rest were unknown. I didn't want to know them.

"You heard everything that happened, everything he said. Is it true?"

"Yes, as far as we know, it is all true."

"Tell me what you aren't sure is true."

"It's all speculation, Victoria."

"I don't give a shit if it's a wild idea you might have. I need information. How am I supposed to do this if I can't put the pieces of the puzzle together? You came to me when he ended him. I chose to do this to get justice. I have murdered fourteen men who nobody fucking missed. I have changed my name so many times I'm not even sure who the fuck I am anymore. I walked away from my life to make this bastard pay. Now, tell me what I want to know, what I need to know, or every single one of you can go fuck yourselves. You don't own me!" I shouted.

"He has his hand in drugs, guns, prostitution, and we are pretty sure the sex trade."

"Paul? Paul Simon? Or is this Marciano?"

"Marciano, Simon, we believe they are one and the same."

"But you don't have one shred of evidence to back up this assumption?"

"No, that's why we want you to get close to him."

"Yeah, well, about that. I'm getting closer than I care to. I cannot have a physical relationship with this man."

One of the men I didn't know stepped forward. "It may be necessary for you to do just that."

I snapped my head to look at him. "Like fucking hell, it will. I will walk away first. You better do your fucking job, because I'm about done with this shit. I haven't even had time to grieve. I have a fucking life waiting for me on the other end of this mess. A mess, I might remind you, that you fucking created. You knew it was a suicide job to begin with, yet you sent him in there. That's on you. I'm not as easy to kill. But this man, this Paul Simon, is bringing to the surface emotions in me that aren't very healthy. You need to figure this shit out and help me. I'm giving you one month and then I am moving on."

Another man stepped forward. "Do not think it is acceptable to threaten us."

I burst out laughing. "Who the fuck are you? No, wait, I don't give a shit who you are. I want the son of a bitch who killed him. If it's Paul Simon, then give me the fucking proof. What he said to me last night should give you a path to go down. So, get off your lazy ass and go down it. You've got twenty-four hours to get me a full report, or I'm giving my notice at the company, and I'm gone. I'm going home."

"Miss Holmes, are you in love with him?"

I didn't even think about what I was doing when my fist connected with his jaw. "I'm in love with my husband. I have been since I was sixteen years old."

"Victoria?"

I turned around to yell at him, when Al said, "Steven remarried. He got a divorce. They are expecting a child at the end of summer."

He could have shot me. I just stood there looking at him. I felt the room tilt, my ears ringing, and then nothing. I passed out.

In my subconscious, in what felt like a dream, I could hear people talking. Some of the voices I recognized, but I was too out of it to connect most of them.

"Jesus fucking Christ. What the hell, Al? Did you have to do it like that?" Jacob said.

"Well, she needed to know. She needed to know she had nothing to go back to. We need her to finish this."

"I always knew you were a heartless bastard."

"Is she all right? She hit her head pretty hard."

"There's no blood."

"Should we take her to the hospital?" another of the men asked.

"You need to tell her everything," Jacob insisted.

The one man who hadn't said anything, who'd stayed in the shadows before I passed out, spoke up. His voice seemed so familiar, but I couldn't be for sure if it really was who I thought, or if my frazzled state had my mind playing tricks on me. "We can't tell her everything. She can never know everything. She needs to do this on her own. She needs to find the truth on her own."

As I was coming to, the voice that I heard that was so familiar to me got quiet again. I swear, I was hearing things. My eyes opened, and there were four men looking at me. I didn't say anything; I just sat up, waiting for the nausea to pass, and then I got up and left.

I wandered aimlessly around for hours trying to grasp what Al had said. Steven remarried. He was having a baby. Something I could never give him. Something I would never know in this life. The tears fell with no effort on my part to stop them. I had no idea where I was or how I got there, but it was getting dark out. Reaching into my purse, I dialed his number.

"Hello," he said. I didn't say anything. "Hello?"

In the background, I heard a woman say, "Honey, who is it?"

"I don't know. Hello."

I fought with everything I had not to talk. I just hung up and buckled over in pain. I managed to dial his number. I'm not even sure how I pulled it from my memory.

"Hello?" he said.

I was crying so bad I could hardly talk. "Please," was all I could get out.

"Suzanne? Are you all right?"

"No, please."

I heard him talking. "Find her. Now." Then back to me. "I'm on my way. God, are you hurt?"

"Yes. No…" I stuttered out. I heard a car door shut.

"I'll be there in five minutes. Don't hang up." He was yelling at someone. "I don't fucking care. Move." Back to me. "It's all right. I'm almost there."

I couldn't stop sobbing. A scream escaped me, and I just let it go. The pain was unmeasurable in my chest. "Oh, God," I cried out.

"I'm here. Where are you, beautiful? Shit."

Then I felt his arms around me, lifting me up. "I've got you. What happened?"

I just put my arms around his neck and let it all go. I couldn't catch my breath. I felt him put me in the car and then climb in, pulling me into his arms. "Take us to Miss Costello's house."

"No!" I screamed. "No!"

"Okay, take us to my house."

He held on to me, his face buried in my neck, mine in his. I couldn't stop crying. It was just like the day I left him. I was devastated, completely unable to form a coherent thought. I felt the car stop, and then he got out, picked me up, and carried me. Before I knew what was happening, he laid on a bed and crawled in with me, pulling me to his side. "I've got you."

I cried myself to sleep. When I woke, I was alone, and it was dark out. I jumped up, not realizing where I was. He was right next to me. "You're at my house. Suzanne, what happened to you?"

I shook my head, and the pain started all over again. I reached for him, pulling myself into his lap. It felt so good to feel his arms around me, to feel his warmth. It had been so long since I'd felt this. *He's married. He's having a child.* I couldn't catch my breath; I was gasping for air.

"Come on, beautiful. Deep breaths come on. In through your nose, out through your mouth." I tried to focus on him, following his breathing until I didn't feel like I was going to suffocate.

What the hell am I doing here? I can't be this weak. I have to leave.

I started looking around the room like a scared rabbit. He sensed my fear. "Hey," he said, bringing my face to his. "You're safe here. Can you tell me what happened?"

I shook my head no, still unable to stop the pain. *How can I tell him? He could very well be the man who did this. I shouldn't be here.* "I'm sorry. I should go. I'm all right." I went to get up.

"Suzanne, you are far from all right. I picked you up off the ground today. Something happened to you. Did someone hurt you?"

"Yes, but not in the way you're thinking. In here." I touched my heart. "I need to go. I can't be here."

"Why? What's wrong with being here? At least you aren't alone."

"You're a very dangerous man," I said so softly I wasn't even sure if I'd said it.

He tilted his head. "Why would you say that?"

"Because you make me feel things. Things I don't want to feel. I can't do this. I am unavailable." Even as I said it, I didn't believe it any longer. He'd married someone else. I pushed away from him and scooted across the bed. Jesus, it was huge. When my feet hit the floor, I moved to the door. He was right behind me.

"If someone hurt you, at least let me take you home. You don't have to stay here."

I froze. "I can't go back there," I whispered.

He put his hand on my shoulder. "Fuck, did Jacob hurt you?"

I pulled away. "No. Please, Paul, I need to not be here. I can't."

"Why, Suzanne? Tell me why."

I just stood there. I could feel the heat coming off his body. I could smell him, and he smelled like heaven. I needed to feel kindness, to feel tenderness. My hand moved on its own, reaching behind me, touching his fingers. He entwined them, and slowly, I moved our hands to my hip. With my other hand, I did the same.

He stepped forward, but he still wasn't touching me. "I feel so alone. So afraid all the time," I whispered. "I don't know what is happening to me anymore."

He bent his head down so I could feel his breath on my shoulder. "I'm right here."

"You're not a nice man. I can't do this with you."

"Meeting you has made me rethink my life. I told you that," he whispered, his breath hot.

"I just need to feel... I just need to feel anything but what I feel now."

"Tell me what you need, beautiful."

I stepped away from him and moved to the bathroom. Shutting the door, I leaned against it. I wanted him. I wanted to feel anything other than this devastation. He could be a murderer. Hell, I *was* a murderer. I moved to the sink, looking at myself in the mirror. I couldn't do this looking like someone else. Reaching up, I pulled off the wig and then washed my face. When I opened the door, he was standing a few feet away. His eyes filled with confusion.

"I had cancer and lost most of my hair," I lied. It didn't matter anymore. The lies were so common that I was losing the truth of my life. It just didn't matter anymore.

He moved to stand in front of me. "You're still beautiful. If I'm being honest, I prefer the red hair. It would explain all the fire you have in you."

My hands moved to his waist, pulling his shirt out of his pants, and I started to unbutton it. When I got to the last button, I looked up at him. He swallowed hard, his Adam's apple moving slowly up and down his throat. I pushed up on my toes and kissed it with an open mouth. When I put my hands into his shirt, touching his chest, his shoulders, sliding his shirt down his arms, I heard his shaky intake of air.

The shirt fell to the floor, and I stepped back to look at him. His chest was so broad, so chiseled. "My God, you're beautiful," I whispered. And he was, with muscles like you see in a magazine, all the way down to the V disappearing into the waistband of his slacks.

His hand came up and wrapped around my neck, his thumb tilting my head to reach his mouth. I'd never experienced a kiss like this. So tender, so gentle, so loving. A kiss a woman could get lost in, and that's just what I wanted, to get lost. Pulling back, he slid my jacket off my shoulders. His touch on my bare shoulder sent shivers down my spine. Trailing his hands down my arms to my hands, he entwined our fingers and stepped back. I went with him willingly. I wanted this with him. He made me feel like no man ever had. Another step, and he stopped, letting go of my hands. He gently lifted my tank top, slowly pulling it up and over my head. His eyes never left mine. I could see the fear in them. He thought I would run. And I was going to run, but not yet.

"My God, Suzanne, you're beautiful," he whispered as he kissed me again, pulling my body to his. I felt his hardness against my stomach.

I pulled back. "I need to tell you something." Not taking my eyes off his, I continued. "My name isn't Suzanne. I think, before we make love, you should know who you are making love to."

He smiled. "You don't feel like a Suzanne."

"I'm trying to reinvent myself. My name is Victoria."

"A beautiful name, a beautiful woman. Thank you for telling me." He kissed me again.

I didn't care. My heart was in pieces; nothing mattered to me anymore. Nothing but this moment with this man. While we kissed, I reached behind me and undid my bra, then I wrapped my arms around his chest. His back was just as defined with muscles as the front of him.

He lifted me up and turned, walking toward the bed. Climbing up, he laid me in the center of it, his body half on me half on the bed. His hand moved down to my hip and then to my thigh, bringing it up over his as he slid his leg between mine. We laid like this kissing for a long time. Nothing was hurried. He was making love to my mouth, keeping his hand locked behind my knee, his other arm holding me close as we shared our mouths. I'd never felt this with another person. There was just us. I think that's what he was doing, taking everything else away so it was just me and him in the bed. No ghosts. No pain. Nothing but two people. Me and him.

When he pulled back, my hand moved to touch his face. I wanted to remember him. I wanted to never forget this moment. I touched his eyes, which he closed. I touched his lips, and he smiled. I'd never noticed his dimples before. I ran my fingertips through them.

We laid there in each other's arms, just looking at one another. I'm not sure if he was making sure all the bad was gone. He smiled a little smile and kissed me again, laying me flat on the bed, his hand moving from my knee to my hip. His fingers pressed into my ass. Then, gently, he moved it up to my waist, his thumb barely touching the bottom of my breast.

Pulling back to look at me, slowly moving his hand up, he slid my bra strap off my shoulder. He didn't look at me when his hand cupped my breast. His eyes closed, and he moaned. I watched him enjoy me. It felt so good to be touched, to be held. My body was alive with tiny little electrical sparks firing off wherever his skin touched mine.

My hands moved along his body, through the hairs on his chest, and it felt wonderful on my fingers. I slowly moved down to his pants, unbuckling his belt and then undoing his button. I pulled his zipper down, never looking away from his eyes.

As I slipped my hand into his pants to touch his ass, he leaned in and kissed me deeply. I pressed my fingers into the rock-hard muscle. He was solid and beautiful, so beautiful. I'd never seen a man like him in my life. Not in person anyway.

He pulled back from our kiss, moving his body, taking my bra all the way off. "Fucking beautiful," he said as he gazed at me.

Shifting his body so his mouth aligned with my breast, he cupped them, moving his tongue so slowly across one and then the other. I felt my back arch, my whole body covered in goose flesh. When he circled his tongue around my nipple, I gasped, and when he took the whole thing between his lips, I couldn't do anything but moan. I felt tension building in my body. *Holy hell.*

He spent plenty of time licking, sucking, and enjoying them. My body shivered with the need for release by the time he was finished. Moving back up my body, he kissed me again for a very long time. My hands managed to get his slacks down past his ass. When I brought them around to touch him, my breath caught when I wrapped my hand around him. He was so thick, so long. I swear, my eyes rolled in my head.

I wanted to give him the same as he gave me. I used my feet to push his pants down his legs, and he pushed them the rest of the way off. I arched my back into him, pushing with my hand on his hip. He walked back on his hands until he was kneeling in front of me. I got up on my knees, my mouth clamping onto one of his nipples. I felt the growl deep in his chest. I moved to the other one, my hand slowly moving over the length of him. My other hand reached for his balls.

When I wrapped them in my hand, they were so big and soft. I moved down his body, licking his seed off the tip, his body shivering as I did. My tongue loved his purple swollen head. Wrapping my lips around him, I drew him into my mouth. The man's whole body jumped. Slowly, I fucked him with my mouth. His ability to hold off was phenomenal. With each movement, I took him deeper and deeper. Opening my throat, I pushed him past the ring in my throat and swallowed.

"Arrggg," he moaned out. Again and again, I took him. So slowly, I massaged his balls, giving them a squeeze each time my nose touched him. It was fantastic to feel him. His hands wrapped around my head.

"I'm going to come," he whispered. I think he wanted me to stop, but I didn't. I took him one more time, squeezing his balls and swallowing. It was like making an angel cry, the groan that escaped him.

The way his body shattered beneath my mouth was life changing. So powerful.

This man altered me. In that moment, he became everything to me. Somehow, I knew he hadn't done this since his wife. Somehow, I knew I changed him, too. I made him feel, just like he made me feel. When I swallowed the last of his seed, his hands slowly moved me back, and he lifted my body onto his thighs. His eyes were full of pent emotion. My fingers ran along his lips. As his gaze met mine, I saw what I needed to see, what I needed to continue. He was like me, afraid of feeling, afraid of living. This man was not who I believed him to be. He moved slowly, kissing me, wrapping me into his body. Laying me back on the bed, he held me like only a lover could.

"So beautiful," he whispered on my lips. His hand cupping my breast, he gently squeezed, his thumb moving across my nipple. He took his time kissing me. There was nothing rushed. Words couldn't describe what was happening between us. I knew I'd never felt like this. I'd never been worshiped like this, and he was worshiping me.

Slowly, he pushed up, his eyes locked with mine as his hand moved to unbutton my jeans and pull the zipper down. Pushing up, I lifted my hips off the bed as he slid my jeans off, leaving my panties on. I watched as his eyes moved down my body. He shook his head as they came to rest on my lace-covered core. My back arched on its own as I felt the heat from his gaze on my body, my insides alive for the first time in my life.

He moved up, sliding his hand under my back, and gently rolled me over. Taking my hands, he put them above my head. For what seemed like an eternity, his mouth explored my body. He kissed, licked, sucked, and nipped at my skin. I felt his fingers move under the lace of my panties, and as he pulled them off, I lifted my hips off the bed. When they were gone, he turned me over carefully, his face at my stomach.

I think he waited for me to look at him before he pushed up. I watched as his eyes moved down to my core. Slowly, shaking his head, he smiled a little smile. "Fucking incredible," he moaned. His fingers trailed up my thighs, gently moving my legs apart. I was giving him everything I had. I didn't even know him, and he was giving me everything he had to give.

When his fingertips brushed along the hair, my body shook. I felt him move, and then I felt the warmth of his breath on me. At first, it was just a gentle brush of his lips along my inner self, then his tongue so gently and sweetly tasting me. "Fuck," he moaned when he drew his tongue back in his mouth.

He licked me just as his lips suckled my core, and I was gone. My back came all the way off the bed. "Mmm," I moaned. His mouth covered me as he drank me up. He took his time with me, slowly taking what I had to give and then making me give it to him again and again. It felt like my body was convulsing.

When he had his fill, he moved up, taking my knee in the crook of his elbow. His mouth covered mine as he so slowly pushed inside of me. My God, the man was huge but gentle. When our hips touched, he let go of my leg, his hands coming to rest on my face. Our eyes locked. Not looking away, he made love to me. So slow, so deep, so long. Our hands caressed each other's faces. Our lips and tongues moved with the rhythm of our bodies. It was never ending. It was perfect. It was mind blowing, life altering emotion.

Tears slowly spilled from my eyes. I felt nothing in this world but this man. There was no sorrow, no fear, not anything but him and the movement of our bodies, the feeling of complete and total annihilation of everything wrong in our lives. Nothing mattered to either of us, but us.

My body tightened. "That's it, beautiful," he whispered as he kissed me while I came, and then his warmth filled me as he gave a final thrust. We laid embracing one another, kissing for a long time. He gently rolled us over, with me on his chest, and he wrapped me in his arms while I cried.

Sleep took me, with his semi-erection still inside of me.

Paul

I was shattered. She was in my arms. Not the woman I thought I was getting to know, but someone totally different. Someone more destroyed than me. But fuck if I wasn't shattered. Not even with my wife had I felt this.

I had no idea who she was, or what her story was, and I didn't care. What I felt in that moment was right. It was the rightest feeling I had ever known. She gave herself to me. I made love to her. I hadn't made love to a woman since my wife, and it was nothing like this.

She felt so tiny in my arms, so perfect. It felt like a dream, a beautiful, wonderful dream. I was terrified of what would happen when she woke. What would become of us? I knew I'd crossed a line here. But fuck if it wasn't the greatest feeling in the world. I took her bare. I didn't even care that she could get pregnant. She felt better than anything I had ever known.

My fate was sealed tonight. Hell, who was I kidding? It was sealed that day in my brother's office. She was destroyed tonight, but she let me in. She let me see her. I kissed her head and let my eyes close.

I woke to the feel of her lips on my nipple. It was still dark out. I was hard nearly instantly. She pushed up, walking her hands up my chest, pushing me down into the mattress as she straddled my hips. I wanted to close my eyes and enjoy her, but somehow, I couldn't do it. I wanted to watch this incredibly beautiful woman make love to me. Her tiny hips rocked slowly on mine. God, she felt incredible. Her soft mews and moans made her all that more alluring. She took my hands from her hips and placed them on her breasts.

They just fit around them. I didn't realize just how full she was. Glorious. Fucking glorious. I was building slowly with her motions. I wanted to kiss her. Wrapping my arms around her, I slowly sat up, my mouth covering hers. She tasted like heaven. Her hands were in my hair, gently pulling it with each rock. We sat like this for so long, kissing and making love. I felt her tighten around me. Her teeth sank into my bottom lip as she let herself go, warming me even further with her release. I followed her. Who wouldn't? She was incredible.

We sat kissing for a long time, not talking. When I felt her move, I released my hold on her and she climbed off me and walked into the bathroom. I fell back on the bed. "Holy shit," I whispered. Never in my life.

I was terrified at the conversation I knew we would have in the morning. I couldn't let her go. I wouldn't let her go. She was who I wanted. I may not be ready for her but fuck if I was going to let her go.

The door opened, and I watched her walk across the room and climb back into bed with me. She snuggled into my side, and I wrapped myself around her, kissing her on the forehead.

◦∽◦

Victoria

When I walked out of the bathroom, my breath hitched in my chest. He was beautiful, so fucking beautiful. I shouldn't have been here, and I wanted to leave. I had every intention of leaving, but when I opened the door, I couldn't. Not yet. He looked so warm and inviting, so beautiful.

I needed to feel safe for a bit. I needed to feel cared for, and the way he made love to me, well, I felt very cared for. As I climbed back into the bed, his arms wrapped around me, pulling me to his side. His warmth was what I needed. What I wanted. I didn't ever want to leave his bed. But I knew, soon, it would be morning and I would have to face what I had done.

I gave him too much information about myself. He knew my real name. I couldn't work for his brother anymore. I'd blown my own cover. Closing my eyes, I really didn't care anymore. For nearly three years, I had been everyone but myself. Tonight, I wanted to be myself. I wanted to be myself with him.

His arms around me, his body around me, I was cocooned like a butterfly, and to be honest, it had never felt better. If my life was different, I would fight for him. But it couldn't be. I was after a murderer, a monster who'd taken a part of me and destroyed my life, changing me.

Is it time to give up the witch hunt? Is this the man who I've hunted? I didn't think he was. I really didn't. His wife was murdered as well, and I was pretty sure it was by the same man.

"Hey, you all right?" he whispered.

"Not sure," I whispered back.

"Do you want to talk?"

I smiled. "No, I'd like to make love again."

Turning on his side, his hand moved up to my face, tilting my head up. "Yeah?" he said in the sexiest baritone voice I'd ever heard.

I nodded as his mouth covered mine. Closing my eyes, I let my body go. His lips and his tongue were magic, loving and skilled. I felt his hand move to my hips, and he slightly turned my body away from him. Sliding it down to my thigh, his whole hand nearly wrapped around it, lifting me onto him.

With feather-light touches, he wisped the hair at my core, sending chills through me. His kiss never faltered. I felt him slowly push inside of me. God, he was so big. He felt so good. I was full, stretched to the limits, but he felt incredible.

After a few minutes, we worked out a rhythm, and for what felt like an hour, we made love, we kissed, we touched. His hands caressed my body everywhere they could reach. Just as my body started to build, his hand slowly moved to my core, his fingers gently pinched my bud, and my body reacted. Shaking, my orgasm ripped through me. I couldn't breathe. I had never felt this.

His hold on me tightened when he realized what was happening to me.

"I. Got. You," he softly grunted out as I felt him fill me with his warmth.

I didn't want to stop the tears when they came this time. He kissed my shoulder, slowly pulling out of me, turning me in his arms. His eyes locked on mine. "I've got you," he whispered as he wiped my tears. My arms wrapped around him, and he pulled me to his chest.

Who is this man? How is any of this possible? Why couldn't this be in another time, in another place? I couldn't stay here any longer. I think I did this so I would have to leave; I know I did. I just wanted to go home. But, for now, I didn't want this cocoon to end. I felt safe here in his arms. I didn't want to talk. I didn't want to do anything but lay in his arms and make love. He made me not feel anything but what was happening between us. Closing my eyes, I let sleep take me.

Paul

I woke to the sweet scent of the woman in my arms, the light from the day coming through the cracks in the drapes. I managed to untangle myself from her, making my way to the bathroom. I stood in front of the mirror looking at myself. My lips were swollen from her kisses. I noticed a mark on my shoulder, which brought a smile to my face. I hadn't had a hickey since I was a teenager, but I'd let her mark every inch of my body if she wanted.

I took care of my business, made my way to the closet to grab a pair of pajama bottoms, and left her to sleep while I made us some food. As I walked into the kitchen, my phone lit up on the counter. "Hello," I said after picking it up.

"Mr. Simon, are you all right?" Max rushed through his words.

I smiled. "I'm fine, Max. Listen, I'm not going anywhere today. Deal with people. I'm turning off my phone. Do not knock on my door or disturb me unless someone dies."

"Sir, your brother has called me several times. He has been trying to get in touch with you."

"Thank you, Max. I'll call him next." I hung up the phone and dialed John. "Hey, brother, what's up?"

"Well, it's nine-thirty, and I haven't heard from you and Miss Costello hasn't come to work yet. I can't get in touch with her either."

I chuckled. "About that, she won't be in today. She's not feeling well."

"Paul, what did you do?"

"I did nothing, brother. I think she has food poisoning or some-thing. She got sick last night on our way home, so I just brought her here, and I've been up most of the night taking care of her. She hasn't thrown up in about two hours, so I'm hoping it's passing."

"You brought her to your house?"

"Yes, is that a problem?"

"Umm, Paul, you've never taken a woman to your house."

I laughed. "She isn't just any woman, John. Don't worry. Listen, I just came out here to make her some tea. I'm shutting my phone off. I'm sure she will be fine and be in tomorrow."

"All right, well, tell her I hope she feels better."

"I will, brother. Talk soon."

I hung up the phone and put the food on plates. When I turned, she was standing at the entrance to the hall, leaning on the wall wearing my shirt, and fuck if she didn't wear it better than I ever could.

"So, I'm sick, eh?" She was smiling.

"It sounded like the right thing to say."

"Whatcha got there?" She moved toward me. God, she was fucking beautiful. Her hair was really red.

"I thought I'd make you breakfast in bed," I said as she took the tray out of my hands and set it on the counter. Running her hands gently up my chest, she wrapped them around my neck.

"Is that right?" She pressed on my shoulders, I lifted her, and she wrapped her legs around me.

"Yes," I moaned as I kissed her. "I think we are going to need some nourishment."

Her mouth covered mine. God, she tasted so good. My hands nearly fit around her tiny thighs. We stood there in the kitchen kissing, my fingers gently touching her core. I wanted to slip my fingers inside her, but she wasn't some whore. She deserved nothing but tenderness. I found her nub. Lifting her hood, I gently brushed it with my fingertip. Her body reacted to me instantly. She didn't make a huge production of her arousal like every other woman I'd been with. It was so intimate. Just the feel of her body and her reactions drove me to continue to make her feel everything. Her legs tightened around my hips as her body started to tremble, her kiss deepening.

She was fucking magnificent. I wanted, no, needed to be inside of her. I let go of her with my other hand and pushed my bottoms down, sliding her down on me as she contracted. Slowly, I turned and stepped to the wall, leaning her against it, her body already moving on me. So slow, so beautiful, so erotic. My hands moved to hold her face. I pulled back as her head leaned on the wall. Her lips were cherry red, wet and swollen, her mouth slightly open as we made love. I don't think I'd ever seen anyone more beautiful than the woman in my arms.

When she felt my body change just as I was about to release, she opened her eyes. Lifting her head, we locked eyes. There were no words; no words needed to be said. We were one and the same. Both holding our secrets, both with torn hearts and souls. The euphoria I felt as I let go buried inside the woman in my arms was mind altering. As my last pulse released, she sensed it and covered my mouth with hers, deeply kissing me. This was a kiss that was imbedded with love.

I should have been scared to my core, but I wasn't. How could I be? I was sealed to this woman. Never would another do for me but her. Our kiss said the same to me. I was the second man she had been with in her life, and I would be the last.

Pulling back, she whispered, "The food is getting cold."

I couldn't help it, I laughed. "I'll make more."

"Just put it in the microwave. Thirty seconds should do it." She released her legs. "I'm going to go to the bathroom."

I set her down and watched her walk away. I pulled up my bottoms and proceeded to warm our food up. As I walked into the bedroom, she was coming out of the bathroom. I waited for her to climb on the bed and then I joined her. We ate, not talking, just looking at one another. When we finished, I put the tray on the floor and laid down. She curled up at my side.

"Thank you," she whispered as her fingers circled my nipple.

"No need to thank me."

"Can I stay here today? I can't go home yet." Her words shocked me.

I rolled over so I could look at her. "Victoria, what happened that hurt you so badly?"

She shook her head. "I can't tell you right now. I can't even process it in my mind. I just need to feel anything other than that. I don't want it in my mind."

"If anyone understands that statement, it's me. You got it, beautiful. We can hide out here for as long as you want," I said tenderly, touching her face. I kissed her sweetly. "I got you, for as long as you need me."

She nodded and pulled herself into my arms. I held her for a long time. I couldn't imagine what hurt her so deeply. Whatever it was, it brought her to me. It opened my heart, the one thing I never believed would work again. Not like this, not so fast. She was becoming a part of my broken soul. If she let me, I would cherish her for the rest of her life.

We lay on the bed holding one another. "You want to take a shower with me?"

"Mmm, I'd like that. I saw your shower. It's huge."

I chuckled. "I'm a big guy. I need room to move."

She giggled as she rolled over, climbing off my bed. "I guess that explains the bed."

Jumping up, I followed her into the bathroom, closing the door behind us. I reached in and turned on the water as she slowly unbuttoned my shirt, my eyes watching every move she made. I'm pretty sure she was seducing me, and fuck if I wasn't going to enjoy it. When she finished, she put her hands to her side and just stood there looking at me. I stepped forward and slowly slipped my shirt off her shoulders. She was so tiny compared to me. Her breasts looked huge from this angle. I ran my fingers down her shoulders to her chest, down along her nipples which hardened even more, to the hair on her core. She slowly tilted her head up, her teeth buried in her lip.

"So fucking beautiful," I moaned out, kissing her.

Pulling back, she moved around me and stepped into the shower. I stood there looking at her. If it was possible, this woman looked even more tempting wet. She leaned against the wall looking at me. Dropping my bottoms on the floor, I stepped in the shower. We just stood with the water running over us, looking at each other. I watched as a small smile crossed her mouth. She reached for the body wash, squirting it in her hand, and moved behind me. "Put your hands on the wall," she whispered as she kissed my back. Who was I to argue with her? I stood with my legs parted slightly as she washed my back, down my ass, to my legs. It was slow and sensual. Never had a woman taken her time with me. Every swipe, every circle she made on my body was so erotic. Her hands left me, and then she moved in front of me, licking my nipples. Nipping one. Her hands started at my shoulders, and I stood watching her, feeling every touch, every fucking sensual touch. She saved my cock for last. By the time she got to it, I was rock hard.

I watched her as she took her time stroking me. Sometimes a firm grip, sometimes a soft grip. When I was on the brink of release, she stopped. After rinsing me off, she reached up and kissed me sweetly then moved her way down my body. *Fuck!* Her hand wrapped around my cock, the other one cupping my balls. Her eyes locked with mine as her head moved, her mouth surrounding me. "Ahh, fuck." She pushed me all the way down her throat, time and time again, swirling her tongue around me and making me crazy, so much so that my body betrayed me and I released to an earth shattering orgasm. Slowly, she stood up, wrapping her hands around my neck and kissing me. I could taste myself on her tongue.

When my body finally calmed down, I pulled out of our kiss. Removing my hands from the wall, I wrapped them around her wet body. I picked her up, leaning her against the wall, and made love to her mouth. She felt like the finest silk. "So beautiful," I whispered on her lips.

Pulling back, she opened her eyes. They were filled with desire. "Let me get you cleaned up," I whispered on her lips, as I set her down.

She smiled and turned back around, placing her hands on the wall. Washing this woman was a religious experience. My hands slid across her skin, setting me on fire. Her breasts were exquisite, wet and soapy. I could feel my cock getting harder. I had no idea how this was happening to me. Our bodies were so in tune that mine fed off hers, and hers off of mine.

I rinsed her off, and we left the shower. As we stood drying off, her hand reached for me, wrapping around my cock. She gently pumped me, pulling her lip between her teeth. I felt like I was in a dream world, like we'd crossed over into the twilight zone or something. Her touch was loving, sensual. *Who is this woman? I can't wait to find out.* When she finished getting me fully hard, she released me and walked out of the room.

I finished drying off, my eyes not leaving her perfect ass. God, she was fucking perfect. My feet moved into the bedroom as she slowly climbed up on my bed

When I laid on the bed next to her, she shook her head and got up. I watched her walk to the bathroom and grab my shirt, then she left the room. I went after her. She was standing in the corner of the dining room, facing the wall with her hands on her mouth, screaming into them. "Hey, beautiful. What happened?" I wanted to grab her, hold her. I watched helplessly as she shook, crying silently in the corner.

Victoria

It was too much, and I couldn't handle it. He was perfect. Everything about him was perfect. The way he touched me, cared for me, made love to me, fucked me; it was all perfect and tender and gentle. I couldn't handle it. I couldn't handle this. With Steven, I knew now it was just sex. I came here to forget him, and I learned that he was already forgotten. The minute Paul touched me, he was forgotten.

This was all so unfair to Paul. He had no idea that when he woke, I would be gone. Never to be found again. I could feel him behind me, the tension rolling off him, and the only thing I could think about was how much this was going to hurt when I left. Just like with Steven, all

I did was leave. I felt my knees buckle, and when I went down, he went down with me.

"Please, Victoria, talk to me."

I turned, putting my hand on his face. "I'm so sorry for this, for doing this. For being here like this," I whispered.

He shook his head. "No, don't be sorry. I'm not. Did I hurt you?"

I shook my head. I needed to leave. I took his hand and stood up. We went back in the bedroom and climbed in bed. I needed for him to sleep so I could leave, because he wouldn't understand. He would want to take me home. But I wasn't going back there. I couldn't. We snuggled up. "I'm just so tired."

He chuckled. "Me too, beautiful. I feel like I could sleep for a week."

Soon, he was sleeping, a little snore escaping his mouth. I moved slowly from his embrace, waiting by the bed to see if he woke. I moved quickly through his room, gathering my clothes. I left my panties; they were dirty and I had a long way to go. I took his shirt and left. I didn't go back to my apartment. I was sure Al and Jacob were waiting for me, so I headed to the airport. Once there, I made my way to the lockers and grabbed my backpack, then went to the bathroom to change my appearance. Once my wig was in place, I headed to British Airways and got a flight out. I was leaving it all behind. I needed to refuel my heart.

CHAPTER SEVEN

PAUL

When I woke, I was alone. Smiling, I stretched and looked at the bathroom door, but it was open, and the light was off. My heart started pounding in my chest. "Victoria," I called out, but only silence greeted me. I got up, turning on the light. "Victoria?" Nothing. I moved to the bathroom to grab my bottoms. As I was walking out, I noticed her white lace panties on the floor. I picked them up, realizing that the rest of her clothes were gone. "No, no, no, beautiful." I turned and ran into the living room. Empty. Spinning around, I looked for a note, something, anything. But there was nothing.

My heart now slamming in my chest, I could hear it beating in my ears. Picking up my phone, I turned it on and called her.

I'm sorry but the number you have dialed has been disconnected. Please try your call again.

"Fuck!" I yelled.

I dialed Max. "Mr. Simon."

"Max, have you seen Miss Costello?"

"No, sir, not since yesterday. Is everything all right?"

"No, she's gone. Ask the guys if anyone saw her leave."

"All right, I'll be up in a few."

I hung up and went to get dressed. I was going to her house. It was the only place she could be. Or the beach... she liked the beach. I opened the door, and Max was standing there. "No one has seen her."

"Send some of the guys to Oak Street Beach and have them search the place. Come on, I need you to take me to her apartment."

"Sir, you don't look so well."

"Max, I know you have only been with me for a few years, and you may not know this, but I was married for a long time. I got myself in a bit too deep with this guy, and when I refused to play his way, he murdered my wife and our unborn child. If I'm being honest, I'm terrified something has happened to her."

"Shit, come on, let's hurry. Even though she can beat my ass, I like her. She's got spunk."

"That she does."

We made it to her building in less than ten minutes. Traffic this late was minimal. When the elevator stopped, I ran out to her door. Knocking, I waited. When the door handle moved, my heart lurched. But it wasn't her who opened the door. Her boyfriend, Jacob, was standing there. "Is she here?" I asked, nearly shouting.

"No, we had a fight yesterday and I haven't seen her. Have you?"

I wanted to hurt the bastard. "Yeah, she called me. She's been at my place until sometime tonight. She was in pretty bad shape. What the hell did you fight about that would destroy her like that?"

Jacob played his part. "We fought about you. Tell me, Mr. Simon, did you fuck my girlfriend?"

"No, like I said, she was a mess." I didn't lie. I didn't fuck her, not really. I made love to her, so if he had asked me that, I wonder if I would have lied. It didn't matter really. "So, you haven't seen her?"

"No, now if you'll excuse me." He went to shut the door.

I pushed back. "You wouldn't mind if I check for myself." It wasn't a question or a suggestion. It was a statement of fact. I stepped into her house while he protested. I moved from room to room, looking, but nothing. Her clothes hung in the closet, her things in the bathroom. Nothing was out of order. I heard voices as I was walking out of her room. When I got to the living room, there were three other men in the room with Jacob. "What the hell is going on?"

"Mr. Simon, my name is Al Bower. I think it's time we had a conversation."

"Do you know where she is?"

"No, we do not, and that is why we need to have a chat. Please." He motioned to the chair in the living room. I sat down, as did they.

"Well, Mr. Bower, I'm sitting. What do you know?"

"I know who killed your wife," he said.

He could have shot me. "What the fuck do you know of my wife?" Man, I was pissed.

He dropped a file on the table. I picked it up, and no one said a word while I read through it. Jesus, they had my entire life in this file. "I was a mark?" I whispered.

"No, you were our prime suspect."

I looked up at him. "Were?"

"Yes, were. We no longer believe you to be this man. Although, we knew of the death of your wife, it wasn't until you told Suzanne the story behind her death that we figured it all out." *He said Suzanne! Her name is Victoria. What the fuck.*

"You said you know who killed her. Who was it?" I was doing everything to hold back my anger.

"A man named Andy Marciano. Do you know this man?" His eyes never left mine.

I was registering what he said. *Fucking Marciano.* "You said, our prime suspect. Who is Miss Costello?"

"I'm afraid, Mr. Simon, I can't tell you that. She must stay protected. Her anonymity is our only assurance she will stay alive."

"What aren't you telling me?" I asked.

"Mr. Simon, there is a contract on her life. But the fact that no one knows what she looks like is the only thing that is keeping her alive."

I threw the file on the table. "That's bullshit. Who would want to hurt her?"

"The only way you are going to have this information is if you agree to help us. She has disappeared while she was with you. We have no idea where she is or who she has become. This is bigger than you know. So, if you want to help us and avoid prosecution for the crimes you have committed, we will agree to give you all the information we are allowed."

I started pacing, running every conversation I had with her through my head, everything she said to me. The pieces to her distress and her frame of mind fell into place. I turned and looked at Jacob. "You're not her boyfriend?" He shook his head at me. "Did she play me?"

"No, Mr. Simon, she fought us tooth and nail concerning you. I ordered her to get close to you, and she refused."

She refused, so she came to me on her own terms. She didn't share what we'd shared together with anyone; instead, she left. What we shared was real. My heart started to hurt. She left to save me, to protect me. *God, beautiful, where did you go?*

"Mr. Simon, if she ran, she did it under cover."

"What does that mean? If? What aren't you saying?"

"Do you agree to help us?" Mr. Bower asked.

I needed to find her. I needed to know if what we shared was part of her job. I already knew the answer, or at least I hoped, but I needed her to confirm it. I'd wanted that bastard to pay since Sylvia was murdered. I just couldn't find him. I had done some things that would warrant prison time.

"You'll clear my charges?" He nodded. "You'll get me out of the shit I'm in?" He nodded again. "When this is done, you'll tell me where she is?"

"I don't know where she is, Mr. Simon."

"You'll help me find her when this is done?"

"I will do everything in my power to help you. Yes."

"Then I'm in. Now, tell me who she is."

"Her name is Victoria." He took a deep breath. I looked around the room at the other men. They were all acting strange. "She is, or was, British Intelligence."

"Are you fucking kidding me?"

"No, Mr. Simon, I am very serious. She was dis-involved, at her request, six years ago when she became pregnant. Unfortunately, although she has no knowledge of this, someone made an attempt on her life in order to control her brother, and she lost the baby. It was such a traumatic accident that left her no longer able to have children."

"So, she's married?"

"No. Well, it will be three years in a few days that her brother and his wife were murdered. His wife was pregnant, and the baby survived. When she received the phone call from MI6, she left her husband, took the baby, and went into hiding. About a year later, we finally caught a break and discovered Andy Marciano as the source of his death. He is an arms dealer, selling out to the highest bidder. When Victoria was informed of our findings, she volunteered to be reinstated." *So, she's after Marciano.*

"Why?"

"Mr. Simon, Victoria holds exceptional skills."

"Yeah, I know. She leveled two of my men without breaking a sweat."

"Yes, but besides her physical attributes, she also has an eidetic memory. She doesn't forget a damn thing she sees."

I closed my eyes, remembering how she looked at me, her fingers tracing my face. She was memorizing me. Her submission to me was real.

"She is close to finding Mr. Marciano, closer than anyone has come."

"Why do you need me?"

Two of the men got up and walked to the door. I watched them, and as I turned my head back to Mr. Bower, he said. "After we analyzed all the information she has gathered in her six months here, we know who he is. Although, we believed him to be you, she was very adamant that it was not you. She was more afraid of you as a man than she was of you being Mr. Marciano. She was the one who brought it to our attention that he or his name was an alias. Like a shell company. Finding him was like looking for a dummy corporation. But we have, in fact, discovered who he is."

I sat there looking at him, my mind running in twenty different directions. "What aren't you saying?"

"There is a great deal, Mr. Simon, that I cannot disclose to you right now." The look in his eyes was saying something different. I needed to figure it out. "Our problem now that Victoria is missing is our access to him. That and the fact that we don't know if she has disappeared on her own accord, or if she was taken. I'm afraid it will be at least a week until we can verify that."

"So, what do you want from me?" *None of this is right. It's a smoke screen, but why?*

He reached in his pocket and handed me a phone. "Do not turn it on unless you need to contact us. Then only send a text to the number programmed into the phone. Afterwards, delete the text and turn the phone off. Keep it someplace safe, and please do not let anyone know you have it." His eyes gave off that look again. *What the fuck am I missing here?* "If we need to contact you, a message will be in your mailbox, and the return address will be the Art Institute."

"What am I supposed to do?"

"Live your life. Continue cleaning up your life. Do what you've been doing and don't tell a living soul what is going on. No one, Mr. Simon, and I mean no one. We will get in touch with you when we have information concerning Victoria."

I shook my head. "No, I need to find her. I need to make sure she is fine." I think my panicked tone sparked something inside him.

"What aren't you telling me, Mr. Simon?"

"Yesterday, when she called me, I found her on her hands and knees on the beach. She was destroyed. What happened to her? I know her frame of mind, and it wasn't her normal self."

I watched as he looked at the other men. One of them nodded. He turned to look at me. "Yesterday, she discovered that her husband had divorced her and remarried and is having a child. She actually fainted when it was confirmed."

My mind whirled a million miles a minute. She came to me because the man she loves wasn't waiting for her. She said that she wasn't available to me, but when she discovered she was, she came to me. She gave herself to me.

I stood up and walked to the door. "Mr. Simon, not a word to anyone."

"No one," I said softly.

"Not a soul," he reinforced.

I walked out of there with more questions than I had answers. *What was I going to do? Where could I start looking?*

CHAPTER EIGHT

VICTORIA

I held it together all the way across the Pacific. It wasn't until I rented a car to drive myself to Surrey, when I got away from the airport, I pulled over. I let the pain out. It took everything I had to walk out of his apartment, to leave him lying in the bed naked and sedate. This pain was worse than when I left Steven.

I still couldn't believe he remarried. I really couldn't blame him, since I just up and left him. I wondered what he would do if I just showed up. Shaking my head, I knew I couldn't do that. I needed to keep moving. I needed to get to my love. I knew there was a price on my head, but I also knew he wasn't looking for me. I pulled myself together, and I drove. Hours passed until I dropped the car off. I jumped in a taxi and headed home. Home to my world, to my beautiful little cottage, to my beautiful little life.

When I pulled up, it was late. Walking up to the house, my heart was racing. It was still as beautiful as the day I bought it. Using my key, I let myself in and made my way through the house to the door that held my heart. Slowly, I opened it. There she was, her tiny body in her big girl bed. I popped my shoes off, pulled my wig off, and crawled in bed with her. My eyes closed, and sleep greeted me with open arms.

When the light from the new day crossed my eyes, I opened them to the feel of a tiny hand on my face. To see her beautiful face next to mine. Her hair was longer, full of curls. Her bedroom door opened as Ruth came in the room. I put my fingers to my lips. I saw her tears as she nodded and left us. My love's face was chubbier, her pouty lips fuller. I looked in her mouth, seeing she had all her teeth. I missed so much on this fucked up mission. But I needed for her to be safe, to stay safe. For Johnathan, I needed her to live a long life.

Her hand moved along my cheek. She was still doing the sucking thing with her little mouth. My tears just came. So innocent, so pure. I would die for her. She opened her eyes and blinked a few times.

"Uh, Momma?" she whispered.

"Hi, beautiful, Happy Birthday," I whispered back.

She threw herself at me, hugging me. I couldn't stop the tears. She had never called me Momma before. She felt so good in my arms, and she smelled like heaven. She pulled back.

"Don't cry, Momma. I love you."

"I love you, too, beautiful. It's your birthday."

"Are you my present?"

"Would it be okay if I was?"

She nodded. "Yes."

I laughed. "Come on, let's go see what Ruth has to eat. I'm so hungry."

She giggled. "Ruth is making panny cakes for me. 'Cause it's my birthday."

"Well, I love panny cakes."

Together, we walked into the kitchen holding hands. Ruth hugged me, and we ate while I told them of my adventure.

"Are you leaving again?" she said with a sad voice.

"Just one more time, and then I am never leaving you again. I just have one more thing to do, and then we will live here in our cottage forever. I promise."

"But you are here now."

"I am, and I am so looking forward to making cookies with you and to walking along the beach."

Her smile said it all for me. She finished her pancakes and got down to go with Ruth to get dressed. I walked over to my backpack and took out her present. I sat it on the little table by the door so she could find it. Ruth walked into the room.

"How are you, my dear?"

I looked at her. "Not so good, but I'm better now. Where's Joanna?"

"She is gathering up all the pictures she's drawn for you."

I smiled. "Ruth, I can't thank you enough for taking care of her."

"It has been my pleasure."

"I'm going to be home for a week or two. Why don't you take a vacation or something?"

She smiled. "I think I might miss you two too much. But I wouldn't mind a few days away. Are you sure?"

"So sure. I just want to reconnect with her. She called me Momma this morning."

Ruth smiled and moved to the kitchen.

I heard Jo running down the hallway. "Momma, where are you?"

"In here, beautiful."

She came running in with her arms full of drawings. We sat on the sofa while she showed me each one and told me what it was. We were there for over an hour. Then we went for a walk on the beach. She had grown so much in the six months I'd been gone. So smart just like her dad. One day, I would tell her about him, when she was old enough to understand.

By the time we got back to the house, Ruth had lunch ready. We ate, laughing and talking, then it was nap time. I wanted to take a shower and feel normal again.

I walked into my room. Nothing had changed; it was a bit dusty but nothing else. I stripped and got in the shower. I didn't want to wash his scent off me, but I needed to feel clean. As I washed my body, my mind kept flashing to his hands on me. To his lips, his body, his mouth. I thought I might have fallen in love with him. The physical part of us was electric. I didn't have the chance to know the mental part of him. It didn't matter. He was just what he was. A way to make the pain stop.

As I sat on my bed, putting lotion on my legs, I kept hearing a crinkling sound like paper being squished. When I pulled back my blanket, I found a few pictures that Jo had drawn. They looked like Ruth and a man. I knew it wasn't me, because Ruth had short brown hair, but the last time Jo saw me, my hair was long and its natural red.

There was one of her and a man, and his hands were on her arms. There was one of Ruth, and she looked like she was crying. Then there was one with the man's hand raised. My heart was racing. *Why are these in my bed? Was Jo so scared that she drew them? Did she think she would get in trouble for drawing them?* She drew so well for a three-year-old. I looked at the door. I took the pictures and put them in my bottom drawer under my sweats, then headed out to watch Ruth. Something was not right, and my three-year-old niece knew it. Of course, she knew it; she was her father's daughter.

Walking into the kitchen, I grabbed a glass of water and sat on the counter. "I'm going to run into town and grab a few things," I said. "Do you need anything?"

"Oh no, dear, but I've called my sister. I'm going to be leaving in the morning. Could you give me a ride into town?"

"Of course." I jumped down. "I'll be back in a little bit."

I went and got in the car. Something was very wrong, because Ruth didn't have a sister. I thought it was her way of telling me something was not right. I drove to town. I wasn't being followed, so I couldn't be sure if I was on the right track or not. I parked and got out of the car. I went to a few stores, bought a phone in one. I sent three messages. Then I went to the hardware store and bought a few things, then to the drug store for a few others. Then to the grocery store for a few more things.

On my way back to the house, I made my plan.

We had a lovely afternoon, then dinner, then cake. Jo didn't find her present, so I put it back in my backpack and took it to my room. I needed to get some supplies for tomorrow. I knew we would be followed. I was so pissed. I was in the bathroom, getting my guns out from behind the claw foot tub, when the phone vibrated in my pocket.

Pulling it out, I checked the message. My heart relaxed a bit. Now to wait for plan A.

I didn't sleep well; in fact, I don't think I slept at all. I found myself looking out the windows all night. *Come on, you fucker. I've waited a long time for this.* I kept thinking, *I should just leave here and leave Jo with Ruth*, but he knew now. He knew about her. I needed to protect her at all costs.

When the sun started rising, I was half-asleep when a glint of light flashed outside. I jerked my head toward it. Grabbing my binoculars, I spied someone sitting in the patch of trees a few hundred yards away. I grabbed my knife and a gun and headed out the back door. I worked my way around behind him. Low and behold, a man with a rifle sat nice and secluded. I listened for a minute to him talking to someone.

"No, no movement yet. No, the boss said to wait until she returns from dropping off the old lady. Not the kid. The kid stays with the old woman. Just the woman. Just stay low. If we screw this up, we are toast."

He had an American accent, and there were two of them. *Well, boys, aren't you in for a surprise?* I made my way back to the house, back to my room. It had been fifteen hours, so everyone should have been here. Now, I hoped my plan worked or I'd be dead.

Paul

I spent the day pacing back and forth. I didn't know what to do. I called John just to talk, but his phone went to voice mail. I called his secretary, but she said he had to suddenly go out of town on business and that he would be back in a day or two.

Not thinking, I didn't ask where he had gone. I couldn't eat. I couldn't sleep. I had nothing. How could one person just disappear into thin air? I sat in the chair by the window in my room looking at my bed. I couldn't bring myself to get in it. I must have dozed off, because when my phone rang, I nearly jumped out of my skin. "Hello."

"Hey, brother, Jill said you called. Everything all right?"

"Oh, yeah, I just had some free time. I thought we'd hang out."

He laughed. "Well, I'm in London. I had some business to finalize. Fucking company decided to sell at the last minute, so I had to get my ass over here."

"Oh, yeah, the one you've been going back and forth about. I remember you going over there a few times."

"Yeah, but hey, I need to go. You sure everything is all right?"

He sounded strange. "Yeah, let's do dinner when you get back."

"Sounds like a plan. We can celebrate my success."

"Deal."

He hung up, and I just sat there looking at my phone. It was one in the afternoon in London. That didn't make sense. My phone chimed with a text message from an out of area number. Swiping to the messages, I opened it.

~Surrey Quay Shopping Mall, Discovery Planet shop. Please, Paul, I need you.

V~

I started a search, only to discover she was in London. My heart jumped. I grabbed my passport and ran out the door. Max dropped me off at my plane, and we took off ten minutes later. Once we were in the air, I got up and started pacing. *How did she get to London? Why was she in London?* She was MI6. Shit, she was British. Closing my eyes, I searched our conversations, trying to pick up a hint of an accent. Nothing, she was good.

I pulled the other cell phone out of my pocket and turned it on. I had WIFI up here and wondered if the phone worked. Once it loaded, there was nothing. Turning it off, I put it back in my pocket and started pacing again.

Was she setting me up? No, that didn't make sense. They knew I wasn't Marciano. But they knew who was. *Did he find her? Did he figure out who she was?* I had eight hours before I'd even be on the ground. I needed to chill the fuck out. I sat back down and tried to relax.

I let my mind wander to us making love. She was glorious. Then the fucking. Listening to her finally get a little vocal. My eyes flew open. She did have a British accent. I could hear her say the word God. I smiled. All the clues were right in front of me. But the one thing I couldn't figure out was why she was working for my brother. Closing my eyes, I tried to get some sleep. I must have dozed off because I jerked awake when the plane touched down. Jesus.

As I was walking through the airport to security, I kept going over the conversation with Bower. He said that they figured out who Marciano was because of the work she did there. But they thought it was me. "Oh my God." It hit me. *'Don't tell anyone.' 'Not a living breathing soul.' 'London.' 'Surrey.'*

My brother was Andy Marciano.

He killed Sylvia.

He killed her brother.

He was there to kill her.

"What the fuck," I whispered.

Oh my God, she is going to kill my brother.

I had to stay calm. She was a trained agent, so I was positive I am not the only one who she called. She wasn't stupid. But she had a child with her. *How old did they say it was?* Three, yes three years old. *How is she going to protect a three-year-old?* I picked up my pace again. Oh my God, this was the longest fucking terminal. It took forever, but I made it through security and stood outside looking for a cab.

Finally, I waved one down. "Can you take me to the Surrey Quay Shopping Mall, please?"

"Sure thing. You here on vacation?"

"No, I'm here to meet my girlfriend." I smiled when I said it. I should have said my future wife, but that would have sounded weird.

Victoria

We had our breakfast and then I changed Jo. "But, Momma, I want to wear a pretty dress."

"But, sweetie, we need to wear jeans and our tennis shoes today. I promise, when we get home, you can wear a pretty dress. Momma will wear one, too. Oh, I know, we can stop and get matching ones at the shops."

That perked her up, so she didn't fight me anymore. When we walked down the hall, Ruth was waiting for us. "Everyone ready now?" Jo smiled and nodded. Ruth looked at me funny, like it was the last time she was going to see me. She shocked me when she grabbed me up in a hug. "You take care now."

I laughed. "Ruth, you'll be back in two days."

"I know, I know." She knelt and grabbed Jo in her arms. I heard her say. "You stay safe, little one."

I didn't say anything. She would get hers for conspiring against me. "You've got everything?" I asked her. She nodded to the door. I thought it a little odd that she was taking such a big bag for just two nights. I wondered what she had in there. "Here, let me get your bag for you."

"Oh, no, I've got it. Don't be silly." She moved over and picked it up.

When we walked out of the house, I made sure to stay one step ahead of her. I put Jo in her car seat and then got in the driver's seat. It took about fifteen minutes to get to town where I dropped Ruth off at the bus stop. I spotted Jacob, who was standing a few feet away from her. I nodded to him, so he knew who she was. We said our goodbyes, and I drove away, headed to Surrey.

Pulling up to the mall, I parked as close to the door as I could get. We went in and shopped for a little bit. As promised, we bought two dresses that matched. "Would you like to go to Discovery Plant and see what's new there?"

I knew she liked the store because Ruth would often take her. Her eyes got big, and she nodded at me. Holding her hand, we made our way to the other side of the mall. I could see the sign up ahead. I was nervous and excited, hoping he would be there waiting for me, for us. The closer we got, the faster my heart beat. When the doorway came into view, my heart sank when I didn't see him waiting for me. *Shit!*

Jo was pulling on my hand. "Come on, Momma. There it is."

I smiled at her big brown eyes. "I know, I see it."

As fast as her little legs would take her, she tugged me through the doors and into the store. She pulled me from one display to the next, entranced by all the cool things. We laughed and giggled as she showed me all her favorite characters. I was so caught up in her excitement that I stopped worrying about Paul. If he didn't come, then we would go to plan B.

I was on my knees while we looked inside a giant fish tank. She had found a fish that looked like Nemo and one that looked like Dory. "Momma, look its Dory."

"I see, she sure is pretty."

"Do you think she will talk to me? Just keep swimming," she sang.

"I'm not so sure fish can talk." His baritone voice sent electricity right through me.

Jo giggled. "She talks in the movie."

"Yes, but I'm not sure she can talk here. What if everyone heard her? It would be crazy in here. People would want to take her home."

I just knelt there looking at him. His eyes met mine. "Hi, beautiful."

"You came," I whispered.

He smiled. "I did."

Jo looked at me. "Momma, is he your friend?"

My eyes moved to hers. "Yes, sweetie, this is my friend, Paul." I looked at Paul. "Paul this is my daughter, Joanna."

He put his hand out to shake hers. "Very nice to meet you," he said, "but I'm more than your momma's friend. I'm her boyfriend."

Jo turned to me. "Momma, what's a boyfriend?"

I laughed. "He's a boy, and he's my friend." That seemed to satisfy her.

"So, this accent is new," he smarted.

I just smiled at him. "I'm sorry I left."

"No, you're not, but I know why you left so I forgive you."

I laughed. "Oh yeah, how do you know?"

"Bower and Jacob told me everything that they could."

My heart jumped. He knew about Steven. I looked at him, my hand reaching to touch his arm. "What we did, it was about us, nothing more."

"I know. We are going to have a long talk." He looked at Jo. "Hey, Joanna, seeing as how this is a special day, would you like to get some ice cream?"

"Only if Momma can come."

He laughed. "Of course, she can come."

We stood up and I took Jo's hand. I watched as Paul reached down and Jo put her other hand in his. Together, we walked out into the courtyard. Jo tugged us along to the ice cream shop where Paul bought her a huge ice cream.

"Joanna, you can't possibly eat all of that."

"Paul is going to help me." She turned to look at him. "Right?"

He laughed. "Right."

They sat there eating, and he kept looking at me. "You should have some. It's really good."

"Momma doesn't like ice cream," Jo said.

I just looked at her and smiled. "How do you know that, sweetheart?"

She smiled as I wiped her chin. "Ruth told me."

"Did she now?"

Jo nodded. My eyes shifted from her to Paul. "We need to talk," I said softly.

His smile touched his eyes. "Oh, I know we do. But, right now, we are having ice cream." His eyes softened. "It'll be fine," he whispered.

Just looking into his eyes, I wanted to believe him, but I knew that wasn't the case. My house was being staked out with men toting high powered rifles. My live-in babysitter had turned me over to Marciano. My niece's life was in danger, and I was sitting here watching the man I might be in love with and my daughter, who isn't actually my daughter, eat ice cream. Life sure was weird.

"Momma, I'm tired."

"All right, then we should get going." I wiped her face.

I stood to pick her up, and Paul stooped down and said to her, "Can I carry you? Momma has to carry all the bags."

She nodded her little head. Paul picked her up, and she snuggled right into his neck. "He smells good, Momma."

I smiled as tears filled my eyes. "I know, baby."

His hand came up, and he wiped my tears. Pulling me into his chest, he whispered, "I was so fucking scared. I think I'm in love with you. Don't do that again, beautiful."

I couldn't talk. I just nodded into his chest.

Jo put her hand on my face. "Don't cry, Momma," she whispered.

"These are happy tears, baby."

She smiled and wrapped her little arm around his neck. "Come on," he whispered, taking my hand. We walked through the mall; it seemed to be the safest place for the minute. "Victoria, why did you leave?"

"Because I didn't want you to be part of the job. I was ordered to get close to you. I refused. I...I..."

"Are you still in love with your husband?" he asked softly.

"Until that day, yes, I believed that I was."

"And now?" His voice was barely above a whisper.

"Now, my heart hurts for you. I gave you me, all of me. I think I'm terrified you don't want me for anything other than what that was."

He stopped, pulling me into his chest. "That was me giving you me. Aww, beautiful, words cannot tell you what that was for me."

I tilted my head up. "So, you want me?" I almost didn't hear my own voice.

His mouth came down on mine, kissing me deeply in a crowded mall. "With all that I am."

The only thing I could do was nod. He put his arm around my shoulder and pulled me to his side, and we started walking. "So, Bower filled me in. My question is, why am I here?"

"I need you to take Jo." I pulled the paper out of my back pocket. "I want to know, if anything happens to me, that you will take her, keep her and raise her?"

He stopped walking. When I looked up at him, I couldn't read his eyes. He looked around then grabbed my hand, leading me to a bench.

We sat down. "Victoria, why would you ask me that? We don't really know each other."

"You're wrong," I whispered. "The safest I've ever felt was in your arms. It's why I came to you. I just needed to feel safe, and somewhere inside of me, somehow, I knew that in your arms was the only place I would feel that way. I know you might think you know what my life has been these past few years, but you only know what Al told you. Jo is comfortable with you. Look at her." I reached up to touch her face. "I can only do this, finish this, if I know she is safe. And she's not. I found drawings stuffed under my covers of Ruth, the woman who's been taking care of her, and a man. That's how I knew something wasn't right. Then, early this morning, I discovered two men sitting in the tree line of my cottage with high powered rifles. I am only here because a deal was made with Ruth and Marciano. She is to get Jo when he kills me. I don't believe that. He is going to kill Jo, as well."

He pulled me into his chest and kissed my forehead.

"There's more. Jacob got Ruth before she got on the bus. She told me she was going to see her sister. I think she was trying to warn me; she doesn't have a sister. My house is wired for sound and with cameras. He knows I know he's here. I just need for her to be in the safest place, and I believe that to be with you." I couldn't stop the tears. "Please, Paul, I can't do this if I know she is in danger."

"Victoria, there are some things I need to tell you. Yes, I will keep her, but you aren't doing this alone."

"I know the team is here. I need to end him."

Shaking his head, he continued. "You are not understanding what I'm saying. I will take Jo, but only if I get her mother, as well. I want a life with you. Bower is clearing my underhanded life. When it's over, I'll have a clean slate, and I want it with you and with Jo. But, and there is always a but, you are not walking into this alone."

"I won't risk your life," I snapped.

He just smiled at me. "You won't be. I know who Marciano is."

I searched his eyes. He was telling me the truth. "Who?"

"Do you have another option for Jo?" he asked softly. I nodded. "Implement it, and we will do this together. I'm not letting you walk away from me this time. I think I'm in love with you, and I am not letting you go. Not today, not tomorrow, and certainly not next week." He pulled me in and kissed me. "Now, let's get this over with. I have this insane need to be inside of you," he whispered.

I felt my face flush as I pulled my phone from my pocket. I sent my text. "Fifteen minutes, on the East side of the mall."

"Well, then, let's get moving. The sooner this ends, the sooner I can make love to you," he whispered in my ear.

I smiled and we made our way to the Eastern doors of the mall. Waiting for us was an old colleague of mine. I hugged her. "Thanks so much for doing this."

"Any day of the week. Johnathan was my friend, as well. I will keep her safe," she said.

"This is Paul Simon. If I don't come back, he will come for her. He has all the paperwork. He'll take her back to America and raise her as his own."

She smiled at him then looked at me. "You are, or were, the best agent we've ever had. I know you will be fine. You know where we'll be."

I handed her the backpack. "Everything is in there. Please, make sure Paul gets it."

He handed Jo over to her, kissing her on the forehead. I hugged my friend and my daughter. Kissing her, I whispered, "I love you to the moon and back." Looking at my friend, I said, "With your life."

She nodded and walked out the door. I couldn't stop the tears as I watched the only person I had left who was my blood walk away. Paul pulled me into his arms. "We will come back. Come on, we have a great deal to talk about."

He tried to turn me away, but I couldn't look away, not until I knew they were fine. I watched a car turn into the lane. Shaking my head, I took off out the door, pulling my gun from the back of my jeans. Paul was right behind me. The back door of the car opened as the car slowed down. When a man got out of the car, I shot him in the chest. Kathy turned to shield Jo. Another man opened the front door, but by this time, I was ten feet from him. I shot him in the head, and the car took off. I kept moving until I got to Kathy and Jo.

"You're not safe. What happened?"

"There was only one person who knew I was coming here," she said.

Paul ran up. "My plane is at Heathrow. Come on." He took Jo. I stopped to look at the men. "Fucking Johnny McDonald. Bastard." I looked at Paul. "Marciano is definitely here."

"I know, come on."

We made our way back to Heathrow via taxis. "Here are the keys to my apartment. I will have a man named Max Hinkle meet you at the airport. He will die protecting you. Stay in my apartment. It's a fortress."

"I think we should fly commercial," Kathy said.

"Too many variables. This plane gets you into a private hanger when you land. No people," I said.

Kathy nodded and they got on the plane. We stood and waited until it took off, then we rented a car.

～

Paul

"I have an apartment in London. I'm going to take us there," I said.

"No, we can't, not now. We need to keep moving." She was in a panic. I watched her reach in her back pocket and pull out a phone. "The cottage is staked out. They got the shooters. We need to go back there." She was reading a text. Then she dialed. "Jacob, talk to me." She hit speaker phone.

"There were four men in the tree line, but we got them all. They are tucked away."

"And my cottage?"

"Too many devices to find them all. We know they are there, so we have a scrambler in place."

"No, leave them alone. He knows I'm here. They tried to get to Kathy and Jo. I killed McDonald and one other goon. We have them stashed, so I know they are safe. We are about a half an hour out. This happens today, do or die. I'm out when it's finished."

"We'll be waiting." The phone went dead.

I didn't say anything; I was lost in my own thoughts. Something wasn't right. "Victoria, I know you are good at your job, and I would trust your instincts before anything else, but I've got a few things to tell you." I pulled over in a little turn around once we were out of the city.

Reaching over, I took her hand. "Come, let's walk. Leave your phone."

She looked at me and dropped her phone in the center compartment. I did the same. We got out of the car and walked out into the English countryside where we sat down facing one another. "Paul, you're freaking me out."

"Yeah, well, I'm going to blow your mind in a minute. Since you left, so much shit has happened. Things I don't think you are aware of. Things you couldn't possibly know, but from what I understand about you, you remember everything you see and hear." She nodded her head. "Okay, after you left, I went to your apartment. Jacob and Bower were there with two other men, who I didn't know and who didn't speak. That is where I agreed to be a part of this, in exchange for clearing my name and then their help to find you when it was over."

"You wanted to find me?" she whispered.

Smiling, I reached up to run my fingers down her cheek. "Yes, beautiful. I'm not letting you go this time."

Leaning in, she kissed me. God, I couldn't stop myself; I pulled her onto my lap and deepened the kiss. We sat like this for more than a few minutes. "Beautiful, if we don't stop, I'm going to make love to you right here." I watched as her face flushed. She climbed off my lap, and I took a deep shuddering breath.

"Anyway, I agreed to everything. But what struck me was what

Bower said to me. Keep in mind that I had, what, twenty-four hours to run every conversation we had over in my head. Things didn't add up. Bower gave me a phone. He told me if I needed to talk, to text then erase. He said that if they needed me, I would get a note in the mail from the Art Institute." She nodded her head. "Well, he was very clear that I was to not tell a living, breathing soul about any of it. He made it a point to say that three different times. Jacob didn't say much. I asked Bower what I should do, and he said that I should just go on living my life, that they would find you and let me know. But what got me and sank in my head was that he said it would take at least a week to confirm you were alive or dead."

I watched her face, her eyes. "They knew where I was," she whispered.

"Yeah, I figured that out, along with a few other things. He told me that I was suspected to be Andy Marciano, but after they analyzed all the information you retrieved, they were wrong, and they knew who he was."

"Why didn't they tell me?"

"Well, I'm not sure. But this is what I figured out, and I thought if we had some time, you might be able to remember what it was you found. He kept referring to your eidetic memory. I remembered the way you studied my face, and that's when I figured out that you being there with me was because you wanted to be there, and you were memorizing my face. But whatever it is you saw, or found, it's in your mind somewhere. Well, before I got your text, I was losing my mind trying to figure out why you left. I called my brother to see if he wanted to hang out because I needed a distraction. But his phone was off. So, I called his secretary, and she told me he had to go out of town on business. Now, John never said anything to me about that. A few minutes after I hung up with her, John called me. We talked, and I played it cool, but then he told me he was in London. It didn't raise any kind of red flag. But when I hung up, you texted me. I had no clue what or where Surrey was, so I looked it up."

"London," she whispered.

I didn't say anything. I was watching her go through everything in her mind. When her eyes locked with mine, she went to open her mouth to talk and I put my fingers on her lips. "While I was on the plane, I put it all together. My brother could be Marciano. But something more happened. When you shot those men today, you had said one of the guy's names, McDonald. When I looked at him, I knew it was Johnny McDonald. I know the guy. He doesn't work for my brother. He is a hired hitman. Don't ask me how I know that, but I do. The other guy I knew, as well. His name is James Times. He is a hired thug. Tell me how you know McDonald."

"While I was working for you and your brother, I had another job. I worked in a dive bar; the same one you were taking me to that day I freaked out on you. I couldn't go there because Jerry would have recognized me, and my cover would have been blown. McDonald, I knew him from there. I knew he was Marciano's main man, but no one had ever seen Marciano so I had no idea who he was. Paul, I never saw your brother in that bar, and I worked there for six months. It's a whore house. I know because Jerry tried to sell me to some guy. I was the only one who didn't have sex with the men for money. I think Jerry was sweet on me."

"I know why I was suspect. I owned that bar, but McDonald was not my guy. You know my guys; you beat the shit out of two of them. So, Marciano was using my bar. This is too much like a set up. I know my brother is involved with this, I just don't know how, but I don't think he is Marciano. His identity is in your mind somewhere. Victoria, I think you've been allowed to live because you hadn't figured it out yet. But he knows now that it's just a matter of time before you do. Sweetheart, he's a part of this. He's on the inside, and he knows you. You know him."

She just sat there in a state of shock, I think. "I need a minute." I watched her get up and pace back and forth. Her eyes closed. "Your brother, the files he gave me, they were your illegitimate businesses. But it didn't make sense to me."

"What other accounts did you work on?" I asked softly.

"Your brother isn't Marciano, but yes, he is involved. He knew who I was."

"He kept telling me to stay away from you, that he needed you. He showed me files, accounts you worked on. He told me to walk away from you. I think he killed my wife because he couldn't kill me. I think you were to fix whatever needed to be fixed and then he was going to kill you. He knew what losing Sylvia did to me. I think he was protecting me."

"Makes sense. You do know that I am going to kill him? He killed my brother and his wife. He nearly killed Jo."

"I know, but I would like to talk to him first."

She nodded and kept walking. Out of nowhere, she spun around. "When they told me about Steven, there was another man in the room, but I couldn't see his face. He was in the shadows. He didn't talk while I was there. I passed out from the shock of it all. When I started to come around, I heard a voice that I didn't know, but it felt familiar to me. He said, *'We can't tell her everything. She can never know everything. She needs to do this on her own. She needs to find the truth on her own.'* I remember now that it was so familiar to me. But with everything that was in my head, I pushed it aside."

Her eyes filled with tears. In the faintest of whispers, she said, "I know who Andy Marciano is."

I was on my feet and she was in my arms. Her whole body was shaking. It took a long time for her to pull away. She put her hands on her knees and threw up all over the place. I didn't know what to do, so I just held her hips. She wiped her mouth and stood up, then it was as if her whole being physically changed in front of me. Her body got stiff; she squared her shoulders. Her head went back, and her eyes closed. She stood there for a minute or two. Opening her eyes, she had a look in them that freaked me out.

"Excuse me for a minute," she said in a dead, cold tone. I watched as she walked away from me, pulling another phone out of her back pocket. I heard it chime as she turned it on. She kept moving further away from me. I could see her dialing the phone, putting it to her ear. She just kept moving. I could hear her voice, but I couldn't make out what she was saying. She hung up and just stood there looking at me. I went to take a step, and she shook her head. I stopped.

We stood staring at each other for a few minutes, and then her phone rang. Her eyes not leaving mine, she listened to whoever was on the other end of the phone. I saw her mouth move, saying, "Thank you," and then she hung up the phone and turned it off. I watched as she took a few deep breaths. Then she started toward me.

"Are you positive your brother won't kill you?" she asked in her dead, cold voice.

"No. Victoria, what just happened?" I touched her arm.

Her whole body was stiff. "Paul, we need to go."

I laughed. "Beautiful, we aren't going anywhere until you tell me what just happened."

"I just figured out that my whole life has been one big fucking lie after another. And I just figured out that it's my life, and I am fucking taking it back. Paul, I think I'm in love with you, and I am trusting that what you said to me is the truth. I need to have some truth."

"Yes, it's truth. I would love nothing more than to spend the rest of my life with you and Jo." I ran my fingers down her cheek. I watched as her eyes closed and she leaned into my hand. "Talk to me, beautiful."

A tear slid down her cheek. "I can't right now. But I will. Just give me some time. Please, don't change your mind."

"Never," I said as I kissed her. "Feel me, beautiful."

"I do. But, right now, I can't trust how I feel. Don't let me go. No matter what you see today, or what you hear, don't let me go. Even if I kill your brother, which I'm not sure I'm not going to do."

"I. Got. You. Beautiful." I had no intentions of ever letting this woman go. I kissed her again. "Come on, let's go end this so we can go get Jo and start our life."

She nodded, I let her go, and we walked back to the car. She stopped and looked at me. "Every single one of those men are dirty. Jacob, Al, and the other two men at my apartment. I need for you to promise me, and mean it, that you won't interfere in this. If I am in grave danger, you will not try and stop it. Promise me, Paul."

I grabbed her, pulling her into my arms. "God, Victoria, I promise. But you promise me you will not put yourself in line to get killed."

Her arms wrapped around me. "I promise," she whispered. "This is going to get bad, Paul, I mean really bad. Death will be everywhere, so be prepared."

I nodded into her head. We released each other and got in the car. "Where do I go?" I asked.

She directed me to her cottage, but we stopped a few hundred yards down the road. She got out of the car and ran to some bushes along the road. When she came back, she was carrying a small duffle bag. Climbing in, she opened the bag and pulled a few guns out and then clip after clip. She slipped them all over her body. "Do you know how to shoot?"

I had a stupid smile on my face. I grabbed her face and kissed her. "Yes." She handed me two guns and a few handfuls of clips.

When we finished, she pulled the phone out of her back pocket, turning it on. I watched as she sent a text. Turning the phone off, she looked at me. "Let's do this. Remember your promise, Paul. You are going to see a part of me that no one sees. Please, don't freak out."

"Got it." If I was being honest, I was about to shit in my pants. How had I found myself going into a gun fight? Fuck.

CHAPTER NINE

VICTORIA

The closer we got, the angrier I got. I hoped that John would not kill his brother. I also hoped he didn't make Paul watch while he killed me. I couldn't let that happen. I found the man I felt I was supposed to be with. He smiled at me. He was so beautiful; this was going to destroy him.

I could see the roof line of the cottage. As we pulled up, there weren't any cars parked around. I hated that I'd have to kill Al and Jacob. But they knew. They knew all along who I was searching for, and they just let me go at it. I think the plan was to see if I could detect Mr. Marciano's footprint in the world of crime.

If everything went according to plan, this would be over before it started. Paul pulled up and parked where I told him. Looking at him, I said, "You promised."

He nodded. "As did you."

I smiled. I wanted to kiss him but I would lose my edge if I did. Opening the car door, I waited for him to join me.

"So, this is where you live?"

"It is. I love it here. There's my garden." I pointed to the lot of land that was my garden. When I had a life here.

"I like it. This cottage is something out of a painting."

I laughed. He got it. "It's why I chose it. It reminds me of Monet's..."

He interrupted me and said, "The Customs House at Varengeville. I have a reproduction of it in my apartment."

"It's one of my favorites," I said as we rounded the cottage.

"Oh my God," he said as he stopped.

I followed his eyes and giggled. "I like the beach."

He burst out laughing. "I should have known."

I looked at him. "How could you have imagined this would be me?"

He pulled me into his chest, whispering, "I'm terrified." Then he kissed me sweetly.

"Me too. You ready?"

He nodded his head, and I said, "Come on, I'll show you the inside."

The minute the door shut I knew what was happening outside. Everything looked normal as we walked up, but nothing was as it seemed. I squeezed Paul's hand when I heard footsteps coming from the kitchen. It was the look on John Simon's face that made me giggle.

"Paul? What the hell are you doing here?"

"Well, we just got married, and Suzanne was showing me her little cottage." He squeezed my hand.

"Mr. Simon, why are you in my house? I don't understand."

His eyes cut through me like razors. "You didn't show up for work. I was here on business, so I thought I'd stop and see why you quit." He had no knowledge of my life here. I had to smile. He just made a major mistake. He was very scared.

"I didn't quit." Turning to Paul, I said, "You didn't tell him, did you?"

"No, I didn't want to tell him on the phone. But he said he was out of town."

I turned back to John. "We are on our honeymoon. We are headed to Spain from here. He was supposed to tell you."

I swear, the man looked like he was going to have a stroke standing in my living room. Paul let go of my hand when John stepped forward to hug him. I heard when he whispered to him, "Did you kill my wife, John?"

I pulled a gun from my jeans and slid my hand down the front of his pants while Paul held on to him. "Don't fucking move," I whispered. "Paul, turn him around." As he turned him, I stepped between them and wrapped my arms around him. I brought a gun up to his chin. "You killed my brother and his wife. You care to tell me why?"

"I can't," he whispered.

I knew he could feel me smile against his neck. "Why? You afraid Marciano is going to kill you?" I giggled. "Don't worry about that, because I'm going to do it for him."

"You are not going to walk out of this house. Neither is my brother. You signed all of our death warrants."

"Nope, just yours and his. The rest of them will spend their lives in prison. Do you even know who Marciano is?"

A man appeared in the doorway of the kitchen. "Did someone say my name?" I closed my eyes. He wasn't the man in the room.

Paul drew one of his guns and pointed it at him. "You couldn't possibly have enough guns or bullets to end this here." He smiled.

I smiled at him. "Would you care to make a wager?" I moved my gun from John's throat and shot the man in the head, immediately shoving the nozzle against John's neck.

His body jerked from the pain of the heated metal. "I can do this all fucking day. Where is Marciano? I know he's fucking here. I know he wouldn't miss this," I yelled out. The fucker was here. He just didn't know that I knew who he was.

"He's not here!" John yelled.

"Oh, John, I know him. I know he's here. He wouldn't miss this. Just like he didn't miss it when my baby died. Just like he didn't miss it when you killed my brother. He was right there watching. He isn't going to miss this. I promise you, he's here. I made sure of it."

"Hey, John," Paul said. "Before we get started, I asked Victoria not to kill you before I had a chance to ask you why you killed my wife."

"Marciano wanted me to kill you, but I couldn't kill you."

"So, you killed my wife and my unborn child?"

"She wasn't any good for you."

"Who are you? Why would you do this shit?"

He laughed. "For the money, brother. And I just love the way the bodies feel when the life drains out of them."

"You're a sick fuck." He leaned into me, whispering in my ear, "I'm all right with you killing him now."

"Thank you, baby."

"Wait, wait, I can make this right."

Shaking my head, I said, "Yeah, no, I don't think you can." I pulled the trigger and shot off his dick. The screams were giving me a headache, so I snapped his neck and dropped him on the floor. It was then that I heard that voice.

"You really think I enjoyed watching your baby die?"

I don't know what happened, but I froze. I think that's what he wanted. It was Paul's hand on my lower back that snapped me back. He loved me. Fight for him. Fight for Jo.

"I know you did. I remember seeing it in your eyes. Why did you do it?"

"I always hated that about you. That you remember everything. I knew, eventually, you were going to die, and I couldn't leave a poor defenseless child in this world alone."

"Ah, but Mr. Marciano, isn't that exactly what's going to happen to you?"

I could feel his rage. Even his voice changed as he laughed. "I don't know what you're talking about."

I giggled, raising my gun. "Oh, you certainly do." I pulled the trigger. The bullet went through the living room wall. I heard him grunt when it went into his shoulder. "You most certainly do."

The front door opened, as did the back door. I yelled, "Don't kill him."

Paul wrapped his arm around me, pulling me against him and stepping back against the wall. I wanted to run in the other room and see his face. But I knew I would just kill him, and I didn't want my house to be the sight of his murder. We stood there listening to the scuffle, punches being thrown, glass being broken. I didn't move. I just leaned into Paul and breathed in his scent.

When I saw him, I heard myself say, "Daddy," and I ran to him, jumping in his arms. The tears just came. I couldn't hold them in any longer.

"Come on, baby girl, let's get you out of here." He scooped me up and carried me out the front door, across the front lawn to the picnic table. "I knew you were a smart girl. How did you know?"

"It's a long story."

"Oh, by the way, you're fired. Never again, Victoria, never again. You've got to raise Jo. This is it. I don't want to see your name cross my desk again."

I nodded. "Did you get them all?"

"We got them. This went deep. He had shit on all of them." Paul cleared his throat, and I smiled. My dad turned around. "Mr. Simon."

"Sir." he nodded.

"I've managed to clean up your life for you, and I'm trusting you're going to do right by my daughter and granddaughter."

Paul looked at me. "If she'll let me. She has a bit of a stubborn streak in her."

My dad laughed. "Yeah, she gets that from her mother. It's good to meet you, son. You make sure to take care of my girls."

"I will do my best, sir, and thank you for all your help."

My dad turned to me. "I suppose you want to take care of this?"

I nodded. "I have to, Daddy. I don't want to, but I have to."

"Good shot, by the way."

"I knew he was there. Hey, do you think you can fix my wall before you go? I don't want to have to explain it to Jo."

He laughed. I heard the struggle across the lawn. "Will you excuse me? I need to take care of something."

When I walked by Paul, he looked at me, his hand coming up to my face. "You all right?"

"I will be. Remember, you promised."

"I did."

As I walked away, I heard my dad say, "What did you promise."

Paul laughed. "Not to interfere."

I heard my dad laughing all the way across the lawn.

"Excuse me, can I have a few minutes please?"

One of the guys let him go. "He's all yours."

"I don't even know what to say to you," I said.

"Don't say a fucking word. This isn't over, you know."

"Yes, it is." I punched him in the stomach. "Why?" I shouted.

Paul went to move, and my dad stopped him. "This needs to happen."

"So I could keep track of you."

"Why did you kill my baby?"

"I didn't want a fucking baby with you."

I drop-kicked him in the jaw. He fell over on the ground.

"Fucking bitch, take the cuffs off me."

I looked up. "Un-cuff him."

"Victoria, NO!" Paul yelled.

My dad grabbed him. "She's got this."

"He's three times her size. He'll kill her."

"He's her ex-husband," my dad said. "He has this coming."

I watched as one of the men un-cuffed him. The minute his hands were free, he swung at me. "I'm going to finally be free of you, you little bitch."

I moved away from him. "Why, Steven? I loved you."

"The only way to control you was to marry you."

"It's a shame, you know, that your child is going to grow up without a father."

He laughed. "There is no child. It was all a ruse. I needed you to lose your focus so I could get the upper hand." I tilted my head. "I knew you were still in love with me. I knew it would devastate you."

I smiled. "What it did was make me realize that there is life after you."

"You have no life. You will never have a life. I'm going to end it here and now." He swung again, but I blocked it and slammed my fist into his stomach. "You think you can hurt me?" he yelled.

I slammed my fist into his throat. He grabbed my arm, twisting it. I felt it snap, and he threw me across the lawn. By the time I got up, he was on me again. He grabbed my broken arm, and when he swung me around, I pushed my knife into his side. He just stood there holding me, looking at me.

"Fuck you," I whispered to him. Pulling the knife out, I pushed it in again, between his ribs, puncturing his lung.

Somehow, he got his hands on my throat and started to choke me. I stabbed him again. Paul screamed out my name just before I started to black out. I managed to get my arm up and slam the knife in his throat. As the world was turning black, I could feel his grip lessening. He went down, and I went with him. The world went black.

Paul

Her father wouldn't let me go. When I heard her arm break, I fought hard against him. For an old man, he was strong. I stood there horrified as the scene unfolded before me, horrified when she stabbed him. He finally let me go when she slammed the knife into his throat. I was too late; he had taken her down.

When I got to her, she was covered in blood and unconscious. Gently, I picked her up. "Oh my God, beautiful. Come on, baby."

"Mr. Simon, please let me look at her," a man said. I didn't want anyone to touch her ever again. "Mr. Simon, I'm a medic. Please, let me check her out."

Gently, I laid her on the ground and sat there watching him check her over. "Her arm is broken, but she is alive. She is going to have a hell of a sore throat when she wakes up. Johnny, call the transport. We should get her to a hospital."

I couldn't look away from her face. She was so pale, so lifeless. I reach my hand out; it was shaking. I don't think I'd ever been so scared. I pressed it to her chest, needing to feel her heartbeat. I kept it there until a helicopter landed in the field. Three men came running up with a gurney and gently lifted her onto it. "Come on," one of them said to me.

I felt like I was having an out of body experience, like I was floating, as I followed them. Turning, I saw her father nod to me.

Two hours later, I found myself pacing the hall outside of the operating room. No one would tell me anything. Finally, someone came out. "Mr. Simon?"

"Yes, how is she?"

He chuckled. *Why would he chuckle?* "She is fine, better than fine. She is in recovery, yelling at everyone to find you. Her arm was pretty badly broken in three places. We had to put a few pins in it, so she is going to be sore for a few days. Her throat is badly bruised, but there was no permanent damage done."

"When can I see her?" I was shaking.

"Come on, I'll take you back there. She is one bossy little woman." He laughed.

"Yeah, she is. I wouldn't have her any other way." I smiled, a bit more relieved knowing she was yelling at everyone.

When the door opened and I saw her tiny body in that huge bed, I nearly lost it. The bruises on her neck were nearly purple. Her arm had a huge cast on it. When our eyes connected, my heart stopped. God, she was so beautiful.

"Hi," she whispered.

"Hi." I moved to the side of the bed of her good arm. "God, beautiful, I was so scared."

"Me too," she whispered. "Are you all right?"

I chuckled. "I'm fine. Nearly shit my pants, but I'm fine."

She laughed. Reaching up, she grabbed my shirt and pulled me down to her mouth. "Kiss me, Paul."

"My pleasure." And kiss her I did. God, she tasted like heaven. She had to stay overnight because of the surgery. She couldn't travel for a few days, and she didn't want Jo to see her neck, so we went to my apartment in London. I carried her in and straight to the bedroom.

"Mr. Simon, are all your beds this big?"

I laughed. "Every damn one of them."

"Hmmm," she smarted.

"What? I'm a big boy."

She laughed. "Oh, I know you are."

I set her down in the middle of the bed. "Can I get you anything? I don't have anything to eat, but I can run to the store or order in."

"We can both go to the store."

I reached up to touch her neck. "Maybe I should go. You sleep. I'll only be about an hour. Then I'll join you."

She smiled. "Will you help me undress. I'm going to need some new clothes."

As we took off her clothes, she had nothing on under the scrubs they let her have. "Jesus, Victoria, you're fucking beautiful."

Smiling at me, she crawled into bed. "Hurry up and get back here," she said so sweetly.

I couldn't help myself; I laid down next to her and pulled her into my arms. Having this cast on her arm made it a bit difficult to snuggle, but I needed to kiss her, to feel her. She slid her hand up my shirt, her mouth covering mine. We lay there kissing for what seemed like hours. I liked this about us. Nothing was hurried, nothing forced. It felt so natural to kiss her. "You taste like heaven," I whispered to her.

"Mmm, go, so you can get back," she whispered, closing her eyes.

I slipped out of the bed and headed to the store. I didn't want to leave her, but we needed supplies. The stores here closed so early. I got a few supplies, and then I stopped off and picked up some clothes for her. I didn't get any panties or bras; she wasn't going to need them just yet. Smiling, I headed back to the apartment.

I put everything away and then went to the bedroom. Dropping my clothes, I climbed into bed behind her, wrapping my arms around her.

"I missed you," she whispered.

"I'm right here, beautiful. Go back to sleep."

Her body relaxed as she fell back asleep. I closed my eyes and followed her. This was my life now. I wanted this so much.

∾

Victoria

When I woke, I was cocooned in his arms. I couldn't remember ever feeling so relaxed, at least, not in a very long time. He sensed I was awake because his arms pulled me a bit closer. I felt his lips on my neck. "Did you sleep well?" he whispered as he made a meal of my shoulder and neck.

"I did," I breathed out. It was more like a moan. "Paul."

"Yeah, baby?"

He shifted my body a little so I was laying partially on his chest. His mouth covered mine. We laid like this kissing for a long time. His hands were gentle on my breasts. So good, he always made me feel. Our kisses were kisses of lovers. Slowly, he moved his hand down my body, across my hip, to my thigh. I loved how his hand nearly fit around my thigh. He slowly slid it up over his, opening me to him.

I couldn't move, my cast lying on his chest, my other arm touching his face. I felt him run himself through me, then slowly, he pushed inside of me and made love to me. It was so intense, so slow, so long. I marveled at how he could stay hard for so long.

His fingers trailed up and down my body, across the hair at my core, his body not missing a stroke. I was so open to him like this; I felt his fingertip gently pass over my bud. My body shook, it felt so good. So erotic, again and again he did it. I felt the tears building in my eyes.

He did it again, and I shattered to pieces. Pulling away from his mouth, I cried out.

"I. Got. You," he moaned as he released. We shook and convulsed together, him holding me, me holding his head.

We didn't talk. I think we both just needed this connection. After everything that happened, we needed just to be this. I needed to be this.

I let myself go and fell back to sleep. I hadn't really slept in nearly three years. Always afraid, always aware. It was over now. I just needed to relax.

Paul

Holding her like this, still inside of her, is a feeling I'd never known. She was so fucking beautiful, so tiny compared to me. Hell compared to any man. Her body fit perfectly with mine. Her scent from her arousal only made me harder. I was so glad I'd taught myself control. I enjoyed her. Her core was so tight but yet so silky, and I loved the way she responded to me. I knew we needed to talk about all this shit, but for now, I was going to love her the best that I could, because she simply deserved the best man I could be.

CHAPTER TEN

PAUL

When she moved and winced, my eyes popped open. "You all right?" I whispered. It was dark out.

"I think the pain meds wore off, and I have to go to the bathroom."

I chuckled. "Come, I'll help you get up. I got you some clothes if you want to get dressed."

We untangled ourselves, and I helped her slide to the edge of the bed. "Can I just wear one of your shirts?"

I kissed her forehead. "You can wear whatever you want. The closet is there." I pointed to the door next to the bathroom. "I'll go make us something to eat and get your pill."

I went to walk away, and she touched my arm lightly. I turned to her. "Hey," I whispered. Her head was down.

"I can't have children," she said so softly.

I pulled her into my arms. "I know, beautiful. It's fine. We have Jo."

"Yeah?"

I reached up to touch her face. "Oh, yeah."

She nodded and walked to the bathroom. I watched her. *Damn, she has the perfect ass.* Shaking my head, smiling, I went to the closet to grab a pair of pajama bottoms, then headed out to the kitchen to get her a pain pill. When I walked back into the bedroom, I heard her crying in the bathroom.

I knocked on the door. "Victoria, can I come in?" She didn't say anything, so I tried the knob. The door was unlocked, so I pushed it open. She was curled within herself, leaning against the back wall. I moved toward her, and she started to shake so I got down on my knees. "Victoria," I whispered. She just shook her head. "Sweetheart, talk to me."

Her eyes landed on mine, and what I saw in them scared the shit out of me. "I don't know who I am anymore. I've told so many lies, I don't know the truth. I didn't have cancer. I cut off all my hair so I could wear those stupid wigs," she cried.

"It's over now. It's all over." I tried to calm her down.

"Is it?" she yelled. "He said it wasn't over. He said it wasn't over, that it wouldn't end here."

"Victoria, you killed him. He can't hurt you anymore. Come on, sweetheart," I said softly and moved toward her. She didn't move, but she let me come to her. I pulled her into my lap. "We are safe now. Jo is safe now. Do you want to go back to Chicago and get her? Max will protect her."

"I need to talk to her, to Max. To Kathy. What if he got to Kathy? She was so willing to help me. I keep playing over in my mind the scene in the parking lot. She didn't even draw her gun. I think she knew what was happening. She was insistent on flying commercial. Jo is still in danger."

"Come on, let's get dressed. I'm afraid I didn't get you any panties or a bra. I didn't think you would need them right away."

She giggled, kissing my neck. "I didn't plan on needing them. It's all right."

We moved to the bedroom, where I helped her put on the jeans I got her. She took one of my shirts out of the closet and put it on, tying it around her waist.

Picking up my phone, I called Max. "Max, listen, don't react. In fact, act like I'm your mother or something. Is Jo still at my apartment?"

"Hi, Mom. Yeah, I'm working. No, don't worry, it's all right."

"Max, she isn't safe. The woman who is with her is a danger to her. She is either going to take her or kill her. You need to figure out a way to get her out of there or contain Kathy. Remember, she is a trained agent just like Victoria."

He laughed. "No, Mom, don't worry about it. All right, I'll call you next week."

"We are on our way back. With your life, Max. With your fucking life."

He disconnected the phone. I turned to look at Victoria. She was dialing her phone. "No, don't." She looked up at me. "If you call her and she knows you are alive, we lose our edge."

She smiled up at me. "Well, Mr. Simon, if I didn't know any better, I'd say you have a knack for this spy shit."

I laughed. "Come on, beautiful, let's get to the airport. We are going to have to charter a plane. If we get on my plane, it will register. Flying commercial won't work either, since our names will be on the manifest."

When we got in the elevator, she looked at me. "You've done this before?"

"I have, yours is not the only life that is full of lies. Victoria, I'm out. Your father got me out. I have more than a billion dollars. We can go anywhere, live anywhere, become anyone."

She shook her head. "I just want to go home and be Victoria Holmes. I'm tired of lying all the time. I'm tired of not being me, of being a liar."

I smiled at her, touching her face. "But you are a beautiful liar."

"I don't want to lie anymore. I want my life back." Her voice dropped. "I want a life with you."

"As I do with you."

I gently pulled her into my arms.

Victoria

We chartered a plane and headed back to Chicago. I couldn't focus on anything. *When was it all going to stop?* I played it over and over in my mind. *What was I missing? Who was I missing it with?* His words rolling over in my mind; I couldn't get them out of my mind.

"Paul, will Max protect her?" I asked.

He chuckled. "Max likes you. He told me that he respected you, so I'm pretty sure he will protect her with his life."

"That's what I'm afraid of," I whispered. "I need to think." I got up and started pacing. Closing my eyes, I ran through every conversation I ever had with him. He'd been Andy Marciano the entire time we were together. *When did he change? How did he change? Was he this man all along?* He said he married me so he could keep an eye on me. *When did we get married?* Right after I joined MI6. He said he hated that I remembered everything, and he married me because of it. *What did Johnathan figure out that ended in his death?*

I started remembering conversations Johnathan and I had right before he died. *Was he trying to tell me something? Did he tell me something?*

I looked at Paul. "What did Al tell you about me?"

"Just that you were married, and you had found out he remarried and was having a child. Why?"

I shook my head. "And that's it?"

I watched him run through the conversation he had with Al. "Wait, he said that you didn't know that the accident you had that caused you to lose your baby was in fact an attempt on your life. A way to control your brother."

I nodded my head. I remembered he kept telling me to be careful, to stay safe. To watch my back. When we were both in MI6, we were a team. He had never said that to me. He knew. He had to know I was in danger. *Who was Kathy in all of this?* She was Johnathan and Elizabeth's friend. More Johnathan's. Her voice popped in my head, the look on her face in the mall. The look on her face when she turned around to see McDonald dead. Her insistence on taking a commercial flight.

I spun around, looking at Paul. "Before I called you, that day at the beach, the day we made love for the first time," he nodded, "I called

Steven. I didn't talk. I just thought I needed to hear his voice. Instead, I heard a woman's voice in the background, asking him who it was. It was Kathy's voice. Kathy is his wife. She is pregnant with his child, and she has Jo."

"Max will not let anything happen to her. I don't think Kathy would do anything if she didn't have the chance. Max won't let her have a chance," he said as he came to me, pulling me in his arms.

"God, Paul, I'm so scared. So ready to be me. All these lies, years of hiding, years of lying, years of not living. So many passing me by."

"Shh, I've lived the same way, beautiful. After Sylvia, I couldn't look at myself in the mirror. I didn't want to see the failure of a man I had become. I couldn't save her. My brother put a blade to her throat right in front of me, and I couldn't do a thing. Victoria, when Steven had his hands around your throat, I think I was more terrified he was going to take you from me."

"My father wouldn't have let him kill me," I whispered.

"Maybe so, but that still didn't lessen my fear. You said you think you're in love with me," he whispered.

"I did," I whispered back. "I do. I've never felt this connected to someone in my life. That day in your brother's office, when you shook my hand, I felt you through my whole body."

He chuckled. "Me too." His hand came up to my face, and he kissed me. "Come on, you need to rest. There's a bed in the back of this plane. We still have five hours to go before we touch down." I nodded to him and let him lead me to the back of the plane. "I got you, beautiful," he whispered into my neck as he wrapped himself around me. Closing my eyes, I let sleep take me. I was in the place I felt the safest.

Paul

Everything was spinning around in my head. She was safely cocooned against my body. I just wasn't sure how safe I could keep her. She was disabled with her broken arm. I just wanted this to be over. Life shouldn't be this hard for someone.

As I lay there holding her, I couldn't help but smile. There is life after death. I said a prayer to Sylvia and thanked her for loving me, for teaching me how to love and be loved. I knew I'd have to tell her of the life I led these past five years. She needed to know everything; I wanted our slates to be clean.

She was all I wanted. Her scent was embedded in my soul. The way she made love with me was incredible. I felt my arms tightening around her, realizing I loved her. I was falling deeper and deeper in love with her. Was this how it happened? Did it happen this fast?

The plane slowed, and I knew we were getting ready to land.

I kissed her head and started to rub her back. "Mmm," she moaned gently, just like when we made love.

I chuckled. "You keep making that noise and we won't be getting off this plane anytime soon."

"Yes, please." She giggled. "Are we here already?"

"Just about. We've started to slow down, and from the pressure in my ears, we are starting our decent."

"Paul, I'm going to need a gun."

I knew she could feel my body tense up. "Max always carries. But do you really? She is contained in my apartment."

"I know, but I am not taking that chance."

"Come on, let's get up and get in our seats."

We sat holding hands until the plane stopped. We went through customs, and Max had a car waiting for us. It took about forty minutes to get to the apartment. Getting out of the car, I leaned in to Denny. "I need your gun."

Without hesitation, he handed it to me. I turned and gave it to Victoria.

"Thank you," she said.

Turning back to Denny, I asked him, "Where's Max?"

"Upstairs, he hasn't left your apartment."

"I need you and two others to follow us up. Hopefully, everyone is sleeping. I don't want any bloodshed, so we need to contain the woman and keep the child safe."

"Sir, it's two in the morning. I think everyone is sleeping."

"Everything is not what it seems. Let's go."

Victoria's body changed the closer we got to the apartment, just like in the field outside her cottage. She was going into work mode. I took a deep breath and closed my eyes. Touching her arm, I leaned into her. "I love you," I whispered so only she could hear.

"Please remember your promise. Protect Jo at all cost."

I kissed her neck as the doors opened.

CHAPTER ELEVEN

VICTORIA

I hoped the element of surprise would be on my side. If my father didn't clean house, then she knew I killed Steven, and she would be waiting for me. She believed me to be dead. She was probably waiting for Steven to come and get her before they ended Jo's life. I could've been wrong, but I wasn't taking any chances.

Paul went to open the door, and I stopped him. "Let me go. Text Max so I don't shoot him. Tell him I am coming in. Give me five minutes and you follow."

"Victoria, we need to do this together. You know it. She is one person and you are hurt. Please."

I knew he was right, and I just loved him for wanting to protect me, to protect Jo. I nodded to him and whispered, "I love you."

He stood there looking at me. I could see the fear in his eyes, but beyond that, I saw it. I saw what I needed to be sure he knew I meant it. Opening the door, Max met us. No one said a word as he led us to the spare room. Walking in, I could see Kathy in bed with Jo. Not what I wanted to see. I walked over to the bed and put the gun to her head, pulling back the hammer. I saw her eyes open. "Get up," I whispered. "Now." She hesitated, and Max reached around me, grabbing her by the throat and lifting her off the bed. Paul put himself between Kathy and Jo.

Picking up Jo, he carried her into his room, telling Denny to protect her with his life.

Max dragged Kathy out into the dining room, putting her in a chair. He pulled out some zip ties and tied her to it. "Victoria, what is going on?"

I sat down across from her. "How long?"

She shook her head. "What? How long what?"

"How long were you fucking my husband?"

Her eyes shot up to Paul. He was watching me. "I have no idea what you are talking about."

"You didn't expect to see me again. You know he was going to kill me. You know the only reason he married me was to control Johnathan."

She laughed. "Are you insane? I know as much about this case as you told me."

I laughed. "Kathy, I know you are, or should I say, were Steven's new wife. I also know you're pregnant."

Her eyes gave her away. "What do you mean, were?"

"He's dead. I killed him. Stabbed him right here." I put my hand on my neck. "Hit his jugular. It took maybe twenty seconds before he bled out. Well, that and he had a bullet hole in him here." I touched my shoulder. "And a few other knife wounds. You should have seen it. He broke my arm, as you can see, and he nearly choked me to death. But I won."

"Impossible, he is three times your size," she said softly.

And there it was. I smiled at her. "You meant nothing to him in the end. He denied you."

She gasped, then visibly collected herself. "Why the fuck couldn't you just die like your brother?"

I stood up and swung, slamming my fist into her face. "Because good always wins," I said.

"You're a fucking hitman for the British government, and you call me a murderer. I wouldn't get too comfortable, Victoria, because this is just the beginning. He wasn't Andy Marciano; he was second in command."

I stood there looking at her. Everything swirled in my mind. It was like a million flashes of light. I had to grab the table it was that bad. I felt Paul touch me, and I shook my head. It felt like the world was tipped off its axis. "I can't breathe," I whispered.

Paul got in my line of vision. "Victoria, look at me." My eyes tried to focus on him. "Come on, beautiful, breathe in through your mouth and out through your nose." I did what he said. "That's it, come on, follow me." It took a few minutes before I could breathe again.

I looked at Max. "Is there someplace you can take her? Someplace you can hold her where she won't get away?"

He looked at Paul, who nodded. Max said, "Yeah."

"Make sure she is fed and well cared for. She is pregnant. She is to be guarded twenty-four seven."

He smiled. "You got it."

"You can't hold me prisoner."

I looked her right in the face. "I'm not holding you, I'm protecting you. If I have you arrested, you're dead. If I let you go, you're dead. If what you just said is the truth, you're dead."

"I see it in your eyes. You know it's the truth, and you know who Marciano is, don't you? Tell me, Victoria. Tell me who he is."

I just stared at her. "Max get her out of here."

They took her away. Paul went to get Denny, and then Max left. I paced the living room while Paul stood in the hallway watching me. I knew who was behind this. I knew, and I didn't want to know. I wanted to believe it was Steven. Hell, I wanted it to be Paul. But it was neither of them. "Nowhere is safe," I mumbled. "Steven was right. This isn't over. It's just begun." I looked at Paul. "You aren't safe. You staked your claim to me. You and Jo aren't safe. There is nowhere you can hide with her. Oh my God." I could feel the tears coming; I could feel my body shake. "This can't be happening. This can't be real. Oh my God."

"Victoria, talk to me, beautiful," he whispered.

I couldn't do anything but stand there looking at him. "This can't be real," I whispered to him. "This can't be real."

Paul

I didn't know what to do. She freaked out. *What the hell is going on?* I thought my life was deceitful, but it was nothing compared to this.

"Hey." I reached out to touch her fingers. Her eyes dropped to our hands. "Come on, let's get some sleep. We will worry about this tomorrow." She nodded, wrapping her fingers in mine. We walked into the bedroom, and she climbed in on one side of Jo and I on the other. We held hands above her head. "I love you, Victoria. No matter what."

She smiled and closed her eyes.

I lay there looking at her, looking at the tiny life between us. This beautiful little girl who warned her mother of the pending danger. These two forces of nature were going to be my life. Jo would call me Daddy, and Victoria would call me her husband. I knew that then, to the depths of my being.

My brother was dead. I needed to close the business and end his sick life. Thinking back, I couldn't believe I never saw it. I never saw how disturbed he was. He murdered my wife right in front of me. *Who does that?* I should've felt some sort of remorse for him, for the loss of him, but I didn't. I couldn't. But if he hadn't done it, I wouldn't know this. I wouldn't know her.

Jo rolled over into Victoria's chest, her broken arm gently pulling her closer. It was probably the most beautiful thing I'd ever seen. I just watched them, Jo's little hand reaching up to touch her face. It's like they hadn't been apart at all, a bond only a mother can have with her child, and I laid witness to it. It was changing me again, my heart expanding for her, for this tiny life that wasn't even a part of me.

I scooted over so I could hold them both. They deserved everything I had to give. We would survive this, all of us, and we would live happily ever after. Closing my eyes, I let sleep pull me under. At least, for now, we were safe. If no one knew what we knew, we were safe.

I don't know how long I slept. Time seemed to have no meaning to us right now, but I had the strange feeling of being watched. When I opened my eyes, a pair of big brown eyes were staring at me. Her smile lit up the whole room.

"Hi, Paul," she whispered. "Momma's sleeping."

"She is. You all right, sweetheart?" I whispered to her.

"I have to go potty."

I smiled. "Come on, I'll help you."

We carefully got off the bed. I carried her to the bathroom and helped her go potty, then we washed her hands. "I'm hungry," she whispered.

We quietly made our way out into the kitchen. She wanted me to make pancakes—well, panny cakes as she called them. So, I sat her on the counter, and we made panny cakes. She seemed to be a very intelligent little girl. I discovered a side of me I was sure was lost. She was so innocent to how the world really was. I could see why Victoria lived in the cottage. A city full of crime was no good for a child. I needed to get her back there. Running in the grass, tending the garden, playing at the beach, that's the life I wanted us to have.

"Should we take these to Momma?" I asked her when we finished.

She nodded her head. Turning, I went to grab the tray, and Victoria was standing in the hallway with tears on her cheeks. I picked up Jo and walked up to her, pulling her into me with my other arm.

Victoria

When I woke up and they were both gone, I must admit I panicked, until I heard the giggles and whispers in the other room. I managed to get out of bed and sneak out to see what they were doing. Low and behold, he had her on the counter and she had convinced him to make pancakes. My heart was full. He had taken to her like she was his own. Watching them, the way she spoke to him so matter of fact, and he just went right along with her.

When he turned and saw me standing there, I saw nothing but love in his eyes, whereas before, I hadn't seen it so clearly. I didn't realize I was crying until he walked over and wrapped me in their embrace and whispered in my ear, "My life is complete. I love you."

I couldn't talk, so I just nodded into his chest.

"Momma, you crying again?" Jo asked, putting her hand on my face.

"I'm just happy, baby."

"Me and Paul made panny cakes."

"I see that. Should we eat them?"

Paul sat her down in a chair, which she had to get on her knees to reach the table. We sat and ate all the pancakes Paul had made. Then I watched as the two of them did the dishes and cleaned up. She didn't ask about my arm or my neck. She was completely content to just be with us. We talked, we drew pretty pictures, and she talked about Max and how he took her to the park. She didn't even ask about Kathy.

We all curled up on the couch and watched her favorite movie. She fell asleep halfway through it, half laying on Paul and half on me. Paul carried her into the second bedroom, the one closest to his.

Paul

I walked out into the hallway, wrapping my arms around her. "I know there is so much we need to talk about, but last night, I was thinking. No one knows what we know, so I think we should just let you heal and come up with a plan. For now, we are safe. Things are calm and no one is out to kill you. Why don't we take Jo back to the cottage and spend the summer there? Let you heal. Let us grow."

"You would leave here?"

I laughed. "Victoria, I am not leaving you. You and Jo are my life now. What's best for her, and you as well, is what I want. You have had a hell of a life. It's time you sit back and live it. No more running. No more lies. No more death. Let's just be happy for a while. When you are healed and at one hundred percent, I will do whatever you want. But she has been without you for so long, and I'm just now getting to be a part of the both of you."

"But your life is here."

"Not anymore. It's with you. I have more money than we could ever spend. We'll take Max and Denny, and we'll go back to Surrey and live there for a bit."

"You mean it?" she whispered.

I nodded. "But I would really like to make love to you."

She smiled at me. "I'd really like that."

"How long does she usually sleep?" I whispered, walking toward the bedroom.

"An hour or so."

"I can work with that. Should we close the door?"

She giggled. "She does know how to open a door."

"Maybe we should wait until she goes to bed tonight." God, I felt awkward.

"Come on, I've got an idea." Smiling, she pulled me into the closet, closed the door, and pushed me against it. We got lost in each other, kissing. Slowly, our clothes left our bodies.

I slid down the door to my knees, so her core was right in front of me. I had to touch her. My hands slid down her body to rest on her ass. Pulling her forward, I buried my face in her fluff, inhaling. "God, you smell like heaven," I moaned. Gently kissing her, I lifted her leg and set her foot on my shoulder. I couldn't stop myself. Her essence was like nothing I'd ever known. Gently, I brought her around and held her while she convulsed on my tongue.

Just as slowly, I picked her foot up, setting it on the floor, and then held her while she lowered and wrapped herself around me, our mouths coming together in a beautiful dance. She made love to me.

With her sweet body gently rocking, I held myself through her orgasm. Laying her on the floor, I made love to her, gently flicking my hips to hit her end. For so long, we moved in perfect harmony, bringing her to the edge of reason as she tightened around me, our mouths pulling apart to look at one another as I emptied myself buried deep inside of her.

"Victoria," I whispered on her lips, holding her. "So beautiful."

"Okay," she moaned.

I chuckled, kissing her deeply. "Okay what, beautiful?"

Her hand was on my face, her eyes dilated and sedate. "Okay, let's go back to the cottage. Let's have this life. I want happy with you," she whispered.

I couldn't contain my smile. I didn't want to contain it. If she wasn't hurt, I would have grabbed her up and spun her around. "Yeah?" I whispered, choked up.

She nodded. "Paul, I love you."

"Aww, beautiful, I love you." We lay on the floor kissing for a little while. "Come on, you need to get cleaned up."

Slowly, I pulled out of her; God, I hated that. I wanted to do nothing but make love to her. I picked her up so she wouldn't struggle with her arm, then watched as she put on one of my shirts. "Can I wear a pair of your boxers?"

I laughed. "Anything you want. But I think they are going to be more like shorts." I grabbed a pair of boxers for her. We walked out of the closet and back into the living room to make our plans. Jo didn't wake up for at least another hour, so we cuddled on the couch.

"You sure you want to do this?" she asked as her hand slid under my shirt, sending fire through my veins directly to my cock.

"I haven't been surer of anything in my whole life. I just need a few days to take care of my brother's finances. Is that all right?"

"Of course, it is. I'm really sorry that I killed him."

"I'm not. He murdered my wife, your brother, and countless other people."

"This isn't over, you know."

"I know, sweetheart, but it is for now. And I want to live in the now. We have at least two months before your arm is healed, and I want to live it to the best of my ability."

"I never really had this, you know?"

"What's that?"

"This feeling of perfection."

I turned on my side so I could look at her. "You deserve nothing less." I kissed her, and she deepened the kiss. It was the giggle that separated us. I felt embarrassed that Jo saw us. My hand was up her shirt, caressing her breast. When I jerked it away, Victoria started laughing.

"Oh my God, you should have seen your face," she laughed.

Sitting up, I was grateful for the long t-shirt I had on to hide my erection. A three-year-old is not something I was used to. But I wouldn't change it for anything in the world. I was looking forward to being a step-in father to this gorgeous little girl.

Climbing on the couch with us, she fixed herself between us. "Momma, is Paul going to be my daddy?"

My heart jumped out of my chest. I saw Victoria struggle to find the words. "Sweetheart, I will be whatever you need or want me to be. We are all in this together. No matter what. Okay?"

She nodded her little head full of curls and kissed my cheek. Turning to Victoria, she whispered, "He smells good."

Victoria burst out laughing, pulling her closer with her broken arm. "I know, baby." She giggled in her ear.

"Momma, can Max take me to the park? He pushes me on the swing."

"Well, how about I get dressed and Paul and I will take you with Max? Maybe we could get some ice cream after."

She nodded and climbed off the couch. I helped Victoria up, and she went in the bedroom to get dressed. Walking out into the living room, she said, "Paul, we are going to have to go shopping. I need some, um, well, you know."

I chuckled. "We can go now. Max is waiting downstairs for us."

~

Victoria

It felt weird walking around with him and Jo. After I lost the baby, I didn't think I would ever feel like a family. Even when I took Jo, I knew I would never love again. Looking at him, I really thought I was in love with him, but how was that possible? I didn't even know him; well, I knew a great deal about the man he portrayed to the world, but the man he was with me, I knew nothing about.

I couldn't help but smile, pretty sure he was thinking the same thing about me.

"You okay?" he asked.

I just nodded, looking at Jo. "Now, you know the rules. No walking away from Momma or Paul or Max. You stay with one of us at all times."

"I know, Momma. Can we get pretty dresses?" She loved her pretty dresses.

I went to answer her, but Paul said, "Well, I think we could find one or two. What do you think, Momma?" I saw the twinkle in his eye. He was going to spoil her, give her any and everything she wanted.

"One or two." I looked at him.

He laughed as we pulled up to Saks. Max opened the door while Paul got Jo out of her car seat, which I didn't realize we had. "Where did that come from?" I asked.

"I bought it for her, Miss Costello," Max said.

I just looked at him. Did all these big badass men buckle and become Jell-O around Jo? "Thank you, Max, but my name is Victoria Holmes, and I'm sorry about hurting you."

His face blushed a bit. "It's not a worry. I'm sure I deserved it."

I nodded as he helped me out of the car and then Jo. Paul came around the other side. "Are we ready?"

All of us walked into the store, Max included. We headed to the lingerie department. I watched as Paul walked up to one of the women at the counter. "This is Miss Holmes. Anything she wants, please put it on my card." He handed her a black credit card.

"Of course, Mr. Simon." She smiled at him.

Turning to me, he said, "You get what you need. I think me and Jo are going to go for a little walk. Will you be all right here on your own?"

I smiled as he gently pulled me to him. Leaning in, I whispered, "I still have Denny's gun. I'll be fine. Don't spoil her too much." I looked at Jo in his arms. She fit so perfectly on his hip. I reached up and touched her face. "Have fun, my love. I'll see you in a little bit."

Her smile said it all for me. Looking past me, she said, "Max, you stay with Momma."

Paul and I looked at each other. We didn't need words to see it in each other's eyes. He said, "How about we all stay here with Momma, and then we will all go together?"

She shook her head, her curls softly hitting the side of his face. "No, Max stay with Momma."

"It's fine, I'll only be a minute," I said, kissing her.

Paul squeezed my side and then let me go. I watched as they walked away. Then I looked at Max who looked a bit uncomfortable. "She's bossy, just like her mother."

I burst out laughing. It took me maybe ten minutes to find enough bras and panties to last a week or so. Then we were off to find Paul and Jo, and find them we did. On the counter were ten new dresses, socks, t-shirts, jeans, shorts, shoes, and underpants.

"Momma, look at all the pretty dresses." She pointed to the counter.

"I see," I said, looking at Paul.

"What? They are all so cute."

I laughed. "Yes, but you can't be doing this."

He pulled me to his side. "I can, and I will. Every little girl should have pretty dresses to wear." He turned to the sales lady, handing her his card. "Could we have these delivered today?"

"Of course, Mr. Simon. We have your address on file."

"Great, there will be more from the toy department, as well."

She nodded and we walked away, heading to the toy department.

"Sir, I can have Denny and the guys take all of this back to the apartment. It might be a better choice, considering."

Paul looked at me, and I nodded. He turned around, looking at the sales girl. "We'll take it with us."

She started to put everything in bags. Denny and another man appeared out of nowhere. I was going to have to ask him about that. We headed to the toy department and bought her a few toys, which Denny and Max carried, then we headed to the park. While Max pushed her on the swings, I walked into Paul's embrace.

"Considering what?" I whispered.

"Considering Kathy. Max used to be CIA. He was shot and he quit. Nearly ended his life before he came to work for me."

"Which brings me to this question. Why do you have four bodyguards?"

He pulled me closer, kissing my forehead, his eyes never leaving Jo. "I lived a bad life, Victoria. You know this. I pissed a great many people off. Just because your father fixed everything doesn't mean a damn thing. I'm going to be gone most of the day tomorrow, cleaning up my brother's life, so I want you to stay inside where Max can keep an eye on you."

I laughed softly. "We really do need to have some serious talks, don't we?"

He chuckled. "Oh, you know we do. Come on, she looks like she is getting tired. Let's go have a nice dinner and then a quiet night. I just want to enjoy the both of you. I want an uncomplicated life with you."

When we got back to the apartment, we had tacos. I had to laugh when we watched Jo try to eat one. It was a mess. I felt bad that his floors and chairs were taking the brunt of it. But, all in all, we laughed more than we fretted.

I gave Jo a bath; well, the best that I could with one arm. Paul helped me get her out, dried off, and into her jammies. We all changed and curled up on the sofa. Jo was sleeping in a matter of minutes. Paul carried her to the bedroom where we tucked her in together.

Instead of going back to the living room, I headed to the bedroom, while he locked up and turned off all the lights. By the time he walked in, I was crawling into bed with his shirt on. His clothes left his body as he walked across the room. When he crawled in bed behind me, I felt his erection on my ass. "You are so fucking beautiful," he whispered into my neck.

Giggling, I turned my head. "No, you are."

Paul

I kissed her, my hand moving up my shirt to caress her perfect chest. I took my time touching her, loving her with my mouth and hands. "God, beautiful, what you make me feel." I moaned as I slid my hand down her stomach. I needed to touch her, to feel her. The truth of what was between us, there's no way two people could feel that and not be in love.

"Take them off," she moaned in my mouth.

I couldn't stop kissing her as I maneuvered my body around hers to slip her panties off. I managed to unbutton my shirt and there she was, all her perfection laid out before me. My hands moved on their own, gently touching her, my fingers totally appreciating the feel of her silky skin. I watched as her back slightly arched, the goose flesh hardening her nipples. Her breath hitched with tiny moans and mews, like no woman who had come before her. I would never stop fighting for her, fighting with her. No matter what laid ahead of us. I believed, if she kept what she knew sealed in her mind, that she would be fine. I needed her to know how I felt about her.

She slowly opened her legs to me, as only she could. I swear she'd been put here on this earth for me alone to worship. God, she was fucking beautiful with her back arched, her nipples peaked, and her luscious core glistening from her release.

I was drawn into her scent. My mouth watered as I slowly made a meal of her. When I finished, I moved up and slid into heaven, my mouth capturing hers to dance a dance only we could dance together. Slowly, I made love to this exquisite woman. Just before she took me over the edge of any reason I knew, I pulled back. "I love you," I whispered on her lips.

With tears in her eyes, she whispered, "I love you."

We let go together, our bodies pulsing as one. Everything in that moment made sense to me. She was all I could ever want. I needed to tell her, to share it with her. Kissing her lightly, I slowly pulled out, curling up next to her, and she wrapped herself around me.

"Victoria," I began. "My life has been something I am so ashamed of, and I can't bear to hold it in anymore. I need to clear my slate and tell you the things I've done."

"I know about it all. I read the file."

"No, baby, you don't. Please, let me tell you." I felt her nod. "I was the owner of a sex club, a BSDM sex club. I would restrain women and have sex with them. It was never against their will, there was always a safe word, but I was not a nice man. Not a gentle lover, if you could even call me that. Rarely was I with the same woman twice. I bought women for my club, and I was always the first to have them. I could never seem to get satisfied. Hell, when I met you, I fucked some poor girl into unconsciousness trying to get you out of my head. That was when I realized that I didn't want that life, that I wanted you. She was the last woman I was with, and that was the night we met.

"Please, keep in mind that I know it hasn't been a long time, but for me, it has. I spent most of my days and nights there, doing nothing really but having sex. Many times a day, but never without a condom, and I made sure I was checked regularly. It was the only way to deal with losing Sylvia. I haven't been satisfied in over five years, not until that first night we spent together. Victoria, I have never felt this way with anyone. I have not been gentle with a woman in a very long time. With you, it's all I want. I'm not sure I could ever really fuck you. You are so much more than that. I sold the club the afternoon I kissed you in your office. I have not kissed a woman since the night my wife died. I have not put my mouth on one. I haven't wanted to. Until you. I can't seem to keep my mouth off you."

She giggled into my chest. "I've only ever been with Steven. What I shared with him was nothing compared to what I feel with you. He never kissed me there. He only ever fucked me. I don't think we ever made love, and if we did, he sucked at it compared to what I feel with you. I don't care what you were before or what you did. It isn't who you are with me. I'm not who I was before, not when I'm with you. Together, we are one. I believe that now. I can see it in your eyes. I felt it that first night. I needed to feel safe.

"Paul, I have never lived my life for me. That first night, that was for me, for you, for us. You gave me something I never knew I was missing in my life. You gave me truth, you gave me trust, and you gave love, and yes, I felt loved. That's why I freaked out. Even when you fucked me, I knew you weren't fucking me because I know what being fucked feels like. You were making love to me, and it hurt so bad because I knew I had to leave. I blew my cover, and I wasn't sure you wanted anymore from me. I mean, your less than stellar introduction scared the shit out of me, but the minute you touched me, I felt you. I just fought it. Giving myself to you was so freeing, so me. Everything I have, all that I am, I give you. Can you feel me?"

"I feel you, Victoria. I felt you then, and I feel you now. I will never let you down. I couldn't take the sadness in your eyes. I've seen so much of it, put there by others that you've trusted and loved, and I couldn't handle being the reason you look like that again. Do you feel me?"

She giggled, kissing my chest. "To the depth of my soul."

Victoria

The scream that shattered our moment had us both moving. Paul nearly broke his neck trying to get his pants on. Me, I grabbed Denny's gun and was out the door before he had time to take a breath. I ran into Jo's room. She was thrashing about in her bed. "No, no, don't hurt her," she cried. Then she screamed out again.

Paul came running in. "Wake her up," he whispered.

I just stood there watching her, listening to the words coming out of her mouth. "No, Momma. Not my momma," she screamed again.

Paul moved around me and picked her up. "Joanna, come on, beautiful. Wake up." I watched in horror as she hit him time and time again. Her little fists fought him. She was screaming at him.

I reached for her, giving Paul my gun. The minute she was in my arms, I whispered, "Beautiful girl, I'm right here." Her head laid on my shoulder, and she burst into tears. "Shh, I'm here, baby. I'm right here. It was just a dream."

Her whole body was shaking. "Come on, bring her to bed with us," he whispered, rubbing her back. "It's all right, beautiful girl. No one is going to hurt Momma."

She picked her head up and turned to Paul, reaching for him. He handed me the gun and took her, wrapping her in his arms. She laid her head on his shoulder. "I'm scared," she whispered.

I had tears in my eyes. "I got you, baby girl. Come on, you want to sleep with us?"

She nodded against his shoulder and we went back to Paul's room. I put the gun away, and he climbed in bed with her. After laying her down, he ran in the closet to put on some pajama bottoms, and I crawled in next to her.

"What happened, baby?" I whispered as I kissed her forehead.

"Bad men were hurting you," she whimpered.

"I'm right here. It was just a dream. We're going to go home in a few days. Back to the cottage, okay?"

She shook her head. "No, Momma. I want to stay here. Can we stay here with Paul?"

He was coming out of the closet. As he climbed into bed on the other side of her, he said, "I'm going to go with you, and so is Max."

She turned in my arms, shaking her head. "No, I don't want to. I want to stay here. Can we stay here, Paul?"

He looked at me, and I nodded. "Of course, we can. Now, come on, let's get back to sleep. It's very late."

She smiled at him and rolled over into my arms. Paul moved over and held us both in his arms. After a few minutes, she was sleeping again.

He chuckled. "I would have never imagined my life would be this."

"What?" I whispered, a bit terrified at what he was going to say.

Looking at me, he touched my face. "So very full."

Smiling, I closed my eyes, and we slept in his arms, wrapped in the feeling of safety. Wrapped in what I hoped to be love.

CHAPTER TWELVE

PAUL

When I opened my eyes, there was a little hand on my face. My life was full. We may never have our own child, but we had this one, and she had already won my heart. They were both so beautiful. I looked over her head to look at Victoria; she had a small smile on her face. God, she was so fucking beautiful. I couldn't believe she loved me, wanted to be with me.

I slowly got out of bed, pulling the door shut behind me. Walking out on the balcony, I called Max. "Listen, I need you and Denny to get up here and go through this apartment with a fine-tooth comb. I want to make sure there are no cameras, no listening devices. I want the locks changed on all the doors, and I want an electronic security system put in with monitors at the doors."

"You got it, boss."

"Thanks." I hung up and called Saks.

I arranged for a decorator to come by and decorate Jo's room. Maybe if it felt like her space, she would feel more comfortable. If she wanted to stay here, she should feel like it was her home. Looking at my bedroom door, I couldn't help but smile. This was her home now, our home.

I called downstairs and asked for a shopper to come and take a grocery list. We needed food, food for a three-year-old. Seeing as how I knew nothing of three-year-olds, I decided to wake up Victoria. As I turned, I felt her hand on my back. "Good morning, beautiful." I pulled her into my arms.

"Good morning. What are you doing out here?" She snuggled into my embrace.

"Well, the guys will be up here scanning for anything that shouldn't be here. I am having all the locks changed and a security system installed. I called Saks, and they are sending someone over to decorate Jo's room after the guys get done. If she wants to stay here, she should feel like this is her home. Oh, and I've got a personal shopper coming to get some groceries in here."

She laughed. "Paul, you don't need to do this."

"Yes, I do. She scared the shit out me last night. She wants to stay here, so I am going to do everything I can to make her feel safe. To make you feel safe."

My hands went to her face, my mouth covering hers. God, the woman could kiss. We stood there until a knock on the door separated us. She giggled when she looked down. "I should get the door. We don't want you scaring the shit out of anyone with this." She grabbed my cock and pumped it a few times. My hips moved into her.

"I want you," I whispered, kissing her again.

"I know. I feel the same way." She let go and walked to the door. I heard her talking to Max and Denny. "I'm going to get changed. You guys do what you need to do. Paul will be out in a minute."

She came into the bedroom, shutting and locking the door, and found me in the closet. I could see it in her eyes. She shut the door and dropped to her knees, pulling my boxers down. She didn't talk; hell, she didn't give me a chance to object. Her hand was on me, and then she was guiding me into her mouth and down her throat. God, it felt so fucking good, I couldn't object. Slowly, she took me. I wanted to hold off and enjoy her, but I was raging. I needed to feel her.

"God, Victoria. I want to be inside you." I watched her take me again. Her nose touched my stomach, and she fucking swallowed. I had no control. My hands reached out to hold myself up as my whole-body fucking shook from my release. I wanted to cry out at her magnificence.

When I emptied myself, she pulled back, looking up at me. "Now, you'll be able to concentrate on what is going on, and you won't be thinking of this."

I chuckled, helping her up. "You want to fucking bet? This is all I am going to be thinking about."

I kissed her, dropping to my knees, slowly pulling her panties off. She put her foot on my shoulder, and I made love to her with my mouth. Time and time again, she shattered in my arms. What a way to start the day. We stood there in the closet and kissed for a few minutes, and then we dressed. When we walked out, Jo was still sleeping in our bed. She looked so tiny.

I left her in the bedroom and went out to find Max and Denny. I handed Max a note.

Start in Jo's room. Not one word. Just search it, scan it, and clear it. Then my office. Work your way through the place. I want our cameras in Jo's room.

He read it and nodded. I went to make some breakfast for us. When I reached the kitchen, Victoria was already cooking, so I sat and watched her. "How late does she usually sleep?"

"Not sure, she's changed a great deal since the last time I've been with her. How do you like your eggs?"

I smiled. I didn't have the heart to tell her I hated eggs. "Scrambled is fine. Can you put some cheese on them?"

She giggled. "Of course. So, are we going to talk about what's going on?"

"Not right now we're not. Right now, I'm going to sit here and watch my woman cook for me."

She laughed, and I mean laughed. "So, I'm your woman now?"

"Fucking right you are," I smarted.

"Uh, Momma, Paul said a naughty word," came a little voice from behind me.

Victoria came around the island. "He did, indeed. Should we put soap in his mouth?" I watched as Jo made a face and shook her head.

"Come on, Paul wants cheese in his eggs. Would like cheese on yours, as well?"

"Yes, please."

She sat Jo next to me. I leaned down. "I'm sorry I said the naughty word. I feel bad."

She smiled. "It's okay. Ruth's friend said a lot of naughty words."

I looked at Victoria, who was frozen, then turned back to Jo. "I'm sorry that her friend said those things."

"He would hit her, too. She would cry. I drew Momma pictures. I didn't like him. He said his name was Uncle John, but he was mean to me."

I picked her up, wrapping my arms around her. "Well, Ruth's friend isn't going to be mean to you anymore because I'm here now, and I am not going to let anything happen to you or your momma."

She smiled at me. "It's okay, Paul. Momma sent him to heaven."

"How do you know that?" I was riveted to my seat. I couldn't take my eyes off her.

"I just do."

I sat her back in her chair and got up to get all of us orange juice. Victoria was just standing by the stove. "Hey, you all right?" I whispered to her.

"No."

"It'll be fine. We can talk later. Come on."

When she picked her head up and looked at me, I nearly lost my breath. She knew, as well as I did, that there was no way Jo could have known that. Something was very wrong.

"Excuse me," Denny said from behind us. Both of us turned. "Mr. Simon, can I talk to you for a minute?"

I turned to look at Victoria, and she nodded. "Hey, beautiful, you want to help me butter the toast?" she asked Jo. I helped Jo off the bar stool and watched her toddle into the kitchen.

I followed Denny down the hall to what would become Jo's room. Max was standing in the hallway. He handed me a note.

We need to talk, someplace else. You shouldn't stay here right now.

Take them and leave. The Seasons. The guys already have the Presidential Suite swept and ready for you.

I looked up at him. He looked a bit freaked out. I just nodded and went back into the dining room where the girls were waiting for me to eat. We sat down and had a lovely breakfast. "Why don't you two get dressed and let's go out for a bit?" I looked at Victoria and nodded toward the bedroom.

Her body changed. She took Jo and headed to her bedroom. Max met her in the hallway, handing her one of the new dresses for Jo. He slightly shook his head. I followed her into the bedroom, getting Denny's gun out of the drawer, and then we left. We walked for a bit and then got in a cab and headed to the Seasons. Neither of us said a word about what was happening. I didn't know what the fuck was happening. We pulled up at the Seasons, and one of my men met me as we walked through the lobby, handing me a key.

We just hung out and watched some cartoons until Jo fell asleep. I carried her to what would be our room and laid her in the huge bed.

Victoria

My mind had been racing all fucking day. *How the hell does she know? Something is so very wrong here. Why are we here? What the hell were Max and Denny doing in the apartment?* I waited for Paul to walk out of the bedroom. When I saw his face, my heart stopped. He was just as scared as I was.

"What hell is going on?' I whispered.

He shook his head. "I asked Max and Denny to clean house. I had them start in Jo's room. I hired a decorator to come in and replicate her room. I thought, if it was like her room at the cottage, she would feel like it was her home." My heart swelled for him. "But he told us to leave. He gave me this."

He handed me a note. "What the hell does this mean?"

"I don't know."

"Is it safe for us here?"

He reached out and took my hand, leading me onto the balcony, pulling me into a hug. "Something is going on. Victoria, do you know who Andy Marciano is?"

"I do. But, Paul, we can't touch him."

"I don't want to touch him. I want to ask you this, and I want you to be honest with me. It's someone you love, isn't it?"

I nodded my head into his chest as the tears started to build up. "I don't think he would hurt me. I think Steven and John were the ones who killed my brother. Steven said a few things to me before I killed him."

"Victoria, do you know what this is about? Why we are here?"

I closed my eyes. I hated to lie. "No." I knew damn well why we were here. I couldn't do this to him. He was not innocent by any means, but he wasn't part of this.

He pulled back from me, looking into my eyes. "I know you know," he whispered, hugging me again. "It's all right. I understand you need to earn trust. But please don't run. Please don't take off on your own. Promise me."

I nodded into his chest. A knock on the door separated us. I watched as Paul walked in and opened the door. Max came in and followed Paul onto the balcony. He looked right at me. "We found canisters of poisonous gas in her room, along with two cameras and three of these." He handed me a small jar of liquid. Inside were three small squares. I knew them instantly.

"What about the rest of the house?" I asked.

"Denny is working on it," he said to me. I nodded and turned to look out over the city.

"I want you to secure my closet as a safe room. No cameras, no listening devices. We need a safe place to talk. How long until we can go back?" Paul asked him.

"We will stay on it, but not until morning. There's one more thing, Victoria." I turned to look at him. He pulled out a small device, what looked to be a phone. When he handed it to me, I realized what it was.

Looking up at him, he nodded. I moved into the room and then the bedroom. Paul and Max followed me.

My hand was shaking. I didn't want this to be truth, but deep inside, I knew it was. I turned on the machine and started to scan my beautiful niece. It was silent until I reached her neck, and then it beeped and a little red light flashed. Closing my eyes, I walked out of the bedroom. Once in the living room, I handed the machine to Max. As he moved it around my body, I heard it beep at the same place as Joanna's. But as he continued down my arm, it beeped three more times. I couldn't stop the tears.

Looking up, I saw the sorrow in Max's eyes. "Don't," I whispered. I couldn't bring myself to look at Paul. I knew what was going on, and I couldn't tell him. I just couldn't. "I need a medic," I said softly to Max. "You were a SEAL, right?" He nodded. "I'm sure you know someone who can be trusted."

Softly, he said, "I know quite a few someone's."

I nodded and walked away. I went in the bedroom, not saying a word to Paul, and crawled into bed with Jo. There was no way this could be fucking happening. I couldn't believe it. That bastard. He would pay for this. I didn't care anymore. I had a few weeks left to heal, and then this was going to end.

Paul

I watched her walk off the balcony. Looking at Max, I asked, "What the hell is going on?"

"Jo and Victoria both have trackers in them."

"What do you mean, in them?"

"Under their skin. I think the beeping in her arm is something else. Sir, we need to get her someplace that is safer than here. What about your lake house? I have a buddy who does private security. I'm going to call him. He's expensive, but he and his brother are the best at what they do. I think we need a secure place." I watched as he leaned in. "I don't think what's in her arm is safe. We need to operate on her arm."

I closed my eyes. "Get it done, Max. I don't care how much it costs. Get it done. She needs to be free of this shit."

"Already on it." I looked at him. "Hey, what can I say? The little one won my heart, and her mother, well, you have to like anyone that size who can kick your ass."

I chuckled. "Yeah, I suppose so. Just let me know when and where."

"It'll be sooner rather than later. I'll pick you up. Joe will be here soon. He was in Chicago doing business. His name is Joe Blackshaw, Blackshaw Security. I told him to meet you here. I'm going to head back to the apartment."

I nodded. "Max, what was in the canisters?"

"Some sort of toxin. I handed it over to FBI. This is bad shit she's into, but I'm going to do everything in my power to get her out of it. No child should have to live like that, and it pisses me off when people threaten or hurt them."

He let himself out as I walked into the bedroom and stood by the door, looking at them. Both of them deserved a great life. I was so lucky to have been given this chance twice. Crawling into bed with them, I closed my eyes just as her hand found mine, and sleep came.

Victoria

When I woke, Paul was lying next to Jo, cocooning us both. His eyes opened a few minutes after mine. I know he felt my body change. "I love you," he mouthed to me. Smiling, I mouthed it back to him. I so wanted a life with him, but I wasn't sure we were going to be able to have it. If anything, he would have Jo. I needed to legally make that a fact. He squeezed my hand and motioned for me to get up. We untangled ourselves from Jo and moved to the living area of our suite.

His arms came around me, his lips sealing themselves over mine. So sweet and gentle our kiss. "I'm so scared, Paul. So very scared."

"You and me both, beautiful. Max has a friend who works in security. He is on his way here now. We'll get to the bottom of this."

"You and I need to have a serious conversation, one where no one is going to be listening in."

"Oh, I know." He wiggled his eyebrows at me, making me giggle. There was a knock on the door. "That would be Joe."

God, he is so fucking beautiful. I can't believe he wants me, loves me. Wants Jo. It's going to hurt leaving him, leaving her. But I have to do it. I have to end this. Why do I have a fucking tracker? Why Jo? Who put the canisters in Paul's house? Maybe it was Kathy, but how did she manage to get them into the country? I think it was done beforehand. Maybe it was Steven. Maybe his plan was to end Kathy all along, end her with Jo and Paul. How did this life get so fucked up?

Paul went to open the door, and I heard talking so I looked up as two very large men walked into the room. My hand naturally moved to the back of my jeans. "Victoria, this is Joe Blackshaw from Blackshaw Security and his brother Al."

"Gentlemen." I nodded.

Joe reached out to shake my hand, and I just smiled at him. "Max seems to trust you. I only have one person here I can trust, and that's Paul. So, excuse me if I'm not so trusting."

He smiled at me. "Understood. Listen, Max explained a little about what is happening. We need to get you to a secure location." He looked at Paul. "I have a crew of men at your lake house securing the location. It should be fine by the time we get there. We should get moving."

Paul turned to me. "Tell me what you feel. Do you think this is what we should be doing?"

"What else do we have? I mean, we have trackers in us. They need to be removed before we go anywhere."

Al moved closer. "I have this here that will fry the circuits in them until we can get them out."

"Well, according to Max, mine is in my neck." I reached behind my head. "Right here."

"May I?" He nodded to me.

I turned around, and he placed a small, cold metal box on my neck. "That should do it." He slipped another thing out of his bag of tricks and scanned my neck. There was no beep. "See, all gone. Mr. Simon, where is yours?"

"It's Paul, and it's not me who has one."

"It's my daughter," I said quietly as I moved toward the bedroom. Al followed me. He walked through the bedroom door, and I nodded to the bed.

"Are you fucking kidding me?"

"Nope, and that is fucked up."

I watched as he quietly made his way to the bed. He put the little box on her neck, looked at me, and nodded as he ran the scanner over her neck, and it stayed silent. We moved back into the living room. "How old is she?" he demanded.

Paul looked at him. "Three."

"Who the fuck does shit like this?"

"Fucked up people. We need to go. I need a place to talk, and I need to find out what the hell is in my arm."

"I'll get Joanna," Paul said. He walked out carrying her, and we all left together.

Paul

Once in the car, we didn't say much. I sat with Jo in my arms and Victoria's hand in mine. She was in her own head. Who the fuck would do this shit? I needed to pay attention to Joe.

"I just got an all clear on your lake house. Nothing out of the ordinary, no cameras or listening devices. We should be safe there. You have a boat house?" I nodded. "I'll have our medic set up in there." He looked at Victoria. "We will get whatever is in your arm out. Do you want to fill me in on what I don't know?"

Victoria looked at Jo. "Not now. When Max gets to the house."

"He is on his way there with Jo's things. He can hang out with Jo while we talk."

Victoria giggled. "I'm sure he doesn't want to play with a three-year-old."

Al looked at her in the rear-view mirror. "Well, if he doesn't, I will."

I watched Joe smile. "My brother has a soft spot for children and abused women."

It took about an hour to reach the lake house. Max met us there, and Jo was awake and ready to go. Max took her down to the beach while Victoria stood on the patio watching them. I assured Joe that she would talk when she was ready. We all just kind of stood around waiting.

"My name is Victoria Holmes, but that's my married name. I am, or was, MI6 Special Ops. My twin brother, Johnathan, was my partner. When I became pregnant six years ago, I quit. I was in a horrible accident which ended my unborn baby's life as well as my ability to have children. I suppose that's irrelevant in the big picture of this fucked up scenario. My brother and his wife were murdered, along with Paul's wife. My sister-in-law was pregnant. Somehow, the baby survived, so I left my husband, took the baby, and went into hiding." She nodded toward the beach. "My daughter, Joanna, is that child. Two years ago, MI6 came to me, telling me that they now had a name and a lead to who killed my brother, who we also believe killed Paul's wife, but at the time I didn't know that. So, I left Joanna in the care of a woman named Ruth Jacobson, a woman who was a retired agent, older, sent by MI6. Who better to trust with the only real thing I had left in this life? I knew there was a contract on my life, and I know it's still out there, but no one ever knew what I looked like. I can change my appearance rather easily, so I was reinstated at MI6 per my request, and I left the only person I had left in this world. I started my investigation. I became the job. Persona after persona, lie after lie, I worked my way to Paul's brother's accounting firm. I was following the paper trail, the money of the man who killed my brother. That is where Paul and I met."

"I wasn't such a nice man."

"I have skills that I don't even want to have. My father always told me I was a natural. I excelled in everything."

I chuckled. "I've seen her take down two of my men without losing her breath. She is definitely a force to be reckoned with."

Victoria turned and looked at me. A small smile crossed her perfect lips. "When I'm mad, I have a hard time controlling it all."

"So, what brought us here?" Joe said.

I noticed Al sitting there, his eyes riveted to her. Not sure I felt comfortable with it.

She turned and looked at Jo and Max for a few minutes before she continued. "I have an eidetic memory. I remember everything I see. It's bothersome most of the time, but apparently, while I was doing the books for Paul's brother, I uncovered the identity of this man who killed my brother. But it was all a set up. I wasn't there to find his identity. I was there to make sure his identity was never found. My ex-husband orchestrated the whole thing. Everyone involved with the op was being blackmailed by him. I'm pretty sure they are all dead now. I know John Simon and Steven Holmes are dead because I killed them. As for the rest of them, I'm not sure. Anyway, it was all a set up. John wasn't this man; he was just the enforcer. He killed my brother and his wife, and Paul's wife. I'm pretty sure he was the one who put the tracker in Joanna. I can't figure out when mine was put in, but it all makes sense now, how Jacob could always find me," she said under her breath. "Anyway, Steven's new wife is, or was, my oldest friend. I gave her Jo to bring to Chicago for safe keeping while I dealt with the man I believed to be the man who killed my brother. Her plan was to kill Jo once I was out of the picture. She's pregnant with Steven's child. We have her stashed someplace."

"Will she talk to us?" Joe asked.

"I don't think so. She has a blood lust for me, and the fact that I killed Steven might make her have a death wish for me. But since we've returned, my mind has brought everything to the surface and I now know the true identity of Andy Marciano, the man who killed my brother."

"Would you be willing to tell me who it is?" Al asked.

"It doesn't matter, in the big picture. He is untouchable by anyone but me, and I'm pretty sure, now that we have gone off the grid by disengaging our trackers, the chances are even less of me being able to get close to him. But I have one last card up my sleeve, and I am banking on it to get me close to him."

"You can't be serious. You cannot go up against someone like that."

I laughed, and they all looked at me. "I'd lay my fortune on the fact that she can kick your ass. I watched her, with a broken arm, take out her ex with one hand while he had her broken arm twisted and his hand wrapped around her throat."

It was kind of funny to see Joe swallow hard. Victoria walked off the porch and headed toward the beach.

"What isn't she telling me?" Joe asked.

"A great deal, if I was a guessing man. She keeps her cards close to her chest. We haven't known each other for very long. She will share when she is ready. I think she is still trying to deal with the fact that she knows this man personally. When she figured it out, she nearly passed out. She was a mess for a few days."

"Tell me about Joanna," Al asked.

"Brilliant child for three. She had a weird dream the other night, said that some men were hurting her momma, and she refuses to go home to England. She also made a comment that scared the shit out of Victoria. She told us that she knew her momma sent my brother to heaven."

"A clairvoyant?" Al said softly.

I shook my head. "Not sure. But it sure was fucking creepy. A clairvoyant sees the future, not the past. But what do I know?"

Joe's phone buzzed. "Doc has the boat house ready. We should get whatever is in her arm out."

My heart stopped. I nodded and headed to the beach. "Hey, beautiful, are you having fun?" I asked Jo.

"Look, Max found some seashells." She held out her little hand.

"Wow, those are beautiful. Maybe we could put them in your room." I knelt on the sand in front of her. "Momma and I have to go have a meeting. Max here is going to stay with you for a little while.

Maybe you two could have a picnic on the beach while you wait for us."

She looked up at Max, nodding her head. I watched as Victoria hugged her. "No matter what happens, baby, you are going to stay with Paul, all right?"

She nodded, putting her hand on her face. "It's all right, Momma."

"I love you, beautiful."

"I love you, too."

We stood there and watched Max follow her down the beach.

"Joe said they were ready for you in the boat house."

She turned into my chest. "Promise me, Paul, that if anything happens you will give her a good life."

I wrapped my arms around her. "Nothing is going to happen. We are going to have a wonderful life together. Just the three of us."

She nodded. "I really am so in love with you. Please promise me."

God, my heart lurched. "I am so in love with you. I promise, Victoria. I so fucking promise." My hands came up to her face, wiping her tears from her cheeks with my thumbs. "I fucking promise," I whispered as I kissed her. We stood there kissing for a few minutes.

"Let's get this over with," she whispered on my lips.

I shook my head. "No, I want to make love to you."

She giggled. "Okay."

We headed back to the house. Walking in, I looked at Joe. "We're going to need about an hour." Victoria turned into my chest and giggled. He just smiled and nodded at me, and we continued to my bedroom.

Walking in, I shut and locked the door. She just stood there looking at me. "An hour, huh?"

I raised my eyebrows at her. "Give or take." I stepped toward her.

It was always a slow dance with us. Our fingers touching, slowly, I undressed her. "Fuck, Victoria," I moaned as I looked at her. She reached up and slid my t-shirt up my chest. I pulled it the rest of the way off as she unbuttoned my jeans, taking her sweet time with my zipper. My cock hurt so much. Her fingertips trailed along it as she pulled down my pants and boxers. On her way down, she inhaled me.

One movement and I was down her throat. She swallowed, and I, Mr. Self-control, was gone. "Aww, fuck, beautiful," I groaned out.

When I looked down at her, she just looked so fucking innocent sitting on her heels looking up at me. Stepping back, I got on my knees, kissing her. "We will survive this," I whispered as we gently kissed.

"I'm scared, Paul. Make me feel safe. Do what only you can do. Love me and make me feel safe."

I picked her up and carried her to the bed, and that is just what I did. I made love to her with my mouth, taking her over the edge three times, and I still couldn't get enough of her ambrosia. Her body was covered in goose flesh, her nipples so hard I was sure she could cut diamonds with them. Looking at her as I knelt between her legs, watching her hips gently rocking into the mattress, my mind emptied of everything except her.

Sliding my hand under her knee, I moved up her body, gently opening her up to me. Just as my mouth touched hers, my cock slid slowly into her tight silken body. I could feel her body arch into mine. So slowly I made love to this siren, this goddess who had become my obsession. I felt her thigh push against me, and I gently rolled us over. She walked herself up my chest, pushing down hard on me, her hips moving in little circles.

"God, Victoria, you feel so good." Her hand taking mine, she put it on her breast. They were perfect.

Wrapping my other arm around her back, I sat up, taking her nipple into my mouth. I felt her tighten around me. Fuck, I was going to lose it. My hand on her hip moved in, and I pressed it against her core. Her eyes opened and looked right into my soul as she released. "Oh, God, Paul," she moaned out. Our eyes locked as we came together. I watched as her eyes filled with tears. "I'm so scared," she whispered.

Wrapping her in my arms, I laid her on her side. "I know, baby. We have to believe this is going to turn out. I can't imagine my life without you in it."

We laid like this kissing for some time. I could feel myself getting harder. My hips just started moving, the feel of her making me harder. "God, Victoria," I moaned as my hips moved faster, harder.

"Fuck me," she whispered on my lips.

Fuck her I did. My arm wrapped around her, anchoring her to me. Her body gave no resistance as my hips slammed into her. Fucking this woman was going to become very addictive. I was done ten minutes after I started, releasing all that I had deep inside of her. She burst into tears, clawing at me to get her closer. We laid there for a long time holding one another.

"I need to clean up," she whispered on my shoulder when the tears stopped.

Pulling out of her was a loss I didn't want. I never wanted to be out of her. My eyes never left her as she walked across the room into the bathroom. I laid on the bed staring at the ceiling. *Please, God, let her be all right.* When the door opened, she climbed back on the bed and kissed me.

"We need to get this over with. The sooner they figure out what's in my arm, the sooner I can heal and then finish this."

Looking at her, I had to say it. I needed to know. "When this is over, Victoria, will you consider becoming my wife? I want a life with you. I want a life raising Jo."

She smiled sweetly, her hand touching mine. "Yes, I will consider it."

I think my smile might have broken my face. Pulling her down on the bed, I kissed her deeply. "I love you, beautiful."

Her good hand on my face, her thumb ran across my lips. "I love you."

We got dressed and headed out to the kitchen. Jo was sitting in a chair eating. "Look, Momma, Max made me mac and cheese from a box. Can you believe they make mac and cheese in a box?"

Victoria burst out laughing. "No, baby, I can't believe that." She sat down next to Jo. "I need to go with these men out to the boat house for a little while."

"I know, Momma. They are going to operate on your arm," she said so matter-of-fact.

"They are, so you be good for Max and take your nap. I'll be back in a little while, then Paul and I will come and sleep with you."

She nodded her little head, her curls bouncing all over. "I love you, Momma." She looked at me. "I love you, too, Paul."

My heart burst. "I love you, too, beautiful."

We all walked out to the boat house. It looked like a fucking operating room. I kissed Victoria, and then Joe made me leave. "If this goes wrong, that little girl is going to need you. Go back to the house and wait for us. Al will go with you."

~

Victoria

I couldn't let go of his hand. We stood there looking at one another. "I'm scared," I whispered.

"We are going to get through this together. We'll have a life after this, together, all three of us." He pulled me into his arms. "Feel me, baby. Feel me."

I nodded into his chest. He had become so important to me in such a short time. Jesus, we just made love like it was the last time we were ever going to make love. I didn't let go of him until my body stopped shaking, and his hold didn't falter until I loosened my grip. Pulling back, he kissed me. "Go," I whispered.

Turning from me, he walked to the door. He paused but didn't turn around. "Joe, we don't know one another, but I am trusting you that this man can do this. We need her."

"I wouldn't be here if I didn't think this was going to work out. I know trust is an issue for the two of you, but you have to start somewhere. Let it be with us. We won't let you down," Joe said gently.

"I love you, Victoria."

"And I love you. Promise me, Paul."

"I promise, beautiful. Hurry back."

I watched as he walked out the door with Al. Joe went over and locked it while two other men sealed the door. "Victoria?" I turned to the man who'd said my name. "My name is Sam McDonald. I'm a surgeon. Whatever is going on with your arm, we will know shortly."

I nodded. "Could you take the tracker out of my neck, as well? And, when you finish, my daughter has one in her neck that I want out."

He nodded. "Come on, let's get you changed and on the table." He guided me to a screen, where I changed into a gown and then got on the table. "Now, you should be out for maybe an hour."

"I don't want to be put out. Please, just use a local. I need to hear and see what you are doing."

"I'm not sure a local will be enough."

I chuckled. "Well, I guess it's going to have to be. If it's too much, I'll let you put me under. I need to know what he did to me." Sam and Joe stood looking at each other. "This is my choice, my body, and it's what I want."

Sam nodded. "Let's get started and get this cast off then." I listened to the saw for a long time while they cut the cast down both sides. "Okay, now, before I take this off, I want to go over a few things. We have no x-rays of what's inside. I have no idea what kind of surgical incisions are here. I'm hoping I can just re-cut and examine. From what I understand, you felt it break. You heard it break?"

"He twisted it back, and it snapped. Well, something snapped. I personally didn't think it needed three separate pins. I mean, it hurt like a bitch, but not like it should have, and two hours of surgery? Does that sound right?"

"It would all depend. Let's get started. You ready for this?" he asked his team. Everyone in the room nodded.

"Joe, can I hold your hand? If we blow up or die from some kind of toxic poison, I really would like to be holding someone's hand."

He smiled behind his mask and reached for my hand. "Thank you," he whispered. "I think I'm a bit freaked out."

I giggled as Sam lifted the cast off my arm. They had set up a mirror so I could look at what they were doing, that and to reflect the light onto my arm. I could see three separate bandages on my arm, two on the side and one on the front of my arm. They were covered in a yellow type of bandage. "Victoria, where was this surgery done?"

"London," I whispered. I could feel the tears coming.

I felt him lift my arm and remove the bottom of the cast. "All right, you are going to feel a few pricks and then a slight stinging sensation." I nodded. Six pricks in all.

Joe squeezed my hand. "This will work. Hopefully, it's nothing and they are just pins."

"What if they are, but still filled with explosives?" I asked.

"That's why I'm here." I turned my head. "My name is Jack Ellis. Explosives are my specialty. I've designed them, disengaged them, and blown some up. I also designed this little baby that will tell us if there are in fact explosives in the metal."

"Can you feel this?" Sam asked. I shook my head. "All right, then let's get started. I'm going to peel back the surgical dressing." I felt the gentle tug on my skin but felt no pain. "Okay, you have six stitches on each incision, which would be right for the insertion of the pins into the bone. This one here on the lower side of your arm looks to be a bit infected. Have you had any pain?"

"Yes, but I've been taking pain medication."

"I'm going to cut the stitches and re-open the wound."

"Wait, I need you to get Denny in here. No offense, but I think I'd like to be put out and I want someone, no offense, who is on our side. Someone I know."

Joe chuckled. "I can do that." He pulled a phone out of his pocket and called the house. "Victoria asked for Denny to come down. She doesn't want to go under without someone here she can trust."

A few minutes later, there was a knock on the door. I watched as two men unsealed it and let him in. He changed into a gown and took Joe's place. I grabbed his hand. "You watch them. Make sure everything is done correctly. I don't think I can stay awake for this."

"Not a problem, Miss Holmes." He squeezed my hand.

Looking at Sam, I said, "Please, don't get us killed. I have a life to live. I'm ready."

Sam covered my face with a mask, and I closed my eyes.

Paul

It fucking killed me to leave her there. I'd never been a man of my word before, so why did I have to be now? Because I fucking loved her, and I needed to build that trust. She needed to know she could trust me, and I needed to know I could be the man to share her so very complicated life with. Pacing in front of the windows, my eyes locked on the boat house. My phone rang in my pocket, scaring the shit out of me.

"Yeah," I snapped.

"Victoria asked for Denny to come down. She doesn't want to go under without someone here she can trust," Joe said.

I smiled, my heart starting to beat again. "He'll be right down." I disconnected the call. Walking outside, I saw him standing guard over the house. "Denny, could you please go down to the boat house? Victoria wants someone there she can trust."

He nodded and headed down. I watched him walk into the building. Now to just wait. Now, I just had my memories until she woke. *Come on, beautiful, you can do this.* Time, it was something I gave up on years ago, but I could feel the hands moving on my watch. I could hear the ticking on the clock in the living room.

I paced the floor like a caged cat, ready to pounce on the first person I saw. Time ticked on with no movement from the boat house. Two hours had passed. Two hours? I looked around, wondering where Jo was. Heading to her bedroom, I found Max sitting on a chair just outside her door.

Pushing the door open, I found her sitting on her bed with her back against the headboard. "Hi, beautiful. Whatcha doing?"

"Momma told me to be a good girl, so I'm being a good girl," she said so sweetly.

"Well, thank you, but I don't think she meant for you to stay in bed all day. Come on, you want to have some ice cream with me?" I put my hand out for her to take.

"I have to go potty," she said as she scooted to the edge of the bed.

I helped her to the potty and waited for her. We held hands and went to the kitchen to have ice cream. "So, Joanna, tell me about your room at the cottage. I thought maybe we could make your room here like that. Maybe we can get you some of the same toys. We could even ask if maybe Denny could go over and get some of your favorite things."

We sat on the barstools eating ice cream and talking about her room. If I was a kid, I would have thought it was some sort of fantasy land. I couldn't help but smile. She was a fantastic child. I was so excited by the time she finished telling me about it, that I wanted to go see it for myself.

We played a game, and then we snuggled on the couch and watched a movie. I couldn't tell you what the hell we watched. But, sometime during the movie, Jo got up on her knees and looked at me. "Momma's awake now. Can we see her?"

I smiled. "Not yet, sweetheart." My heart raced in my chest. Now, at least, we'd have some answers. "Max?" I called out.

"Yes, sir?" He was in the dining room.

"I'm going to go down to the boat house. Victoria is awake. Will you stay here with Jo?"

"Sure." He looked at Jo. "Hey, little one, you want to go down to the beach?"

She shook her little head. "No, I want to wait for Momma."

"Well, then, we will wait for Momma." He sat in the chair.

"I'll be back with her in a little bit," I told Jo, kissing her on the head.

I was halfway to the boat house when Joe walked out. He met me on the lawn. "There weren't any pins in her arm. They were explosives, just like we thought, but not anything we've ever seen before. Some highly toxic nerve gas. The one in her neck was a tracker with some kind of poison to kill her in case the nerve gas didn't work."

I turned and looked at the house. My feet were moving, and Joe was right behind me. Running in, I picked up Jo. "Come on, sweetheart, we need to take you to Momma." I ran across the lawn with Joe and Max following me.

When we got in the boat house, Victoria was sitting on the bed. Jo reached for her. Victoria smiled at her. "Hey, beautiful."

"Momma, I was a good girl, just like you told me to be."

"That's wonderful. Sam here is going to give you a shot and make you go to sleep for a little while."

"Is he going to take that thing out of my neck? Uncle John put it in there. He said it was in case I got lost."

Victoria looked up at me. "Yes, baby, he is."

Twenty minutes later, with Jo in my arms and Victoria slowly walking next to me, we climbed into bed and held each other. We waited for Jo to wake up and for Sam to figure out what the hell was in their bodies.

CHAPTER THIRTEEN

PAUL

I laid here holding her hand, looking at her beautiful face while she slept. I looked down at this incredible child lying between us, with her small bandage on her neck. *Who the hell was my brother? Why would he hurt or want to hurt a child, this child, my child?* The more I thought about it, the angrier I got. My mission in this life had now become them, to protect them, to give them the best possible life.

My eyes traveled up to her face, meeting her incredible blue eyes. I saw the tears built up in them. Reaching up, I gently wiped them away. I wanted nothing more than to hold her, kiss her, and make her feel nothing but me.

Slowly, she got up, walking around to my side of the bed. Taking my hand, she led me into the closet. It seemed to be the place we always ended up. When I closed the door, she turned and walked into my chest. "Paul," she got out before she completely broke. I slid down the door, pulling her into my lap, and held her.

"I got you, beautiful," I whispered into her neck. She felt like heaven in my arms. I held her while she let it all go.

"I'm sorry," she sobbed out.

"No, don't be. There is nothing to be sorry for. I am here because I can't not be here. You have become everything to me. Both of you. I don't care what we have to face, we will do it together."

She nodded into my chest.

Victoria

I found that the only place I seemed to be able to find solace was in his arms. I just could not comprehend why someone would do this to Jo, to me. *What the hell?* It wasn't so much as someone, but the someone. I needed to end this. I knew that my arm wasn't broken the way they said it was. It was my forearm, not my upper arm. They casted me the way they did because of what they put in me.

As I sat in his arms, I knew that was where I was supposed to be—with him, having a life with him. There was still so much we needed to learn about each other. But, for now, I just wanted this. I just wanted normal. I wanted what every woman on the planet did—the love of a good man and a happy life.

"Are you a good man, Paul?" I whispered.

"I want to be, but I haven't been. Victoria, I will not hurt you."

"I know. I just want to know if you're a good man."

"I haven't wanted to be a good man for a long time. I didn't give a shit about anyone or anything except myself and my brother. Then I met you. You took my breath away, and it scared the shit out of me. That day that you slapped me across the face for kissing you, I knew then that I was going to have to change who I was if I stood a chance in hell of ever having you. I began that day to clean up my life, to become the best man I could, simply because you deserve nothing less."

"Thank you."

He chuckled. "For what?"

"For kissing me that day. I really wanted you. I fought it so hard. I'm grateful that you feel the same way. I just don't know what I would do right now without you. Without this. For so long, I've lived a life that wasn't mine. My life with Steven was a lie. It destroyed me to leave him. I hoped that when it was all over, I could go back and explain it all to him. You know, make him understand. But he orchestrated this whole fucking thing. My whole life, Paul, has been nothing but lies, and I am the biggest lie of them all."

He chuckled, his fingers turning my head up, his lips pressing against mine. "Perhaps, but you are the most beautiful liar I've ever known." He deepened his kiss.

Pulling back, I looked him in the eyes. "Steven's last name was Holmes, not mine. My last name is Parker."

"Victoria Parker, nice to meet you. I'm Paul Alexander Simon." He kissed me. "I really want to make love to you right now," he moaned in my mouth.

"Mmm, and I want you to make love to me." His hand moved under my shirt to cup my breast.

"Come on, you haven't had anything to eat. We need to feed you, and hopefully, Jo will be getting up soon."

We made our way to the kitchen, leaving Max to sit with Jo. "Do you think he minds being a babysitter?" I had to ask.

"Believe it or not, he insisted."

We had sandwiches and just sat on the couch for a bit. Joe came in and sat looking at me before he spoke. "You both are very lucky. The tracker in your neck had a nerve agent in it. Remotely released. Jack is trying to locate the source."

"I know where it came from," I said quietly. They both looked at me. "What was in my arm?"

"Apparently, one of the pins was an explosive device, and the other two were filled with some kind of chemical weapon. Victoria, the amount of explosive in the canister was more than enough to end your life as well as people within a twenty-foot radius. The chemicals in the other two are not known to us yet. I came in here to ask you if you would be all right with me calling in some friends of mine. This is huge, chemical warfare huge. I don't think any of us have ever seen anything like this. Like I said before, you need to trust us or we can't help you."

I sat there looking at him, reading his eyes. He was a trustworthy man. "I need to end this. I know who did this, and I need for it to be over. I'm the only one who knows who did this. You or your friends will not get close to him. I can."

"How can you be so sure of that?" Joe asked.

I couldn't tell him. I couldn't say anything yet. I needed a plan. I need to make sure Jo was safe, and right then she was not. "I can't tell you right now. I need to make sure Joanna is safe. If she had the same toxins in her body as I did, then she was some sort of insurance policy that I would do what I was told to do. If that's the case, then I am the only one who can do this. He will see you coming a mile away. I need for her to survive this. She is just a baby. She beat the odds by surviving the death of her mother, and I need to make sure she does just that."

"I have an idea. I'm not sure how you will feel about this, but I have a place to stash her, making her as safe as she is with you."

"I'm not sure she would leave me."

"She will go with Max," Paul said softly.

I turned my head and looked at him. "She is so little."

"Victoria, I would stash her with my mother."

I giggled. "I'm sure your mother wants a three-year-old hanging around."

Joe laughed. "I have five brothers, and not one of us has children. Trust me, she would love it. Why don't I call her, talk to her, and then have my little brother bring her here? She can hang out with Jo so they can get to know one another."

I nodded. I needed this to be over. "You can call your friends, as well. I'm going to need some help. I don't want to die." Turning my head, I looked at Paul. "I want that life you keep talking about."

He smiled. "And a great life it will be."

Paul

The next few hours were a blur. Victoria and Jo cuddled in my bed, while Joe and his team worked to isolate the toxins. Joe's mother, Sally, came and was in the kitchen making brownies and cookies. She was excited to meet Joanna, but they stayed in the bedroom talking and holding one another. I wanted to be a part of that, but I knew Victoria had been away from her for so long.

Max came walking out with Jo in his arms. "Victoria is in the shower, and Jo is hungry," Max said.

I smiled. "Jo, I want you to meet my friend, Sally. She came here to meet you and to hang out with you."

Jo smiled at me. "I know why she is here, Paul. Momma told me."

I couldn't help but smile as I took her tiny hand and kissed it. I introduced Jo to Sally, and they were thick as thieves' minutes after. Looking at Max, I said, "I'm going to take a shower." He nodded and smiled.

When I walked into my room, I made sure the door was locked. Victoria was in the bathroom, but I didn't hear the shower, so I made my way in there. She was in the tub. "I can't get my arm wet, but I needed to feel clean," she whispered.

"Can I join you?" She nodded and scooted up while I dropped my clothes. Climbing in behind her, I wrapped my arms around her, pulling her against my chest. "I've never taken a bath with someone before."

She giggled. "Paul, out of all those women, did you bring any of them home with you?"

"No, not one of them. You are the only woman since my wife that has been in my bed."

"I'm sorry your brother killed her."

"Yeah, me too. But they say that people die for a reason. If I hadn't known her, I wouldn't know how to love you."

"That's nice to say. I suppose the same goes for Steven. If all this mess hadn't happened, I wouldn't be here in America and I would have never met you. I'm grateful for you, and I am so thankful that you were so very persistent in having me."

I chuckled. "I think, even if none of this had happened, that I would have found you."

"You think?" she whispered.

I kissed her neck. "Oh, I think."

We had a lovely bath, just sitting in the water holding another, until the water went cold. Getting out, I couldn't help but watch her dry herself off.

"What's going on in your head?" I asked.

"I'm terrified," she admitted softly.

I dropped my towel and pulled her into my arms. "I'm with you all the way."

"Paul, that's what scares me the most. I think, in order for this to work, I am going to need you to help me. But I can't do it. I can't risk your life as well as mine. Jo deserves to be happy. She deserves to have a life, one filled with love and happiness."

"I made a promise to you, and I plan on keeping it. I don't need to go with you. I want to go with you, but you're right. Jo needs to stay safe. I don't like knowing you are going to go out there and possibly not come back. But I understand it."

She wrapped her arms around me. "I really do love you, love this. I love the idea of a life with you."

I kissed her head. "We will have those things. I promise."

Shaking her head, she pulled away from me. "Make love to me." She looked at me. "You're so beautiful and I need to feel. I need to feel us instead of this mess."

Gently, I picked her up and took my time loving her. When we finished, she lay content in my arms. I felt her move up my body, her breath warm on my ear. "I'm afraid I'm going to have to kill more people. Can you live with knowing I'm a murderer?"

"If I'm being honest, I try not to think about it. As far as I am concerned, it's either kill or be killed. Victoria, if I was in the same position, I would do the same thing."

She snuggled closer to me. "You might have no choice, Paul. Can you pull the trigger if you have to?"

"If it was to protect you and Jo, fucking right I will. Without hesitating. You, in such a short time, have become my life. Your father," I felt her tense up when I mentioned him, "gave me back my life. Hey, while I'm thinking about it, how did he do that?"

She pulled away from me and got out of bed. I watched as she walked to the bathroom. When she came out, she went in the closet and put on a pair of my pajama bottoms and a t-shirt. When she walked out, she looked at me. "I need time to myself. I need to think."

I nodded to her and watched her walk out of the room. I wanted to go with her. I wanted, no needed, to make her understand that she wasn't alone. But I didn't. I got up, dressed, and went to find Jo. She was in the kitchen with Sally and Max, having a good time making cookies.

"Hi, Paul. We made cake, and now we are making cookies." She was beaming.

"Well, that's wonderful. We can have some after we have dinner." I smiled at her then turned to look out the window. Victoria was headed toward the beach. Even dressed in my clothes, she was magnificent.

∾

Victoria

I wasn't sure what I was supposed to do with all the information in my brain. Looking out at the water, my mind was like a whirlwind of information. Every single moment in my life came to a point. It was all a lie, all training for this moment in time. I needed to be the machine I was trained to be. Kathy held more answers than not. She had information I didn't have, that I could only speculate on. I'd never gone into a mission without every possible piece of information.

Turning, I looked at the house. I needed to talk to her. I needed to trust Paul and tell him what I knew. I could see him standing in the window watching me. I suspected he knew something was wrong. *How long until my arm heals?* The break was nothing, but I was worried about the stitches. It could be used as a weapon against me. As I searched my brain, my eyes closed. *A week, maybe two.* I needed information.

When I opened my eyes, I saw Paul, Joe, and Al on the deck with five other men I didn't know, but I was pretty sure they were there to pick my brain. Shaking my head, I turned around and walked along the beach.

Time was not my friend here. The more time that passed, the more danger we were in, especially with the trackers. I just couldn't figure out why the explosives were in my arm. *What did he want me to do? Could he have killed me? He killed my brother, but did he? Or was Johnathan killed to control him? Would I have been sacrificed as well? Did he know? Does he know?*

When I came back across the house along the beach, I noticed one of Joe's men standing guard over me. I couldn't help but wonder if they thought I would take off. But with no bra, no panties, dressed in clothes that were literally five times my size, and barefoot, where in the hell could I go? I giggled.

I sat down and pushed my feet into the sand. I was going to have to do this. I'd probably have to kill him. I didn't want to, but he was willing to kill me, to kill Jo. Hell, he even went so far as to attempt to kill Paul. *Who does that shit?* I needed answers. I needed to know, or did I already know? I knew it was him; it was the only thing that made sense. *How is it possible to hide in plain sight like that for so many years?* It must've been exhausting, keeping everything covered.

Before I knew it, the sky was getting darker. It was time to go and see Jo, see how she was getting along with Sally. I had no choice but to trust Joe and his crew. I needed help. I wasn't naive enough to think I could do it on my own. I would be walking into the den of death; I had no doubt. It was time to go see what the hell kind of cards they had up their sleeves, and to see who they were. As I stood, the water looked so inviting. It was fully dark out, well nearly. They wouldn't be able to see me.

Dropping my pants, I stepped toward the water. I pulled the t-shirt off and threw it behind me then headed out into the water. I knew I had antibiotics in me, so my arm would be fine. I didn't care. I just needed to swim. I hadn't realized how far out I was until I turned to see the lights in the house. The lake was really calming. I headed back to the shore. As I got close, I could see someone standing on the shore and smiled. I would know that body anywhere. Paul was waiting for me with a huge towel in his hands. As I walked out of the lake, he smiled, but it didn't reach his eyes.

Paul

I nearly had a stroke when she dropped her clothes and walked into the lake. I mean, there were at least twenty men keeping watch over her. My heart raced as she lifted her shirt. A few of the men groaned behind me. *Yeah, look, you bastards. She is mine.* I went in the house and grabbed a giant beach towel out of the hall closet and headed down to the water.

As she walked out of the water, my cock was instantly fucking hard. The look in her eyes was one of pure sex. She smiled a little smile as she got closer. I knew all those men behind me could see her. I walked into the water, wrapping the towel around her as she pressed herself against me.

"I see you," she whispered, her hand coming to rest on my cock.

I chuckled as I covered her mouth with mine. Pulling back, I whispered, "Up until this moment, I wanted to throttle you. But now, all I want to do is make love to you, then fuck you."

She giggled. "I'm yours. They can look all they want. My heart belongs to you."

I picked her up, and she wrapped her legs around me. "Victoria," I whispered on her lips. We stood there for a few minutes kissing. She released her legs, and I set her down, wrapping the towel around her. "Come on, there are some people who want to talk to you, and Jo is waiting for dinner. She made cake."

It was good to hear her laugh. I grabbed her clothes as we headed back to the house. As she walked up onto the deck, she nodded to the men sitting around. "Gentlemen, I need to shower and then have dinner with my daughter. So, if you'll excuse us for about an hour, I'm all yours."

Joe smiled at her. "Do what you need to do. We aren't going anywhere. I'll have Doc re-bandage your arm. Might want to get a new cast on it, as well."

Nodding, we went in the house and straight to the bedroom. I watched her drop the towel and walk that perfect ass into the bathroom. My cock hurt from wanting her. I couldn't help myself. I suppose, on one level, I was a pervert, but I wanted her.

She was standing in the shower with her hands on the wall. I shut and locked the door, dropped my clothes, and stepped into the shower with her. "Victoria," I whispered as I put my hands next to hers on the wall.

She leaned back against me. "Paul, I don't want to feel." My hands moved on their own, touching her everywhere I could. I felt her move her hands around and wrap around me. "I need you," she moaned.

"Put your hands on the tile, Victoria."

She released me, her hands moving to the wall. I slipped my leg between hers and bent my knees, finding her. "You have an incredible ass," I whispered as I pushed up inside of her. I pulled her hips back a bit and proceeded to make love to her.

"Paul," she moaned as I slowly moved in and out of her. "Fuck me."

I almost didn't hear her. I moved a bit faster, pushed a bit harder. God, she felt magnificent. I wasn't going to last long at this rate. I felt her contract. "Oh, God, beautiful, I'm going to lose it."

Just as I said it, she let go. I felt her warmth encase me. I couldn't stop myself as I spilled all that I was deep inside of her. My hands pulled her back against my chest. "You beautiful woman, I love you." Her head lay back on my chest as I slipped out of her, wrapping her in my arms.

We washed and got out. "I had some clothes delivered from Saks for you. Bras and panties as well."

She smiled at me. "Thank you." I watched as she got dressed. I threw on a pair of jeans commando and a t-shirt. We walked out bare-foot and had a lovely dinner with Jo.

"This is the best cake I've ever had, Joanna. Thank you." I smiled at her.

"I mixed it up and baked it all by myself." She was proud. "Momma, will you read me a story before I go to bed?"

"Of course, do you have one in mind?"

Jo nodded, climbing off the chair, and we watched as she ran down the hall to her room. She came back with a story book in her hand. "This one," she said, handing it to Victoria.

"Well, come on then. Let's get you a bath and into your jammies, and we can snuggle up and have us a read."

As the two of them walked hand in hand down the hall, I cleared off the table and put the dishes in the dishwasher. I grabbed a beer and headed out to the patio, where the guys were finishing their burgers.

Joe looked at me. "Is everything all right?"

"Not sure, she hasn't said a word. She is giving Jo a bath and then reading her a story, so about another half an hour. Do you have a game plan?"

One of the men sitting at the table spoke. "I think the exchange of information would help us figure one out."

I stood there looking at him.

Victoria

I laid in bed with Jo for a long time after she fell asleep, looking at her. I couldn't help but think she knew more than I believed her to. But how did you question a three-year-old? You didn't. She couldn't be involved in this.

I got out of the bed, kissing her on the forehead. "I love you, beau-tiful," I whispered. As I walked out of her room, Max was sitting in a chair across the hall.

"Max, I can't thank you enough for your devotion to Jo."

He smiled at me. "I know we got off on the wrong foot, but no child deserves what has happened to her."

I smiled at him. "Thank you."

He nodded and I headed out to the deck. I had to remember to keep my cards close to my chest. No need giving them all the information I had. When I walked out, Doc walked up to me. "Let me get you bandaged up and that cast re-set while we talk." He led me over to a chair where he had everything waiting.

Introductions took place. The five men who had arrived were, in fact, FBI and CIA. "I guess the place to begin is with the information you have, Miss Holmes."

"My name is Victoria Parker."

"Miss Parker." He paused and looked at the papers in front of him. Lifting his head, he stared at me.

I laughed. "I think this would be easier if I knew who you all were." I looked at the man staring at me.

"My name is James Little. Parker?"

"Yes, my father, Jerry Parker, is the head of MI6. He has been for the past fifteen years." I happened to look at Paul. His eyes spoke fear to me. "Mr. Little, obviously, you are here because you are at an impasse. You believe that Steven Holmes was in fact Andy Marciano. You believe I took him out, and that this is over. I suppose the fact that I had some kind of chemical weapon implanted in my arm set off your red flags, and now, you are sitting here torn between arresting me or using me. I just want to be clear here. You are not going to use me. I'm the one who will be, in fact, using you. I can't do this alone. You want me to end this? Well, I'm not going to do that for you; I am doing it for me, for my daughter. One of those trackers was injected into her neck. Whoever did that planned on using her to control me. She would have been killed along with me when I complied. You need to understand one thing in the big picture here. You don't own me. You don't control me. You don't get to dictate what I do, where I do it, and how I do it. I am the only one sitting here who knows the true identity of Andy Marciano. I am the only one sitting here who has the ability to get close to him. Do we understand one another?"

No one said a word. I looked at Paul, noting the smile on his face. The men talked in whispered voices, and I watched as Doc re-casted my arm.

"Miss Parker," Mr. Little began.

"Victoria," I interrupted him.

"Victoria, we have decided to play this your way for now."

I burst out laughing. "Not to sound like a bitch, Mr. Little, but you don't really have a choice. But I'm not doing this for free. I have a few stipulations of my own."

"Victoria, you really aren't in a position to make demands. We can and will arrest you for espionage and for bringing chemical weapons into this country illegally."

Doc finished with my arm, and I stood. Leaning on the table, I looked Mr. Little in the eyes. "Don't think for one minute that you can threaten me or scare me into believing a fucking word coming out of your mouth. If you arrest me, I'll be dead the minute you close the cell door. This isn't something that can be washed under the rug. You know it, and I know it. You do not own me." I pushed off the table and walked off the deck, headed toward the beach.

I heard their voices, but I couldn't make out what they were saying. A few minutes after I sat down on the beach, Paul was sitting next to me. He put his arm around my waist, pulling me onto his lap. "You are not alone, beautiful."

I wrapped my arms around him. "Why are all men so arrogant?"

He laughed. "I think it has to do with our genetic makeup. We think, or believe, that we are superior because women are generally the weaker sex."

"Paul, I'm scared. I don't think I've ever been this scared before. I can't do anything until these stitches come out of my arm, so we have a few weeks before we can move on this. Are you sure we are safe here?"

"Aww, baby, I'm not sure. But we have plenty of men to watch out for us. Joe has more men coming tonight. We have the FBI and the

CIA to look out for us, as well. I suppose we are as safe as we can be. No one knows what I'm about to tell you. This house has a safe room. I didn't put it in. The man who owned it before me did. It's in my office, so if anything happens, at least we can get Jo to some kind of safe place."

"Paul, I'm tired. I need to sleep."

His hands never stopped moving up and down my back. "Come on. We can go to bed. These guys aren't going anywhere."

We got up and walked back to the house. When we walked up the stairs, eleven heads turned to look at me. "Miss Parker, we will do as you ask. Let's get started with the exchange of information."

I smiled at him. "I am going to bed. I can't and won't do anything until my stitches come out. Having these wounds on my arm is a weakness I don't need or want. If you want to give me your file, I will read it and you can come back tomorrow around one in the afternoon when Jo takes her nap. Otherwise, I am going to bed."

"I'm sorry, Miss Parker, but we need to discuss this now. Not tomorrow, not the day after, but now," Mr. Little said. I watched as two of the men stood up.

"You've got that wrong. I am going to bed, and if you want to try and stop me then try. But you don't own me, and if you want to push me, I will disappear and take my knowledge with me." I turned to walk away, and one man reached out and grabbed my arm. I spun around, slamming my casted fist into his throat. He went down as the other man grabbed me around the waist. I slammed my head into his face, breaking his nose. He let me go, and I turned, cracking him across the face with my cast. When he fell on the deck, I spun to look at Mr. Little. "Don't fucking touch me again. You want to arrest me, do it. But don't fucking touch me or believe you can manhandle me in anyway."

He smiled at me. "I guess I underestimated you, Miss Parker. My apologies." He handed me the file. "I will see you tomorrow at one."

Joe and Al were standing a few feet from me smiling. Joe looked at Mr. Little. "James, you told me you could do this without force. She has the means to do this job, as you can see. You need to back off. This is a two-way street. If you can't or won't stick to your word, I will personally help her disappear. I gave her my word that she can trust you. I guess I was wrong in believing you were on the up and up. Get the hell out of here. Either you are with us or not. I was under the impression that capturing, possibly putting the biggest fucking arms dealer out of business was on the top of the list in this fucking war against terrorists. But again, I am reminded why I no longer work for you or this fucking government. There are some people left on this planet who matter. You are way out of line."

I smiled at him. "Thank you, Joe. I've dealt with men like him my whole life. It's an ego thing. Most men just can't handle a woman like me. I'm all right with it, as long as they don't mind getting their asses handed to them by a woman who weighs a hundred and ten pounds." I turned and looked at Mr. Little. "I would suggest you leave, and when you come back, you might want to have a change of attitude. Remember, Mr. Little, I don't need you to do this. I'm already resigned to the fact that this is a suicide mission, so your threats don't bother me. I will end this, and I am the only one who can. Otherwise, you wouldn't be here."

I took the file and Paul's hand. He paused and said to everyone at the table, "I, at one time, was all about controlling a woman, until I met this one. If one of you or your men touch her again, I will not be held responsible for my actions. It is never acceptable to harm a woman."

We walked into the house. "I want to check on Jo," I said. We went together. Denny was outside her room. "Where's Max?"

"Sleeping in the chair in her room."

We went in and I kissed her on the forehead. Then we went into our room. I tossed the file on the bed and went to change. Paul didn't say anything. He was sitting in the chair when I came out of the bathroom. Walking up to him, I climbed on his lap, laying my head on his chest.

His arms wrapped around me. "You all right?" he asked softly.

"No, and I'm worried about you."

He chuckled. "Why me?"

"Because I know that men have a hard time with a strong woman. I'm pig-headed and mean when pissed off."

"Listen to me," he pulled me back putting his hands on my face, "for the past five years, I have objectified women and brought them to their knees. I've tied them up, took away their free will, and used them for my own gratification. I do not, nor will I ever have a problem with your strength. I know part of your back story, and you amaze me with how you manage to keep it all together. The way you handle yourself is unfortunately the only way anyone will take you seriously. I will never underestimate you. I will never take you for granted. You are a precious gift to me, and I plan on cherishing you for as long as I'm alive."

"Yeah?"

"Oh, hell yeah. Come on, beautiful, let's get some sleep."

He stood up, picking me up with him climbing on the bed, then he laid me down and went to change. When he came back to bed, we kissed for a long time, gently touching one another. We didn't make love; it wasn't about that. It was about us connecting, letting the other know where our hearts were.

CHAPTER FOURTEEN

PAUL

I laid there holding her in my arms while she slept, wondering what the hell was going to happen with us. *Who is this man she hunts?* I had gone through just about every conversation we'd had, and I could only come to one conclusion. I needed to be strong for her. I didn't want her to do this alone, and I thought I might have a plan on how I could do this with her. But I knew she would deny me. Her first priority was Jo, and I promised her that I would give her a full and beautiful life.

Unable to sleep, I got up and made my way to Jo's room. She was the most important person in this fucked up plan. She looked so angelic cuddled up with her bunny. Max snored in the chair across the room.

I made my way into the living room, pouring myself a glass of scotch. The whole thing was fucked up. I felt like I'd walked into some super spy novel. I couldn't even begin to imagine how Victoria had survived her life.

Walking out on the deck, I stood leaning on the railing, looking out at the lake. The lights in the boathouse were still on. I wondered what was going on, so I headed down. When I walked in, there were fifteen men sitting around a table. Mr. Little and his goon squad were there, as well.

"Mr. Simon," he said. I looked at the guy whose face Victoria broke. He didn't look happy.

"Mr. Little, what are your intentions toward Victoria?"

"I'm going to help her bring this man to an end."

"And then what?" I needed to know.

"And then it's over."

I stood there just looking at these men. Al stood up and walked over to me. "Can we talk?" he asked softly. I nodded and we walked out. Halfway across the lawn, he stopped. "Listen, I know these guys, and there is something more going on here. Joe and I are trying to find out what. But something is not right. I'm thinking that perhaps you guys should just disappear and let this go. We are talking about chemical warfare here. This isn't just about one man; it's about a chain of people. Taking out this guy isn't going to end this. It's just going to put a bigger target on her back. It will never end. Her life will never be her life. I know some guys who aren't legal, if you get my drift, who can make you disappear."

I chuckled. "I'm a billionaire. It's kind of hard to disappear with that kind of money."

"It's not really. It will take some time, but I can make it happen. Listen, we are going on the assumption that she isn't going to do anything until her arm heals. Doc already said he could delay it as long as we need. Let us do this for you, for her, for that little girl. It can be done. You know it can. You have been swimming in the back pools of legality for years. You know there are ways to disappear."

He was right. "I'll talk to Victoria."

"Do it where there aren't any ears around. With these guys, anything is possible." He turned and walked back to the boat house. I knew exactly what he was saying. The house could have ears. I walked back in and wrote Max a note, then headed back to Jo's room and gave it to him. I went into our room and woke Victoria.

Putting my finger to my lips to let her know not to talk, I led her into my office, shutting and locking the door. I didn't turn on the lights. I triggered the safe room door, and we went inside.

"What's going on?" she asked.

I took a deep breath. "I just had the weirdest conversation with Al. He seems to think this is a bad idea. Victoria, taking this man down isn't going to end this. Al told me that we are dealing with chemical warfare here. This person isn't the head of the snake, and by killing him, it would only put more of a target on your head. Have you had a chance to read that file yet?"

She stood there looking at me, shaking her head. "Paul, can you live with this? Can you live with knowing that the man who ordered your wife's death, your unborn child's death, is going to just walk free?"

My heart broke when she put it that way. "Victoria, I've thought long and hard about how I feel about revenge, and that is just what this is. Revenge. There will be no justice for this man. You and I both know it. Death won't be payment enough for what he has done, and it isn't going to stop this. Maybe, before all the lies, it might have had some impact on the bigger picture, but you probably already know that he wasn't the one who put those explosives in your arm. I mean, how many more people are they doing this to? It's not just him, baby. We have each other now, and because of the sick and twisted shit that has taken place in both of our lives, we have found each other. We have Joanna to consider in all of this. Yes, I want justice for Sylvia's murder, more than you will ever know. But I love you now, and I love Jo. I want the happiness this bastard stole from me, and I want it with you and Joanna. I can make my peace with it, simply because, as fucked up as it is, it brought me you. I'm terrified that you are going to be murdered as well, possibly even Jo."

She sat in the chair, leaning her arms on her legs. "I've been thinking about it as well. I want to confront him. I want to make him pay for what he has done, but I'm not so sure he is the one who ordered the death of my brother or your wife. I think it was bigger. Can we do this? Can we just disappear?"

I knelt in front of her. "I think we can. Like I said, I'm in this shit, or at least, was in this shit, but not to this extent. I'm sure I've pissed off more than a few people, hence Max, Denny, and the guys. They are trained killers. My past isn't a place I wanted to be. When I met you, I

179

knew I was done with it all. But that doesn't mean it was, or is, an easy transition. Hence the henchmen." I chuckled, putting my hands on her arms. "Victoria, we can become new people, have new lives, and just live out the rest of them raising Jo and being happy. I want to make you happy. I want to have a life with you. Do I want to run away like a scared rabbit? Hell no, I want to fight, but I don't think we are going to win this fight."

She just sat there looking at me. Her hand came up to touch my face. "Paul, I really think I'm in love with you. Deeply in love with you."

Pulling her off the chair onto my lap, I kissed her. She had become everything to me. There weren't words to explain how deeply I felt for this woman. We kissed so slowly and for so long. She tasted so damn good. Pulling back, I whispered, "The minute I touched you in my brother's office, I knew I would want no other. I feel the same way."

Her hand moved to my side, and she slowly pulled my shirt over my head, kissing me. I needed to touch her, to feel her against my body. I pulled her shirt off then wrapped my arms around her. I wanted nothing more than to feel her. The moan that escaped me was deep. "So beautiful," I whispered on her lips.

We sat like this, with her on my lap, kissing. I never really knew how much I enjoyed kissing someone until I met her. My hands gently touched her beautiful porcelain skin. There was nothing like the feel of her in all of the world. I needed her to know that this was what I wanted for the rest of my life. Putting my hands under her arms, I slowly lifted her to stand in front of me and pressed my face into her core. She was heaven. Her fingers ran through my hair, pulling ever so lightly against my skull. With my hands on her ass, I slipped my fingers into the waistband of her shorts, gently pulling them down. I tilted my head up to look at her as she stepped out of them, her beautiful red fluff glistening. Just knowing she was wet because of me made me harder.

Pushing up on my knees, I undid my jeans, sliding them off. I sat back on my heels and gently brought her down on me. With her hands on my face, she surrounded me with her silken center, my eyes rolling in my head when she took all of me. Our mouths met, and our beautiful slow dance began. My arms wrapped around her, holding her still so I could kiss her.

"I love you," she moaned in my mouth. "I'll do whatever you think is best. I don't want this to end. I want a life with you, always."

Every dream I'd ever had, ever wanted, ever desired to feel was this woman. She was all I could ever dream for. "I love you, Victoria."

Laying her back, I made love to her, our eyes locking every now and again, her hands on my face, on my back, my chest. As I felt her tighten, she let go and pulled everything from me. Never had a woman been able to do this to me. Even Sylvia couldn't do this.

We laid there looking at one another, spent and sedate. "Victoria, what you make me feel."

"I know. I don't want to lose you. I don't want to go through this life without you," she whispered. I watched as tears fell silently from her eyes. "I don't want to die. I want a life." She paused. "Let's do this. Let's just go and be happy."

I couldn't do anything but kiss her. I could feel myself start to get hard again as she slowly moved her hips against me. Smiling, I said, "You're insatiable. "

"Not yet," she giggled.

My hips started to move, and in a matter of seconds, I was rock hard, buried deep inside of her. My hips flicked hard when I hit her end. It was a slow rhythm, a slow fucking, and it was beyond anything. For so long, we laid on the floor. I loved how she wasn't about being a showman. I loved how we felt together, her gentle mews, her soft moans. The feel of her body as it shuddered and spasmed was part of what drove me to be better.

She felt so fucking good. It's when she clamped down on my shoulder as she exploded that sent me over the edge. "Fuck, Jesus, Victoria," I whispered on her lips.

She smiled as I swiped my tongue along hers. Rolling over, I pulled her on top of me. She laid her head on my chest. "Your heart is racing."

I couldn't help but laugh. "It's you who does this to me. We've got a few weeks to get this right. We need to play along with them while Joe and Al help us."

"Paul, I don't have any contacts. All the passports I have are known now."

"I told you I was a bad man. I'm sure I can get us some. The question is, where should we go?"

"I don't care, someplace with seasons and a lake. I need a beach."

"If we disappear here in the States, we don't need passports, but I think we should have them, just in case."

She nodded. "Agreed."

"Come on, beautiful. There's a bathroom through that door over there." I nodded to the other side of the small room.

As I watched her stand, she was glorious to say the least. Picking up her pajamas, she moved away from me. I just laid here looking at the ceiling. Hopefully, this would work so we could be free and have a happy life. I got up and dressed as she came out of the bathroom. I checked the monitors, and we left the safe room, making our way back to check on Jo. Max was sitting in the chair.

I walked to the bedroom door as Victoria was walking out. She had the file with her. "I'm going to read some of this now that I'm awake." She smiled.

Kissing her temple, I followed her out into the living room. We got comfortable on the couch and started reading. "They have a great deal of information here," she whispered.

"It seems to be a list of everything you've done."

"I noticed that."

As we read, there was no more information than we already had. It seemed to me that it was a list of Victoria's crimes, my brother's involvement, and very little on Steven or the famed Andy Marciano. "Victoria, this is a file on you, not a file on what they want to achieve."

She closed the file and dropped it on the table, turning to me. "I'm tired, Paul. So many lies, so much revenge. I want to go to bed. Come to bed with me."

I smiled. "Come on, beautiful, let's go snuggle with Jo."

I took her hand, and we made our way back to get Jo in her room.

Denny had changed places with Max and was sitting in the chair reading. He nodded to us as we walked in and got Jo, then we went back to our room where I locked the door. We climbed into bed, and I held them both in my arms. Together, they were still so small. I looked at her, and even in the dark, she was beautiful. "I love you."

"I love you," she whispered back as her eyes closed.

Smiling, I let sleep take me. She owned me.

Victoria

I woke up to a tickling on my nose. When I opened my eyes, Jo was completely snuggled into my chest, her light fluffy curls tickling my nose. My smile was automatic. Paul was so relaxed, his face so defined and so sculpted. He was like a beautiful painting. I felt lucky to have found him. He was right; I needed to just let this go. I would just have to play the part and let him figure out the rest. I needed to know what real information they had on Marciano. My thoughts were distracted by the gentle sucking sound coming from Jo. I knew she was scared and confused by all of this. She was just a little girl. Tilting my head down, I took a deep breath, breathing her wonderful scent in. My smile seemed to come more easily now that I had her with me. Now that I had Paul. Opening my eyes, I was greeted with his turquoise blue eyes looking right into my soul. They spoke volumes to me without ever needing to say a word. The hand that was wrapped around Jo moved to his face.

"Thank you for loving me, loving us."

He smiled. "Come on, beautiful, let me make us breakfast."

A little voice said, "Can we have panny cakes?"

We both burst out laughing. "We can have anything you'd like," he said as Jo rolled over to hug his neck.

There weren't words to describe how I felt right then. We were becoming a family, something I always wanted but never believed I would have. We all piled out of bed, and I took Jo into her room and got her dressed, then she and Paul went to the kitchen while I took a shower.

When I walked into the kitchen, Jo was on the counter, and she and Paul were in a heated discussion on the best way to flip a pancake. My heart was full as I sat down to watch the two of them. It was music to my ears to hear them laughing. I didn't ever want to be apart from them. Then and there, I made up my mind. I was done. Revenge was best served cold. He didn't know I knew his identity, so I decided to keep it that way. No one would ever know what I knew.

The door opened, and I turned to see Joe and Al walking in. I wasn't sure I was comfortable with the fact that these men had open access to the house.

Joe nodded to me, and Al sat down next to me, sliding a small piece of paper to me. Looking down, I read it.

We have a problem.

I shook my head, looking up as Paul set a plate down. "Gentlemen, if you would excuse us, we are going to have breakfast," he said.

They both nodded and left to go on the patio. Looking at me, Paul smiled. He sat Jo in the chair next to me, and he sat on the other side. We talked and laughed while we had our pancakes.

"Momma, can Max take me to the beach today?"

I smiled. "Well, I don't know what Max is doing today, but if he is busy, Paul and I will take you."

"Momma, those men are not nice," she said.

Okay, she freaked me out, more than a little. "What men are you talking about?"

"Those men in the boat house. I don't like them." I watched her stuff a bite of pancake in her mouth.

"Well, they are going to be leaving today, so you don't have to worry about them."

Max was in the hallway and came in, handing something to Paul. "I would love to take you down to the beach when you are done with your breakfast," he said to Jo.

She smiled. "I'm done. Momma, can I go now?"

"Of course. Be mindful of Max."

When the two of them walked out the door, Paul set a little glass vile on the counter in front of me. It had water in it and was filled with listening devices. Shaking my head, I picked it up and slipped it into my pocket. We didn't say anything to each other; we just cleaned up the mess and walked out on the balcony.

"Where are your friends?" I asked Joe and Al.

Al nodded toward the boat house, and I turned to see Mr. Little and his four companions walking across the lawn. I went back in the house and picked up the file. When I walked back out, I said softly to Joe and Al, "Are you with us?"

They both nodded. I sat down, and Paul sat next to me, taking my hand in his. I looked at him, nodding. I was going to play the game; these men were going to be lucky to walk away with their lives. No one owned me. No one controlled me.

Mr. Little sat across from me. "Good Morning, Victoria. I trust you slept well."

I laughed. "Apparently, you know exactly how well I slept." I set the vile on the table. "Seems you don't trust me, Mr. Little. Either that or you are some sick and twisted man who likes to listen in on people making love." I watched as a slight blush moved across his face. I didn't give him time to respond. "I've read your file. Seems it's a list of crimes I've committed, especially the ones in this country. I don't know what kind of game you are playing but trying to scare me isn't going to work. You see, the monster that you want to believe that you are, well, let me just inform you that you are an insect in comparison to the monster that I want. Mr. Little, if you are going to continually try and intimidate me because I am a woman, you are wasting your time. No one owns me. I am not for sale, and no one controls me. I am MI6, and if you arrest me, you run the risk of alienating the British Government, and I know that is not something you want to do. Now, I would like the real file, or you will be doing this on your own. You're aware of the men I have killed, and you know that you or any one of these men couldn't have done it. So, either give me the file or get the hell out of here."

"Miss Parker," he began.

I laughed. "I'm not stupid, Mr. Little. Beginning your sentence like that, almost always, is ended with a threat. Don't threaten me, Mr. Little, because I can guarantee you will not like my response."

He sat there looking at me. "Miss Parker, you do realize that we are FBI and CIA? We don't abide by the common laws of this country. We pretty much can and will protect the borders by any means possible."

I giggled. "So, are you saying, Mr. Little, that I am a threat? Me, little old five-feet-two, one hundred and ten pounds of woman is a threat to this country?"

"What I'm saying, Miss Parker, is that you walked into this country with chemical weapons surgically implanted into your arm, putting this country in grave danger."

Paul laughed, and Mr. Little's head snapped toward him. "Across the borders, through your homeland security. Tell me, Mr. Little. Are you pissed because you couldn't or failed to detect what was in her arm? This has nothing to do with what was in her arm, as it does with you trying to get that little bit of egg off your face. You know as well as everyone at this table that it was Max who figured it out, not you and our so called first line of defense against terrorism. Don't come into my house and threaten my future wife unless you've got something more substantial, because trust me, when I tell you this, it is going to blow up in your face."

I turned to look at him, whispering, "You still want to marry me?"

He smiled. "With everything that I am. I want to adopt Jo, too."

I had to fight the tears building in my eyes. I turned my head, looking at Mr. Little. "I have a life to live here, so either give me the real file or get out. I am so over this battle of testosterone here. You see I don't have any, so I guess I win."

I swear, I could see steam coming out of the man's ears. He slid a file across the table to me. "We'll be back tomorrow afternoon at one."

I watched as he picked up the glass vile, along with the file he had given me yesterday, and they all walked away. Al followed them out, and Joe sat down looking at me.

"Who are you?" he asked softly.

I burst out laughing. "Would you believe me if I told you that I was your worst nightmare?"

He nodded. "Yeah, as a matter of fact, I would. I have never seen anyone take control of such a serious situation like you just did. These guys are out for blood."

"Joe, no offense, but they know who I am, or at least, who they think I am. No one knows me, not completely. People only have what's on paper and the whispers that they have heard. Andy Marciano is the only person who knows the real me, and right now, it seems he is going to live a very long life. Al said you would help us. Is that still the case?"

"It is, and it would be an honor. But I must ask, are you sure?"

I looked past him to the beach. "More than you will ever know," I said softly. "Sometimes in this life, some things are far more important than revenge. I am confident that I will eventually have my justice, just not anytime soon. Now, if you'll excuse me, I'll leave you two to figure out the fine points of this plan." I turned to Paul. "I'm going to play with our daughter."

His smile said it all to me. He nodded and I got up and headed to the beach.

Paul

"She is one hell of a woman," Joe said.

I chuckled. "I've never known anyone like her. She keeps her cards very close to her chest."

"She hasn't told you anything?"

Shaking my head, I told him, "Nope, and before you ask, I have no intentions whatsoever on trying to get her to expose them. She doesn't work like that. When and if she wants to share, she does. I know enough about her to know that no other woman on this planet will ever own me like she does."

"How long have you known her?"

"A few weeks. I have never met someone so strong, yet so tender and loving all at the same time. I watched her kill a man three times her size, with a broken arm twisted behind her back and his hand squeezing her throat to the point of blacking out. She is a force to be reckoned with, and I think your friends know better than to piss her off."

"I was amazed at how she took two of them out simultaneously." He chuckled. "Al wants me to offer her a job. I think he is smitten with her."

"No offense, Paul, but my brother is right. I think I have a thing for your future wife." Al sat down. "Our friends are gone."

"Well, Al, thank you for the compliment. I am one lucky man to have her love me. Offer her the job. I don't make her decisions for her. I'll support whatever she needs to do. My job in all of this is to love her, nothing more, and she makes it easy to do so." I looked past Joe to see her looking at me. When I smiled, she smiled back.

"How about we figure out how to get the three of you out of this first?"

I nodded. We spent the better part of three hours hashing out a plan. Victoria and Jo came in and made us all lunch. We sat around laughing, and then Victoria and Jo went to take a nap while Joe, Al, and myself talked some more. When we finished, I made my way to the bedroom. I needed to touch her, to feel her next to me.

Kissing her gently on the forehead, she turned her head. I nodded toward the closet. Her smile said it all for me. I spent the next hour making love to her on the floor. When we finished, we dressed, climbed into bed with Jo, and crashed.

CHAPTER FIFTEEN

VICTORIA

I liked that he needed to touch me the way he did. I'd read the file on him, and he had told me some of what his life was like. He had been nothing but gentle and kind. I was, however, curious about this other life he led. *Does he still have those thoughts? Those desires?* He definitely was not lacking in stamina.

I couldn't help thinking about Steven. He never took the time to take care with me. I think the longest we ever fucked was maybe ten minutes, and he was getting frustrated that he couldn't come. But, then again, I was sure he was fucking Kathy at the time.

My thoughts spun in a circle as my life with him played out in my mind. The looks they shared… I just thought my best friend was being kind to my husband. I was grateful he liked my friend. *Son-of-a-bitch.*

I moved to get up, and Paul touched my arm. I turned, looking at him, and shook my head. I made my way out to the deck. My feet took me to the beach. I noticed Denny was a few feet behind me. It didn't bother me. I felt a bit safer with him there. I just walked up and down the short strip of sand, letting my life play out.

There was so much that I hadn't pieced together. Conversations that were hushed when I was close. The looks, the phone calls. The job. Steven was a financial advisor *for Andy Marciano.* He killed my brother. *But why? If it wasn't for Marciano, then who? Did Johnathan figure out who Steven was?* Kathy would have these answers. I needed to talk to her. I needed to have a few more pieces to this puzzle and to figure out how and why this was happening to me. *What do I know? What do I know that I don't know I know?*

Mr. Little, I think, knew more than what he was letting on. I was pretty sure Paul had figured out a few pieces of this puzzle as well. I looked back to the lake house. Al was watching me from the deck. It was in me to finish this. *How can I walk away without knowing why my brother was murdered? Why was Joanna left alive? Why was I left alive?*

I walked up on the deck and bent to whisper in Al's ear. "I need you to take me to Kathy. Something is wrong. Running isn't going to make us safe. Knowledge is."

He nodded. "Get your shoes."

I went in the house and grabbed my shoes. I wrote Paul a note.

Please don't freak out. I will be back. I'm with Al.

I love you

V.

On the way out the door, I handed the note to Denny. He nodded and we left, me and Al in one car, Joe and another guy in another car, and then two other men in another car. I chuckled when I realized they were all identical and all had smoked windows. We split up and drove around for a while. I heard Al's phone vibrate, and then we headed to Kathy, pulling up a few minutes later to a pretty big house with a gate and men with guns everywhere.

When we got out, I looked at Al. "Really?"

"Well, you told Max to make sure she was comfortable."

"Not this comfortable." I smiled.

He laughed. "She isn't exactly living large here."

Shaking my head, I followed him into the house. There were men posted in different places. I took in my surroundings. I really needed to trust these guys. They had a fucking army of men, who I was pretty sure were all ex-military. Al led me to the basement, which was decked out with a pool table, foosball, pinball machines, and a big screen tv. *Boys and their toys.*

Through another door, there were two men sitting in chairs and a monitor on the desk. I could see Kathy sleeping on a bed. "See, she's safe."

I smiled at him. "Is there sound?" He nodded. "Turn it off. I'd like to go in alone if you don't mind. She won't talk if you are there."

He opened the door, and I walked in. I sat in the chair next to the bed and waited for her to wake up. When Paul looked at me for a long period of time while I was sleeping, I sensed it and woke up. He was going to be pissed that I did this without him, but I needed to know. I needed to figure this out.

A few minutes after I sat down, she rolled over. "What do you want?"

I smiled at her. "Are you being fed?"

"What difference does it make? I'm never getting out of here."

"Kathy, you are here for your safety, well, and you had every intention on killing Joanna and me. But I can forgive that."

"What do you want, Victoria?"

"I want you to answer some questions. I want to know what you know, and I really want to know how long you were fucking Steven."

"I can't tell you anything. I don't know anything, and eight years."

I chuckled. "I figured as much. You have information you don't know you have, as all of us do. The difference between you and me is mine stays buried in my mind. I know shit I don't even know I know until it's necessary to know it. I've been programmed to do a job. I just haven't figured out what that job is, but you are going to help me figure it out."

She laughed. "What are you talking about, programmed?"

"By Steven. That's why he married me. It wasn't to control Johnathan; it was to control me. He told me, I just didn't understand what it meant. Tell me about the hushed conversations that took place in my house between you, Steven, and Johnathan."

"They were just missions, work shit. You weren't MI6 anymore, so you weren't privy to the information. At least, that's what Steven said."

"Tell me about the accident that killed my baby. Why would Steven kill our child?"

She sat there looking at me, shaking her head. "Steven didn't do it. He was destroyed by what happened. I know, I was there. He was so freaked out, even scared. Victoria, honestly, he had nothing to do with that."

"What about Johnathan? Did he order Simon to kill him?"

She nodded. "Johnathan figured out who Marciano was, and he knew that Steven was his second in command."

"Do you know who he is?"

She shook her head. "No, I didn't find out until after Johnathan was killed that Steven was his second in command. By then, I was already in too deep to get out."

"Were you supposed to kill Joanna?"

"No, I was supposed to deliver her to Johnny McDonald. Well, to let him take her from me if you called. But you killed him in the parking lot. I had a backup plan. I was told, if it went all wrong, to lose her in the airport and just walk away. But you put me on that private plane, then that guy Max took my phone from me and threw it out the window. So, I had no clue what was going to happen next."

"Did you know about the tracker in her neck?"

"Yes, Steven said it was so they could find her."

"Did you know that I had one as well?"

She nodded. "When you passed out in the Art Gallery, Steven injected it into your neck. He said that way he could keep track of you and your progress."

"What was the point of me being at Simon and Simon?"

"To see if you could discover Steven's footprint, Marciano's footprint."

"Who did McDonald work for, Steven or Marciano?"

"Marciano. I worked for Steven. John Simon worked for Steven."

"Did you know that there was a deadly poison in those trackers?"

"No."

I sat there looking at her. I could see it in her eyes that she was telling me the truth. "Who put the canisters of poisonous gas in Paul's house?"

"John did. He said that Paul was getting too attached to you, and he needed a backup plan in case you two got together. He did it after Paul met you in the office and you quit. Apparently, Paul has a way with women and can manipulate them to do whatever he wants. He's a bad man, Victoria."

"I know, I read his file."

She shook her head. "That file was put together just for you. All the bad shit was left out. Steven planned this."

She believed she was telling the truth, which brought up a great many more questions. "Have you seen this file?"

She nodded. "John had a copy, and there was a copy at the Art Museum. Steven hid it there in case I needed some ammunition."

"Where is this file, Kathy?" I felt myself getting angry.

"Instead of going in the room where you would meet, take a left, and it's in a crate against the back wall. The crate has the words 'Milan, Italy 1852' stamped on it. Everything you want to know about Paul Simon is there."

"What did Steven want me to figure out on my own?"

"He knew that what he was doing was known by Marciano. He needed you to figure out who he was. I think he believed that you could save him. But Bower slipped and told you we were married."

"What was he doing?" I could feel my blood boiling. I did exactly what Marciano wanted me to do. I ended Steven and John.

"He was actually trying to expose Marciano. This is bigger than you can imagine, Victoria. You will never be safe." She leaned in and whispered, "Never."

I sat there looking at her for a long time. I stood up. "I'll be back, Kathy." Walking over to the door, I knocked. Al opened it, and we left the house, heading back to the lake house.

"You all right?" Al asked.

"Did you listen in?" He shook his head. "Did you record it?" He shook his head.

"Trust needs start somewhere," he said.

Joe said the same thing to me. "What do you know, Al, that you aren't telling me?"

"I know a great deal. Trust needs to start somewhere."

I laughed. "I suppose it does. Well, then, let's start here. Will you take me to the Art Institute?"

He nodded. We didn't say anything as he drove through the city. I thought about everything Kathy had said, and everything she didn't say. *Why did Steven try and kill me? Did he want me to kill him? Was he hoping I would save Kathy and their child? What the hell was going on?*

We pulled up to the Art Institute. "I'll be back in a few minutes."

"I can't let you do this alone. Trust, all right?"

I sat there looking at him. His eyes were kind, even if his body was a lethal weapon. I needed to trust someone so I nodded. Together, we got out of the car. He followed me as I walked into the curator's office. There was no one there, so I just walked through the door that led me to the room where I would meet Al and Jacob. Standing in front of the door, I turned to the left. The shadows gave me the creeps. Kathy's words echoed in my head. *"Never."* I reached behind me and pulled Denny's gun out of my pants.

I took a step and stopped, looking at the gun in my hand. Turning, I looked at Al then at the gun. I popped the cartridge out, slid one of the bullets out. I looked at it, then at Al. He was staring at my hand. His head came up, and I saw something I wasn't sure I was prepared to see. I saw fear.

He took the gun from my hand, along with the clip, sliding it back in. Then he handed me his gun and nodded his head. Turning, I made my way to the far wall. Just as Kathy said, there was the crate with *Milan, Italy 1852* stamped on the side. My heart, I swear it skipped a beat. I think, for the first time in my life, I was truly scared. I mean, really scared, frozen in fear scared. I reached for the crate, but Al put his hand on my shoulder.

"Wait," he said. "This could be a trap."

I closed my eyes. Was I that desperate that I was making mistakes? I was not this person. *What the hell is wrong with me?* Terrified of what lay within the stupid box, I handed Al my gun and checked the outside of the crate. Nothing seemed to be out of the ordinary. Al handed me a little metal case. He flipped a switch on it.

I knew what it was, and I scanned the entire crate. Not one red light. Looking at Al, he said, "Let me do it. That little girl needs you."

I swallowed and nodded. "You sure?"

He chuckled. "Not really, but I just want to say something to you before I do this. Just in case." I smiled at him. "I think you are incredible. I've never met a woman like you before. I wanted to offer you a job with us, and I am insanely attracted to you. Like crazy attracted."

The smile stayed on my face. "Thank you. If this all works out, I think I'd like to work with you guys, and I already knew that."

He nodded, smiling at me. "Now, get over there, just in case." He tipped his head toward the office. "If this goes badly, tell my mother and my brothers that I love them."

"Al, thank you." I made my way back to the office but stood where I could still see him. I realized my hands were a bit shaky. Would Steven really booby trap it?

"All right, here we go," Al said.

I closed my eyes, turning my back to him. I heard the top of the crate as he set it on the floor. I turned around, opening my eyes. He was walking toward me with the file in his hands. I noticed he had black gloves on. He handed me a pair. "These are special gloves. Be careful. There could be something on the paper."

Taking the gloves, I put them on my hands and took the file from him. We made our way outside and back to the car, but we got in a different one, with Joe driving. No one said a word. I was in the backseat alone, my hands shaking. *Do I really want to open this? Do I really want to know who he really is? Could any of it be true?*

"Take me back to where Kathy is, please. I need to do this alone," I said softly.

"Paul called. He's worried about you," Joe said.

"As he should be," I said under my breath. "I can't talk to him right now. What did you tell him?"

"That you were talking to Kathy," Joe said.

"You didn't tell him I was at the Art Institute?" I looked at him in the rearview mirror. He shook his head. "You've both mentioned trust to me on many different occasions. Something tells me that you have an idea of what's in this file. Am I about to be destroyed?"

Joe took a deep breath. "I am going on the assumption that you and Paul have had conversations concerning your lives apart from one another." I nodded. "I have no knowledge of what he has told you, but you are a very intelligent woman, and I think that perhaps you might already know what's in that file."

Well, that was very cryptic. We pulled up to the house and through the gate. Al opened my door for me and then led me through the house to an office. "You can use this room. It's Paul's office, so I'm sure there aren't any cameras in here."

I looked at him. "This is Paul's house?" He nodded. I walked in, shutting the door, then set the file on the desk before carefully taking off the gloves. I needed to think.

What did I know about Paul? I smiled. I knew that he made me feel alive. *Could he be deeper into this mess than he lets on?* He told me that he was not a nice man, that he was deep into this shit. *What shit? Arms dealing? Sex trade? Drugs? Prostitution?* These things I already knew. I looked at the file on the table. *But do I really?* "This could all be a set up," I whispered. I would need to verify everything. How could I do that? I opened the door, and Al was standing there.

I walked up to him, standing on my tippy toes, and he bent down so I could whisper in his ear. "You talked about trust." I felt his hand on my hip. "If there are things in that file that I don't know, will you be able to verify it?" I felt him nod. "I have no other choice but to trust you, Al. Paul is with my daughter right now."

"She is safe," he whispered in my ear. His voice sent chills down my spine.

We both pulled back, and he mouthed the word *trust* to me. I nodded and walked back into the room, shutting the door. Sitting down at the desk, I put the gloves back on, took a deep breath, and opened the file.

Paul

When she walked out of the room, I had to fight with myself not to follow her. She had a look of confusion in her eyes, something I didn't think I'd seen on her before. I knew she knew things she wasn't really sure she knew, and I wasn't so sure I was comfortable with that. I needed her to know the truth, but even for me, it would be a lot to take in at one time.

I promised her I would make sure Jo was safe, was taken care of. I couldn't go off the deep end here. Her father said he got me out. Being who he is, he had to have kept track of his daughter, so it would be logical to think he would know who she was sleeping with. But then again, I was their prime suspect, or was I their smoke screen to the truth?

Do I know things I'm not sure I know? I casually got up and made my way out into the living room. Denny handed me a note. Looking at it, my heart stopped. "Shit," I said. "No one went with her?"

"Joe and Al and a few other guys."

She knew now about my house. She knew more than I wanted her to know yet. Not that I didn't plan on telling her, I just wanted to take my time. I paced in front of the window, looking out at the beach. This was going to be bad.

Hours passed as I paced. Jo had gotten up and was now on the beach with Max and Denny. I was clueless until the door opened and she walked in. I just stopped; my eyes locked onto hers. I couldn't read them, but I could read her body language. She was in work mode; her body was the same as the day we walked into her cottage.

We stood there for a long time, neither of us moving, our eyes locked in a soul-searching embrace. She was looking for the trust she had when she walked out the door, and I was looking for the love I saw in hers. I would never hurt her; she had to know that. Fuck, I wished she would say something. I almost smiled; she was probably thinking the same thing. But we didn't. It was Jo who broke the stare down.

"Momma, look what Max found on the beach."

Victoria's eyes moved, and she smiled. I could still tell her senses were at full attention. "Oh, my goodness, that's beautiful. Come on, let's put it in your room."

Jo was all smiles, and I smiled at her as they walked by. I reached out to touch Victoria, but she stepped away from me. Closing my eyes, I think for the first time in a long time, I felt fear. I couldn't lose her. I didn't want to lose her. I went out and stood on the balcony, leaning on the railing and looking out at the lake. I was pretty sure she knew the truth. I should have told her; it should have been the first thing I'd done. So fucking stupid of me to think she was never going to figure it out. "Fuck," I said to myself. "So fucking stupid."

It was time to deal with this. I turned around and she was standing there looking at me. I nearly chuckled; she scared the shit out of me. Her eyes were far from kind. They were far from comforting. They were deadly. I opened my mouth to say something, but no words came out. I wasn't sure what I could say to make her understand. She just shook her head and turned to walk away. I didn't want her to walk away, so I reached out, gently grabbing her arm.

She stopped moving and looked down at my hand. "Don't," she whispered. I let her go and watched her walk into the house.

"Fuck," I whispered. There was a knock on the door. I walked over to open it. Sally and Joe were standing there. "Come on in." I smiled. Jo liked Sally.

Joe smiled at me, and I nodded. I heard Joanna behind me. "Hi, Sally. Momma said I was going to play at your house today. Can we bake some cookies?"

Sally smiled. "Of course, we can."

I turned to look at Victoria. "Thanks for this," she said to Sally.

"Don't worry, it's my pleasure. I just wish these boys would give me some grandchildren." She looked at Jo. "You ready?"

"I am. Momma put some clean clothes in my backpack. She said I was going to stay overnight with you."

"Yes, you are. But if you want to come back home, you let me know and I will bring you, okay?"

Jo nodded. "I'm not scared. Momma is mad at Paul, and she is going to yell at him, so she wants to make sure I don't hear them," she whispered to Sally.

I swallowed hard, my eyes moving to Victoria. She crouched down to hug Joanna. "You be good. If you want me to come and get you, just let Sally know."

Joanna placed her hand on Victoria's face. "It's all right, Momma, Paul is a good guy."

Victoria smiled. "I love you."

"I love you, too," Joanna said. Turning, she looked at me. I got down on my knees. "Don't yell at Momma."

I smiled. "I won't. I promise. You go and have some fun."

She threw her arms around my neck. Then she walked out the door with Sally and Joe. Victoria looked at Max and Denny. "Could you please leave us alone?" They nodded and headed to different parts of the house. "No, I mean, could you please leave?"

Max stood there looking at me, and I nodded. Whatever she had to say was not going to be good. I stayed on my knees as everyone left. She turned and went into the kitchen. I heard her banging cabinets and pots around. I got up and made my way in there. Sitting at the breakfast bar, I watched as she made something to eat.

"Jo told me you were a good guy. I am not inclined to believe her."

"Victoria," I whispered.

"No, don't even. You know who he is. You know because you work for him. You are part of this mess. You are an arms dealer. Did you have anything to do with the explosives in my arm? Is that how Max knew they were in there?"

"When Jo said she didn't want to go back to England, something didn't feel right. So, I asked Max to clean house. When he found the canisters in Jo's room, it scared the shit out of me. I had a gut feeling that something wasn't right, but I had no idea that he did that to you. But, to be honest, I don't believe it was him, Victoria."

She put her hand up to stop me from talking. "You knew all along why I was working for your brother?"

"I knew someone was hired, but I had no idea it was you."

"But, when we met, you knew who I was?"

"No, the puzzle didn't complete itself until you left. By then, I was so in love with you, I would have done anything to stop it all. But I can't, Victoria. I can't."

She laughed. "Oh, I know you can't. Little knows who you are?"

"I would imagine he does, but he hasn't let on that he does."

"So, this is how you knew McDonald? This is why Marciano used your club?"

"Yes." I swallowed hard. I couldn't lose her. I wouldn't. I stood up.

"No!" she yelled. "No, don't touch me. Nowhere does this make anything we did acceptable. You knew about your brother? You knew he killed Johnathan? You knew he killed your wife? How is it possible that you can stand there and think any of this is acceptable? I spent my life detesting men like you, killing men like you, trying to save this fucking planet from assholes like you. When, Paul, is it acceptable to put a gun in the hands of a child? For profit, no less."

"Victoria, I told you I lost my mind when Sylvia was killed. I wanted revenge."

She burst out laughing. "So, instead, you go to work for the very man who had her murdered."

"I didn't know it was him," I shouted.

"But you knew in England, and then you just walked the fuck away and lied to me. You fucking lied to me."

I shook my head. "No, I didn't lie to you. Not once. I just haven't told you everything about me. So much has happened, when was there time?"

She laughed again. "There was plenty of time to fuck me, though, right? But no time to tell me the truth?"

"I didn't lie to you. Not once."

"An omission of truth is a lie. I have been nothing but honest with you. I trusted you, and you sit at the right hand of the very man who single-handedly ended my twin brother, my only friend, the only man who I could completely trust."

"Victoria, I love you," I whispered.

"No!" she shouted, shoving past me. "No! You don't have the right to say that to me."

She walked toward the deck, so I followed her. "Where are you going?"

"As far away from you as I can," she shouted.

I grabbed her by the arm. I knew she was going to hit me, but I didn't care. I deserved every bit of what she gave me. She spun around, and I grabbed her arm, wrapping mine around her. "I fucking love you," I whispered on her lips. "You own me."

"I don't fucking..." was all she got out before I kissed her.

She kissed me back for about ten seconds, and then I felt her knee slam into my groin. The pain was so intense, I nearly threw up. When I let her go, she punched me in the face, shoving me to the deck. "Don't fucking touch me!"

As she stormed off the deck, I couldn't see straight. I couldn't breathe. Who knew getting kneed in the fucking balls when you had an erection hurt worse than if you didn't?

Al chuckled as he helped me up. "She is one pissed off woman. You should have told her," he said, helping me into a chair. "I'll get you some ice for that."

I sat there watching her walk toward the beach. Denny tried to stop her, and she laid him out on the lawn. She kept walking right into the water then swam out. Al came back with two bags of ice, one for my balls and one for my eye. Sitting down, he chuckled.

"Not funny. Deserved, but not funny. Fuck," I said as I put the ice on my cock.

We sat there not saying a word. I couldn't take my eyes off her. She must have felt so betrayed, knowing what she now knew and me not telling her. I closed my eyes and put my head back, struggling with my emotions. "Keep an eye on her please." I got up and went to the bedroom. I crawled into bed with my ice and didn't even try to stop it when tears came.

I never imagined I would find her, the woman to open my heart again. I didn't want to lose her, but I thought I might have already. Jo told her I was a good man, so maybe she would know that in her heart. I loved her beyond any feeling or emotion I could explain. After lying there for a while, I felt her. Opening my eyes, I saw her standing in the doorway looking at me. She was so angry and so hurt.

She walked into the bathroom, and a few minutes later, I heard the shower turn on. I got up and made my way in there. She stood with her hands against the wall. I watched as she pulled one down to cover her mouth. Then I heard her muffled scream. My clothes were off my body in record speed, and I was wrapping my arms around her.

"I'm so sorry I didn't tell you. Victoria, I am so in love with you. Please, know that. Please, beautiful."

I'd never begged for anything in my life. I'd never wanted anything more than I wanted this woman. She laid her head back on my chest. "I can't do this," she sobbed out. I felt her pull away. I didn't want to let her go, but I had to. She walked out of the shower, leaving me standing there feeling completely empty.

Turning off the water, I got out and wrapped a towel around me. I went into the closet to grab some clothes. She was sitting on the bench with her knees pulled up to her chest. I got down on my knees in front of her, but I didn't touch her. "I don't know what to say, except that I'm right here, beautiful. I'm not going anywhere. I love you."

Her eyes were so cold, so unfeeling. She shook her head. "You lied to me. It's the worst betrayal," she whispered.

"I know. I just couldn't figure out a way to tell you. I knew you would eventually find out, but I couldn't tell you. I didn't know how. I promise you, Victoria, I didn't know how." I was sincere.

She just sat there looking at me, her eyes filled with tears. Slowly, they fell from her eyes onto her perfect cheeks. I wanted to hold her in my arms and help her through this, but she needed to come to me. She needed to know within herself that she could trust me. I didn't move, didn't look away. If I could say everything I wanted and needed to say with my eyes, she would see it, feel it. She had to.

Her eyes softened, and she nodded a small nod. My hands grabbed her, pulling into my arms. "God, Victoria, I love you. You have to know that."

She started sobbing. "I do. I do know it. I'm so sorry, Paul, so sorry for hurting you like that."

I shook my head. "I deserved that and more. It's my own fault for not telling you." I thought I would die when her arms wrapped around me. "I love you," I whispered as I kissed her head. "In such a short time, you've become everything to me. I just want us to be happy, to live the life we both have been robbed of."

"Me too," she whispered against my neck, kissing me lightly.

"Oh, God, beautiful," I moaned as she drew the skin on my neck into her mouth.

As she released it, she whispered, "Paul, I need to not feel this. I need you so much. Make me forget."

I pulled her head back and kissed her. I loved the way she tasted. I loved everything about her. I pushed up on my knees, and she wrapped her legs around me. I stood up, carrying her to our bed, and it was our bed. It would always be ours. Climbing on, I gently laid her down. Pulling back, I undid her towel. Her hands moved to mine, and she pulled it away, trailing her fingers along my cock. "I'm so sorry I hurt you."

I shook my head, kissing her. I couldn't stop myself; she was heaven on earth. We had no worries in this room, in this bed. Slowly and gently, my mouth gladly covered every inch of her beautiful body. I just couldn't get enough of her scent, her taste, her essence. Her quiet mews and the way her body reacted to my touch was such a turn-on. Once upon a time, I loved and needed to hear a woman scream, but now, knowing her, it was so much more just to feel the truth her body told under my touch.

Victoria

Laying in his arms was the most alive I had ever felt. The way he made me feel was like nothing I had ever known. Well, considering he was only the second man I'd ever been with, that's not saying much. I knew I hurt him that afternoon. I looked at his sleeping face, watching his eye turn purple. I felt bad, really, but not that bad. He failed to tell me who he really was.

Still, I couldn't believe he knew. We could never tell anyone. I wanted a life with him, with Joanna. I couldn't sleep, so I managed to get out of bed without disturbing him. I knew he was worried, scared to death about everything. I was, too, but not as much as I believed he was. I just wished there was some way to end this with our lives intact.

I put on some clothes and headed out onto the deck. I checked my phone to make sure Joanna was doing good. She hadn't texted me or called. I was still nervous about letting her go, but I trusted Al. Not sure about Joe, but Al, I believe, had a good soul.

Mr. Little hadn't come by today, so that had me a bit on edge. Al came walking up from the boathouse. "Everything all right?" he asked gently.

"It's getting there. This is all so fucked up. How is everything coming along with our disappearance from this life?"

"My guy is working on it. At some point, we are going to need some pictures for passports, driver's licenses, things like that."

I nodded. "I have a red wig I can wear. I just want to be me again. Let my hair grow back. Too many people have seen me like this." I reached up and flicked my short hair. "Listen, I think getting lost in America is the way we want to go. Someplace with a lake, a beach, a cottage, nothing big. Two, maybe three bedrooms, and someplace where we have all the seasons. Maybe a bit of land."

He nodded. "I think we can do that for you. Well, it's getting late, so I'm going to get some sleep. Little will be back tomorrow, so be ready."

I laughed. "That man has something up his sleeve."

"Yes, he does, but from what I've seen, you can handle him."

Smiling, I said, "Oh, you know it. I just don't want to have to kill him. I don't think that would go over well."

Al burst out laughing. "No, it wouldn't, but believe it or not, we have a plan in place just in case that happens." He smiled and walked off the deck. I sat there watching him go.

Kathy was right. I was never going to be safe. I needed to trust Paul, but I wasn't so sure I could. My phone vibrated on the table. I picked it up, swiping it on, finding a text message from an unknown number. Opening it up, I read it.

Art

My heart started racing. I looked at the time. Ten thirty. I got up and headed to the boat house. "Al, can I talk to you?" I walked outside and headed toward the driveway. "I need you to take me someplace, right now."

We walked to the car, and he started driving. "Where we going?"

"Same place as this afternoon."

He looked at me. "Victoria, do you know what you are doing?"

"Yes and no. I'm going to need your gun."

"I'm going with you."

"You can't. I need to do this alone."

"I can't let you do that."

"Well, you are going to have to know that I can take care of myself. Joanna is safe, and so is Paul. If anything happens to me, that is all I care about right now."

We pulled up in front of the Art Institute, and my phone vibrated. I swiped it open.

Back door

"Can you go around to the back?"

As I got out of the car, he handed me his gun. "You have ten minutes, then I'm calling for back up and coming in after you."

I giggled. "I could be dead in ten minutes. I don't believe I am going to be, but please don't put yourself in harm's way. If this is what I think it is, I shouldn't be longer than ten minutes. Just, please, stay here. I would like to know that I didn't take one of your mother's sons with me. If I don't come back, please tell Paul I love him and remind him that he promised me."

"You'll be back, because if you're not, everyone in that building will be dead before the sun comes up."

"Thank you, for everything, Al." I got out of the car and headed through the gates. When I made it to the back door, I reached for the handle, expecting it to be locked, but it wasn't.

When I walked in, I heard his voice. "Hello, Victoria. Thank you for coming." I just stood there. I knew there were guns pointed at me. I also knew that whoever pulled the trigger would be dead seconds after. "I think it's time we had a talk."

"I have three questions I want answered. Did you have Johnathan and Paul's wife killed? Were you responsible for the death of my baby? Did you have those chemical weapons put in my arm?"

"No, to all three of them."

"Then I have nothing to discuss with you. The more knowledge I have, or that people think I have, makes the target on my back bigger. I want a life with the man I love and with Joanna."

"That's why I'm here."

"Don't expect me to believe one word that comes out of your mouth. You are here to see if what you believe is true. I am walking away. I want nothing to do with you. Just let me go, and you can continue to live the life you have made for yourself. I just don't care anymore. He loves me. I choose him. I choose Joanna. It's done. Karma is a bitch, and it will find you, but it won't be me on the other end."

I turned around. As I put my hand on the knob, I heard him say, "I love you."

Shaking my head, I had to fight back the tears. I just opened the door and walked out. Al was still sitting in the car, and he didn't look so well. I opened the door and got in. "It's done. Take me home." I didn't look back. I didn't care. I handed Al his gun, and he took me back to the lake house.

When I walked in the door, Paul came flying out of the kitchen. "Where the hell have you been?" When I picked up my head, his whole body changed. He grabbed me, wrapping me in his arms. Al nodded and headed back to the boat house.

I wanted to be held by him, but not at that moment. I pushed on his chest. "I can't." He let me go, and I walked out the door headed to the beach. I just needed to be alone. I needed… hell, I don't know what I needed, but I didn't need him to hold me. Sitting down, I pushed my feet into the sand.

My heart still slamming in my chest, I didn't want to believe it. I couldn't. *How did I not know?* I hated when things worked out unexpectedly. I never made the connection, but then, how would anyone make that connection? It was never a thought that entered my mind.

I needed to let Kathy go. I couldn't be responsible for what happened to her. She betrayed me, just like Steven did. What would happen to her would happen. I'd give her the option to go where she wanted. I just didn't care anymore. The tears just fell from my eyes. It was over. I couldn't look back. I couldn't let this get in the way of the rest of my life. I didn't trust him, wasn't sure I believed him either. *How is any of this possible?* I felt my stomach turn over. I rolled onto my knees as my stomach turned and the contents rose up fast. Again and again, I heaved, until there was nothing. But my stomach didn't stop. It hurt, I hurt, my heart hurt. I didn't plan on the scream coming, but it came from deep inside of me. I didn't try to cover it up like I'd done for the past three years. I just let it go, again and again. I knew there were ten men standing looking at me. Slowly, I felt them walking away. When the sobs came, I felt his arms lift me off the sand.

"I got you, beautiful," he whispered. "I got you."

He carried me to the house where he crawled into bed with me, holding me, wrapping me in his cocoon. I cried myself to sleep in his arms, his hold never failing me. When I woke, he was right there, kissing my forehead. "I got you, beautiful," he whispered.

I unwrapped myself from him and went to use the bathroom. When I walked out, he was sitting on the end of the bed. I walked up to him, wrapping my arms around his head and pulling him to my stomach. He held me tightly, then I walked out of the bedroom, put my shoes, walked out the front door, and took off running. I don't know how far or how long I ran, but when I stopped, I only stopped because my legs wouldn't move anymore. I laid in the grass and cried some more. I think I might have had some kind of nervous breakdown. I couldn't find control. I couldn't get control.

I heard a car stop along the road. I didn't bother to open my eyes. I felt arms pick me up and hold me. I knew who it was. "I'm so sorry," he said.

Shaking my head, I cried, "I hate you so much. You have taken everything that I love from me. There is nothing you can do or say that will fix this between us. Please, just let me go. Let me be happy."

"I promise you, your life is yours. I will protect you to my dying day."

"You know you can't protect me. If you could, none of this would have happened."

"Victoria, you will have your life. Please, go home and have your life. I promise, I will never look for you again. You won't have to look over your shoulder ever again. Go be happy. He loves you like you deserve. Raise Joanna, be happy."

He hugged me tightly, whispering, "Goodbye, Victoria," as he kissed me on the forehead. He sat me down on the grass, and then he was gone. I didn't open my eyes until I knew the car was gone. I couldn't look at him. I couldn't look in his eyes and believe his lies. I knew, one day, I was going to end his life. He knew it, too.

Getting up, I took off running again. I ended up miles from the lake house. I found a gas station and asked if I could use their phone to make a call.

"Hello?" Paul sounded panicked.

"I need you," was all I said.

"Where are you beautiful?"

"I don't know." I looked at the guy at the counter, handing him the phone. He told Paul where I was. Hanging up, I thanked him and walked out the door to sit on the curb.

So much had happened, so much that I really didn't know what to do with it all. I think I just needed to take this opportunity to have a life with Paul and Joanna. I knew it would always be in question, and I knew that he couldn't make a promise like that. There was a price on my head. I will never be the one that got away. Eventually, it would come; my only hope was that Joanna survived.

A car pulled up. I heard the door open, but I couldn't pick my head up. I didn't have it in me to fight anymore. I was done. He picked me up. "God, beautiful, how did you get here? Come on, I got you." He sat me in the car. After closing the door, he got in the other side and pulled me into his arms.

"We have to go now. It's time to go. We need to get Joanna and go."

"Let's go home," he whispered.

"No!" I yelled. "We need to go now. Not later, not tomorrow, now. We need to get Joanna and go now." I picked my head up and looked at Al. "Now."

He nodded. "I know where."

Paul pulled me to him. I could feel his heart slamming in his chest. "What happened?" he whispered into my neck.

I shook my head. "I need to get Joanna. We need to leave now." I pulled back, turning to Al. "Park a few blocks away. How many men belong to you?"

"Three, one in the house, one on the front porch, one on the back."

"I need a knife," I said softly.

"Victoria, what is going on?"

"I need to get her out of there. We are not safe."

Al handed me a knife. "You have one, as well?" I asked.

He nodded. I looked at Paul. "Do you have your phone?" He nodded. "When Al texts you, come to the house." Al proceeded to tell him where the house was. He pulled up one block over, and I kissed Paul. "We'll be back," I whispered. "I love you."

Before he could say anything or stop me, I was out the door with Al behind me. I followed him through the neighborhood. Unfortunately, I was right in assuming the house was being watched. He knew these men would lose their lives. Six in all, positioned in different places. We moved with stealth, backtracking, zig-zagging across the streets. None of them knew what was happening. When we finished, we moved to the house from the back. Al found the seventh guy in the backyard. I found the eighth in the bushes just around the front of the house. His guys were oblivious to what was happening. Glad I wasn't one of them.

We moved into the house, not making a sound. To my surprise,

Joanna was sleeping in a room alone. I went in and picked her up while Al stayed just outside the door. We didn't bother calling Paul. We moved out the back door. The man posted there pulled his gun on Al before I ever made it out the door.

"I can't let you do that," he said.

Al was fast as he swung his hand across the guy's throat. He grabbed my arm, and we were moving through the yard. He went over the fence first. I handed him Joanna. She was awake but didn't say a word or move. She let us hand her back and forth. Al found yet another guy parked on the street as we came out of the yard. Jo and I waited by the side of the house while he took care of it. He managed to grab a walkie talkie out of the guy's car.

As we moved through the neighborhood back to Paul, we listened for any signs that there was any left. No chatter. As we approached the car, Al grabbed my hand and pulled me behind some bushes. There was someone in the car with Paul. I handed Joanna to Al.

Shaking her head, she whispered, "No, Momma, don't go. Stay with me." Reaching for me, I took her back into my arms and we knelt to wait.

Al pulled his phone out and sent a text. We waited for a few minutes then he touched my shoulder and tilted his head for us to move. I followed him through yard after yard, him going over the fences first, me handing him Jo and then following him. Block after block, we moved. Finally, we came to a car. He opened the back door, and I got in with Jo. Al got in next to me.

We drove for hours, but I had no clue where we were going. This was the time that trust needed to be given. I didn't know these two men, but I needed to trust them. I needed to protect Jo, and if that meant running from Paul, then that's what I needed to do. I was confused about what he was doing in that car, though I was pretty sure I know who it was. *But why? Why would this happen?*

We pulled up to a house that was a little bit more than moderate in size. Al helped me out, and we went in. He led me to a bedroom where I put Jo down, then he handed me a monitor and we made our way back downstairs. Joe was standing at an island in the kitchen.

He handed me an envelope. Opening it, I found our new identities. My heart broke. Paul wasn't involved in this.

"You are safe here. I have a client who lives on this lake. He bought this house, and I've put a million dollars in a bank account for you under this name. You and Jo can live your lives out here. No one will ever find you."

"Why would a complete stranger do that?" I asked, looking at my new name.

"His wife was in hiding for years, trying to stay alive. She had a madman trying to find her and kill her. I went to him and explained a bit of your story to him. You are now invisible, untraceable. No one is going to find you, Victoria. No one."

I felt the tears. "What about Paul?" I whispered.

"I don't know yet. There are things about him that don't add up. I was hired to make sure you and Joanna were safe. He may have hired me, but my brother is the reason I did this," Joe said.

I looked at Al. "Why?"

"Our only sister was murdered by her husband. He was an abuser. We didn't know because she was too afraid, too proud to tell us. You are too proud to ask for our help," Al said.

Joe smiled. "We have this thing for strong women who are too damn proud to ask for help. Trust, Victoria, we all need someone to trust. We don't always get it right, but we all need to do it. You can trust us. If and when Paul clears, we will bring him to you. But, please remember, he is not to be trusted right now."

"The car I took has listening devices in it. If he lies to us, he won't ever find you. That little girl up there is what's important. She can grow up here. You'll be safe," Al said softly.

"Thank you. I'm really tired. Are you going to stay until morning?"

He shook his head. "No, we will stay for a while, but we will be gone before morning. Here are your keys to this house. There is a car in the garage. It's all in your new name. Your bank information, the deed to the house, everything you need to start over is right in that envelope. The fridge is stocked as well as the pantry. Everything is done. Have a good life." He slid a phone across the counter to me. "My number and Al's number are in there. Don't hesitate if you need us. Enjoy your freedom. You deserve it. Now, go to bed."

I walked around the counter and hugged him. "Thank you."

He smiled, passing me off to Al. "Above and beyond," I whispered.

"Hopefully, I won't ever see you again. But know that I am always here if you need me."

I wiped the tears from my face and walked out of the room. Climbing into bed with Jo, I crashed.

CHAPTER SIXTEEN

PAUL

It killed me to let her go, but I had to trust that Al would keep her safe. A few minutes after they left, the car door opened.

"Don't," he said.

As I sat there looking at him, everything made sense. He was here to see her. "What do you want? You told me I was out."

"You did the right thing by hiring Blackshaw. They can get her out, keep her safe. She is gone now. You won't ever find her."

I reached for the door handle. "I fucking love her."

His hand wrapped around my wrist. "You will get her killed. She is all I have left in this world, and I can't let that happen. I set this up so they would get her out. You will never know how deep this goes. I tried to get you out, and I thought I did, but fucking Little has you by the balls. Let Joe Blackshaw help you. If he can't erase this, I'm afraid you will never see her again."

"How can you do this? Doesn't her happiness mean anything to you?"

He chuckled. "Paul, I am doing this so she can be happy. Her life means more to me than her happiness with you. She will end you herself if she believes Joanna is in danger. Let her go for now. Let them save her. Let this ride itself out."

"How can you sit here, knowing you are ripping her heart out by taking her away?"

"That's just it. I'm not taking her anywhere. I have no idea where she is going. I don't want to know. Your guy, Denny, is on my payroll. Victoria figured it out. She is smart, Paul, and she would have, if she hasn't already, figured out you. It wasn't supposed to be like this. You weren't supposed to fall in love with her."

"I didn't know who she was. You failed to tell me. I didn't know until it was too late. I'm done with this life. She and Joanna are all I want."

"I wanted my son not to die, but he did. I wanted not to be dragged into this fucking life, but I made a mistake, like you, and I had no choice. I'm giving you a choice now. Being who I am, I am giving you a choice."

"I choose her. I choose them. I want what was taken from me five years ago. I want my fucking happiness with her. Do what you have to do."

"Don't resort to your old life. This could take time, lots of time. Just know that Blackshaw has her secure."

"How do you know that?"

"Because I know Blackshaw. He is straight and hardcore. That man would end your life if he thought you were going to hurt her. Their only sister was murdered by her husband. Their sole focus is to protect women and children."

"So, he is on your payroll?"

He laughed. "I wish he could be bought. Those boys have skills, and his men aren't easily swayed. Do what you need to do to end this. I will do what I need to do. Blackshaw will let you know when there is no footprint of you left. Victoria's is already gone. She is a ghost and will remain one for the rest of her life. It's the only thing I have left to give her."

"Does she know you are here?"

"Yes, I've spoken to her. She knows."

I put my head down. There was nothing I could do. "Get out," I said to him. "Just get the fuck out."

He nodded and opened the door. When he shut it, the tears just came. I don't know how long I sat there, but when I finished, I started the car and went back to the lake house. When I made it to the bedroom, I don't know why I thought she'd be there, but she wasn't. I didn't even bother getting undressed. I just fell on the bed and went to sleep.

Victoria

I woke to feel a tiny hand on my face. Opening my eyes, I was greeted with a beautiful smile. "Momma, why did we leave Paul?"

I pulled her into my arms. "He has some things to do still. But this is our new house. How about we make some panny cakes and explore? Maybe go shopping and get some new clothes?"

"Then is Paul coming?"

"I don't know, baby. I don't know if he is ever coming, but it's okay. We're safe here. And guess what? There is a beach in our backyard."

Her eyes lit up. We spent our day exploring the house. There were four bedrooms and a fancy basement. We discovered there were clothes in the closets and toys for Joanna. Joe was right; everything we needed was here. We wandered into the yard, and there were more toys out there. We walked to the beach and sat in the sand. We took a nap on the big couch in the living room watching a movie.

Me, well, I was always scanning the horizon. Having lived my life always wondering what was next, it was a bit difficult to relax. In the past three years, the only place that relaxed me was in his arms. There, I felt safe, complete, and loved.

Days passed. Soon weeks had taken us by storm. We laughed, we played, and we lived. After three months, I found myself not looking to the horizon. I actually believed that we were going to be okay. Joanna didn't ask about Paul after that first day.

Summer was coming to an end, and it was time for her to start school. They had a pre-kinder class, so I took our new paperwork and enrolled her. She would go three days a week from eight in the morning until noon. I was nervous letting her go, but her eyes were big and she was so excited.

On the first day, I walked out of the school with tears in my eyes. I couldn't leave her, so I sat in the car and waited for the day to be over. This went on for the first two weeks. Eventually, I drove away, but not without a heavy heart. This, too, became our routine, our life. I had never had this before. But I soon relaxed enough to enjoy the excitement in her eyes, the energy she had when she would run out of school with her newest art project. Our fridge at home had become her art gallery.

It took me two months before I could sleep away from her, but Joe and Al were right. He was right. My life was my own. I had to believe that no one was coming for us.

I had met my neighbors, Jake and Jenna Aberdeen, the man who did this for me. They had a lovely set of twins and were the kindest of people. Our life had become exactly that, our life.

Paul

It was maddening not being with them, waiting for trouble to disappear. I missed her so much. Al had let me know they were good, finally relaxed. Joanna had started pre-kinder and was as happy as could be.

Me, well, my life was shit. Marciano was still on the big list, but Little stopped asking me where Victoria was. Now, it was him threatening me, trying to force me to tell him what I knew. I think this was a test of sorts, to see if I was worthy of Victoria, to see if I could keep her safe.

It was coming up on Thanksgiving when Little decided he was done with me and this was a lost cause. I had been away from Victoria and Joanna for nearly six months. My heart ached for them. I was hoping that Christmas wouldn't go by without us being together. I'd managed to move the majority of my money to an off-shore account, under a name that Joe gave me. My first name was still Paul, and he assured me that Victoria and Joanna had kept theirs. I wondered if they had the same last name as my new identity. I wanted to ask Joe but thought better of it. I hadn't said her name or made reference to her since she left.

We had one conversation where I think Al wanted to kill me when I told him it was Marciano in the car with me. But, other than that, nothing. I just got little bits of information from Joe. I couldn't fill a piece of paper with the info he had given me, but that was all right. As long as they were safe and alive, I would bide my time. One day, I would be with them. We would be a family. Reaching in my pocket, my fingers touched the ring I bought for her. I knew she would be my wife one day.

CHAPTER SEVENTEEN

VICTORIA

Joanna was so excited about her Christmas concert. We had to go buy her a beautiful new dress, of course, and she looked adorable in it. They had two weeks off of school for the holiday, and we were looking forward to playing in the snow. We had already built a small snowman in the yard, with a carrot nose and all. She named him Jupiter, after the planet she was fascinated with that week. She knew them all.

I woke up when she came in my room. "Momma, we have to get up. Today is the day for my school concert."

Looking at the clock, I smiled. "Joanna, it's six in the morning. School doesn't start for two more hours." I reached for her, pulling her in bed with me.

"But, Momma, today is a special day."

"Oh, it is, is it?"

She nodded her head. "It is."

I laughed and cuddled with her until the alarm went off. "Come on then, let's get some breakfast and then get you dressed."

She ran into the living room and turned to the tree. "Momma, are you sure Santa is going to find us?"

"Well, you sent him a letter, so I think he will."

It felt good to know that these were the things she was worried about. Simple, childish things, not who was going to kill us. We had become very comfortable with our life.

We had breakfast and then got dressed, and I dropped her off at school. As I was turning to walk away, she said. "Don't forget, Momma, the concert is after school."

"I won't forget." I hugged her. It made me wonder why she would say that. I never forgot anything. I watched her hang up her jacket and walk into her classroom then made my way out to the car, not paying attention. When I stepped off the curb, I looked up and nearly had a heart attack.

I was frozen. I couldn't move. My eyes searched the background then landed on him.

"Hi, beautiful," he said softly.

"How did you find us?" I didn't mean to sound so threatening, but Al had promised.

He looked past me. Slowly, I turned around, and Al was walking up. I shook my head. I couldn't do this, not here. Not in front of her school. "No," I said. Moving to the driver side of the car, I got in and locked the door. My hands were shaking as I pushed the fob in and started it. I drove away. I couldn't breathe. I made it home and into the garage, shutting the door. I knew we would never be safe. I'd let my guard down, and now, we'd have to leave again.

I was so distraught; I didn't notice the garage door open. It wasn't until my door opened and he pulled me into his arms. "I got you, beautiful."

It felt so good to feel his arms around me. It felt like I belonged in them. But I knew that wasn't possible. "Why? Why would you do this to me? Why would you put us in danger again?"

"Victoria, there is no more danger. I'm free of this. It's over for us. No one is looking for us. I did everything Joe and Al wanted me to do. I am here, forever, if you want me. Do you still want a life with me?" He sounded so sad.

I pushed on his chest and scrambled away from him. I don't know how I managed to get to my feet. "You fucking son of a bitch.

Why?" I screamed. "Why would you do this to me? Get out. Get the fuck out."

"Victoria," Al said, and I snapped my head toward him. "Remember when I told you the car was wired?" I nodded. "He didn't lie. He told us everything."

I looked back at Paul, who had tears in his eyes. "They know?"

He shook his head. "No, I didn't tell them that. I only told them what was said. I would never do that. I want this. I want this life. I made a promise to you, and I intend to keep it. I love you."

"No!" I shouted. "No! Get out. Our life is good and happy and peaceful. No!" I couldn't control the shaking; my whole body was traumatized. *What the hell is wrong with me?* I took a few deep breaths. I looked at Al. "Why? Why would you lie to me? Why?" I shook my head. "I need to go. I need to get Joanna." I moved toward the car.

"No!" Paul shouted. I stopped. "Victoria, it's over. No one is coming for us. It's done. Do you really think they would bring me here if it wasn't? I did everything they wanted, everything everyone wanted. I am done, free, just like you, just like Joanna. We can have our life now." His voice got really soft. "Do you still want a life with me?"

My heart froze. For so many nights, I had missed him. I'd craved his touch. I wanted nothing more than to be with him, to love him, to have him love me. I looked at Al and then Joe.

Al nodded. "It's the truth. It's over," he said softly.

I looked at Paul. "No more running?" He shook his head. "No more fighting?" He shook his head. "Our lives are our lives?" He nodded.

"I love you, beautiful. Let me come home. I miss you so much. I miss Joanna."

"Joanna." I looked at my phone. "I have to go. It's her Christmas Concert." I moved toward the car. Paul just stood there. "Get in if you're coming. I promised her I wouldn't miss it." He smiled and got in.

I couldn't talk. I didn't want to talk. When we got out of the car at the school, he touched my hand, wanting to hold it, but I pulled away. I wasn't ready to let him in yet. I needed more answers, but I needed to be with Jo more. I found some seats a few rows from the stage. Pulling out my phone, I got comfortable. I could feel Paul looking at me.

"What?" I asked him softly.

Leaning in, he whispered, "Your hair is longer."

I shook my head. "Just because you are here means nothing. There is much to be said."

"Yes, there is, and I don't care if I have to sleep on the couch. I'm not going anywhere."

I smiled, looking at him. "Don't be ridiculous. We have a spare room."

He laughed. "Good to know."

Just then, the teacher walked out on stage. "Good afternoon, everyone. Today, as you all know, is the last day of school for the Christmas break. We would like to present to you our 3-K Christmas program." Joanna's class walked out on stage, and everyone clapped. I got my phone ready to video record it. When Joanna walked up to the front of the stage, her teacher smiled at her, handing her the microphone. She started talking, reciting *T'was the Night Before Christmas*, just like we'd been practicing for weeks. Tears flowed from my eyes. God, she was so beautiful, so smart.

When she finished, the place erupted in applause. Paul was whistling, and I was yelling. She just stood there with a huge smile on her face. When everyone calmed down, she looked right at Paul and said in the microphone, "I want to tell my daddy welcome home. Welcome home, Daddy." My heart stopped in my chest.

He got up and walked to the stage, my phone still recording. She walked to edge of the stage and wrapped her arms around his neck. He hugged her while the audience cheered.

"Thank you, beautiful," he whispered in her neck.

He let her go, and she ran back to her spot, and the concert began. Paul didn't say anything when he sat back down. In fact, he didn't say anything while we waited for Jo to gather her things. Her face lit up when she came out of school to see us waiting for her. She ran right into Paul's arms. "I knew you would come home," she said. "Momma, I told you today was a special day. I have a daddy now."

I fought the tears. "Yes, you do. Come on, it's cold. Let's get home."

I happened to glace at Paul, who wiped his tears away before Joanna could see them. He put her in her car seat, and we went home. Paul and I didn't talk; all conversation was between him and Joanna. She told him about everything we'd done since we left him. She made sure she let him know that she wrote Santa a letter and that he would find her.

Once in the house, I took her upstairs to change and to snuggle in for a nap. When I came back downstairs, Paul was sitting at the counter with a cup of coffee.

"Victoria," he began, standing.

I put my hand up. "Why were you in the car with him?"

"He was there to talk to me."

"Obviously."

"He told me that he set the whole thing up to get you and Joanna out. That I needed to stay behind so my footprint in all of this could be erased like yours. He was the one who made this all possible for you."

"Are you telling me Joe and Al are on his payroll?" I was getting pissed.

"No, he said he wished they could be bought. But Denny was."

"I know, the gun he gave me had blanks in it."

He cursed under his breath. "He told me that if Joe couldn't erase me, I would never see you two again. It was all he had left to give you. Victoria, I stayed away. I have been nothing these past months. I love you." I watched him stand and move toward me.

Shaking my head, I moved away. "No, I can't do this again. We've just gotten used to being here without you. I can't do this."

His voice got very soft. "Victoria, I love you." He dropped to his knee. "Will you marry me?"

He had a ring in his hand. "What?" I gasped.

"The minute I touched you, you changed me. I want a life with you. I want to love you and Jo for the rest of my days. Please, will you marry me?"

I didn't know what to do, what to say. I just stood there. I shook my head. "Too much water under the bridge, Paul. I can't risk her. What I want, what I feel doesn't matter. Only she matters. She is all I have left in this world."

He stood, moving rather quickly, and pulled me into his arms. "No, Victoria, you have me. You will always have me. Both of you will always have me." It felt so good to be in his arms, to feel the warmth of him. God, he smelled so good. "Don't you understand what I feel for you? I haven't been able to function. I haven't slept properly in months. I wake up and you aren't there. My closet is just a closet now. I'm here, beautiful, and we are safe. We can have our life now, the life we both wanted, full of love and happiness." My arms moved on their own to wrap around him. "Oh, God, beautiful. I love you so much."

"Can we do this? Can we really have this?"

"Yes, baby, we can. Marry me and let's be happy."

I nodded my head against his chest. Pulling back, he picked up my left hand, slipping a ring on my finger. "I love you," he whispered in my mouth as he kissed me.

I knew Al wouldn't have brought him here if he was still connected to all of our old mess. I had to believe he was a good man. Joanna knew he was coming. She'd called him Daddy. *Can this be my life? Can we be happy? Are we really safe?*

When his lips touched mine, as always, my mind went blank and there was nothing in it but him and me. There was nothing but the feeling of him. "I love you," I moaned in his mouth.

He pulled back, putting his forehead on mine. "I have missed you. Missed this. God, Victoria, I've never known love like this. Both of you fill me with such joy."

I smiled. "Is this real? Are we really going to have this life?"

"Yes, beautiful. Yes, we are. Al and Joe made sure we have the same name; we are legally married. Well, the paperwork says we are. I want to get married now, just the three of us here today. We can marry each other. When I make love to you, I want to make love to my wife."

I giggled. "They were sure I would say yes?"

"I think they know that what we feel is rare and real. Victoria, I have never wanted, needed, or desired anything in my life until I met you and Joanna. To me, nothing else matters. Please, believe me."

Putting my forehead on his, my fingers touching his face, I told him, "I believe you."

Slowly, we lowered to the floor, his mouth covering mine as he laid me back. We laid on the floor in the kitchen kissing and holding one another. Just like that first night, he didn't touch me other than holding my leg in his hand and just kissing me. We shared deep lingering looks. I think he was making sure I was with him. He erased every bit of doubt. He was the only one who could kiss me like that. For what seemed like hours, we made love with our mouths.

Pulling back, I put my hands on his face. "I need you to tell me some things," I whispered.

He smiled. "Whatever you need to know."

"I want to know about your life in the world of sex."

I giggled when I saw his reaction. "Victoria, it's not something I'm comfortable telling you. It was what it was, nothing more. There was no emotion, nothing."

"It's something to me. I've been with two men my whole life. I want to know."

He sat up, pulling me with him. "Victoria, what is this about?"

I felt myself blush. "It's nothing," I said, dismissing it. I went to stand up, feeling a bit of a fool.

"Hey," he grabbed my arm, "talk to me. Tell me what's going on in your head."

I pulled my arm away and stood up, going to the fridge to look for something to make for dinner. "It's nothing, really," I said softly as I pulled some chicken out, setting it on the counter.

When I turned around, he was standing behind me. "You need to be able to talk to me. We are in this together now. I'm not going anywhere. Why is it important to you?"

"I... I..." I just couldn't bring myself to say it.

He smiled. "When Sylvia was killed, and I figured out that it was intentional, I kind of lost my mind. I wandered into the club because I wanted to feel something. I was so angry, and I wanted, no needed, to control something. Everything was so out of control. I met a woman there named Charlotte. She introduced me to the whole bondage lifestyle. I can't tell you how empowering it was to have that kind of control over something, someone." He took a deep breath. "I hadn't had sex for a long time, and five minutes after I fucked her, I was done. I was embarrassed actually." He chuckled. "She laughed at me. She egged me on to hurt her. The more I slapped her ass, the harder I got. The more I inflicted the pain, the longer I stayed hard. Eventually, I could withstand holding off my orgasm for a good hour. It was like tantric sex. I figured out that if I brought myself to the edge, time and time again, when I finally let myself go, it was beyond belief. I learned to control myself, basically by controlling the person I was with."

"So, you enjoy being a dominant?" I whispered.

His hand came up and wrapped around my neck. "I enjoyed feeling in control. I lived for it until I met you. Until you showed me that the only way to feel is to let go of the control. So, I suppose, for me, the control was about not feeling anything for anyone but me. It was all about me. I didn't give a shit about anyone but me. One thing led to another, and I bought the club. I lived in that club. I fucked at least four times a day, sometimes more. It was, to me, a competition with myself; each time I wanted to last longer than the time before. When I met you, when we shook hands, I wanted to control you. I wanted to tie you up and spank your ass until it was bright red, and I so wanted to fuck you hard." I swallowed hard. "But you changed me, because deep down inside, I knew I would never be able to hurt you, and I knew that I didn't want to. Victoria," his voice was softer and gentler, "I wanted to make love to you. I needed to make love to you. Even when I fucked you the day you left, I didn't fuck you. It was love. It was love, beautiful. When you left, it was a wake-up call for me. I knew I would never be with another woman. Making love to you is all I want to do."

"What if I want you to fuck me hard?" I closed my eyes, unable to believe I was asking such a question.

His lips gently brushed across mine. "I'm not sure I can do that."

"Why?" I whispered. *God, I can't believe I asking him this. What the hell is wrong with me?*

"Aww, beautiful, I love you. You aren't some whore who chose that for her life or was forced into that life. You are to be my wife. I could never do that to you, treat you so disrespectfully."

"Can you live like that? Without that control? Without that dominance?"

"Baby, I have been living without it all for a long time now. I don't desire to go backwards in this life. We are moving forward, and forward for me is loving my wife, making love to my wife, watching and feeling as my wife makes love to me."

My hands moved up his arms to his neck, pulling him down to meet my mouth. I pressed on his shoulders, and he picked me up, sitting me on the counter. We stayed like this kissing and touching until a little voice interrupted us.

"Momma," Jo said.

Smiling, I turned my head as Paul lifted her into my arms. "Yes, beautiful, did you have a nice rest?"

She nodded, turning in my arms to look at Paul. "Are you staying here with us now?"

He looked at me. "Yes, beautiful, I am."

"Will you be my daddy then?" she asked a bit softer.

His eyes moved to her, his hand coming up to run his knuckles along her cheek. "I will be whatever you need me to be. If being your daddy is what you want, then I'm your guy."

She turned her head, looking at me. "Momma, I want Paul as my daddy."

I smiled. "Well, that's a good thing then." I giggled when she crinkled her little face up. "Paul wants to marry us today. Would that be all right?"

She nodded. "I have a momma and a daddy. Santa did get my letter."

Paul hugged us both. "He will get every letter you write."

Paul

I stood by the Christmas tree waiting for Victoria and Joanna to walk down the stairs. We were going to have a private ceremony, bonding ourselves together as a family. Legally, on paper, we were already married, but we wanted to have a ceremony for us.

Joanna came down the stairs first in a beautiful dress, her smile brighter than anytime I'd ever seen it. She came running up to me when she hit the floor. I scooped her up in my arms, and she wrapped her arms around my neck. When I looked up, Victoria came walking down the stairs in a simple white dress that hugged every delicious curve she had.

"My God, you look stunning," I whispered. I bent and put Joanna down as Victoria walked up. I wasn't sure what I should do, so I took her hands in mine. "I don't know where to begin."

"Then let me start," she whispered. "I never knew what it meant to love someone until I met you. Every day that we were apart was the worst day. I never knew that I could love someone the way I love you. I can't thank you enough for loving me, for loving us, for being so gentle with us, and for fighting for us. I will love you through good times, through bad times, and for the rest of my life. Today, I take you as my husband, to live this life we both want so much. I love you."

Joanna spoke next. "Paul," I knelt down in front of her, her tiny hand coming to rest on my face, "You love my momma?"

I nodded. "Yes, baby, I do, and I love you, too."

She smiled. "Will you be my daddy forever?"

"I will, baby. I most certainly will."

She nodded, so I kissed her on the cheek and stood. "Victoria, I floated through this life for years before that day in John's office. It was that day that I knew God had smiled on me. I knew the minute I turned around and looked into these blue eyes of yours that I was given a second chance at life, at love. I promise to never falter in my love for you. I promise to never let you down and to take care of you, always. Today, I take you as my wife, to live this life both of us want so much. I love you." My hands shaking, I reached up and kissed her.

Then I got down on my knees and took Jo's hands in mine. "Today, I promise to be your daddy and everything else you need me to be, your friend, your protector, your everything. I bought this for you." I reached into my pocket and pulled out the box, opening it up.

She looked inside. "Look, Momma, it's three rings."

"Yes, there's one for you, one for Momma, and one for me. It means we are a family now and for always. Can I put it on your neck?" She nodded. I fumbled with it. I couldn't believe how nervous I was.

Joanna put her hand on mine. "It's all right, Daddy."

I chuckled as the chain came free. I slipped the necklace holding her ring on her neck. "There you go, it's official now. I'm your daddy."

She smiled the sweetest smile. "I always knew you would be."

I laughed and hugged her. Picking her up, I stood and wrapped my arm around Victoria who had tears streaming down her cheeks. "My life is complete now," I whispered to them both, and we put our rings on one another's fingers.

We had a wonderful afternoon and dinner. I read Joanna a bedtime story, and when she fell asleep, I tucked her in, grabbing the monitor off the dresser. I went to find my new wife, who was cleaning up the dinner dishes when I walked into the kitchen.

"Would you like a glass of wine or something?" I asked.

Smiling, she said, "No, Paul, I don't want a drink."

"Do you want to watch a movie?" I smiled at her, bending to kiss her neck.

"No, no movie," she whispered.

"What do you want to do, Victoria?"

"I want to make love to my husband," she said breathlessly as she turned to face me. "Take me to bed, Paul. I need you."

I carried her to our room, gently kicking the door closed. Slowly, our mouths locked in a lover's kiss. God, I'd missed her. I'd missed this. Moving to the bed, I set her down. She pulled my sweater up over my head, then my t-shirt. Her hands slowly touching me, she paused for a minute to roll my nipples between her fingers. My cock wanted nothing but a release, and I nearly did as her fingertips brushed my head as she undid my jeans.

Unable to stand it anymore, my hands moved slowly, pulling her shirt off her. Fuck if she wasn't pure heaven to me. Looking at her, I hadn't realized I was crying until she reached up and touched my face. "You are so beautiful," I whispered. I had to kiss her; I needed to kiss her. As my mouth covered hers, I was lost in her taste, in her touch. I'd never felt a kiss like the kisses we shared. This woman in my arms was heaven on earth. Her skin was like silk, and I couldn't wait to taste every part of her. God, how I'd missed this with her. Lifting her up, I crawled onto our bed, moving to the center, gently laying her down.

I couldn't stop kissing her, our mouths moving in a gentle tantric state. The emotions that were imbedded in my soul where she was concerned were strong and deep. I was complete. Sliding my hand down her side, not touching her glorious breasts, to her hip, then to her thigh, I gently slid it up my leg to my hip as I pushed mine between hers. She was so tiny yet so strong. My hand nearly fit around her thigh.

I nearly lost my resolve when her hands slowly moved down my back and then around to free me from my jeans. "Ahhh," I moaned in her mouth as she wrapped her fingers around me. If she moved her hand, I was going to lose it.

"Let it go, baby. I got you," she whispered as she slowly and gently pumped me.

I could feel my hips move with her hand, her hip bone pressing into the space between my cock and my hip, applying pressure that I wasn't aware was a pleasure spot. I couldn't stop myself as my orgasm ripped through me, literally taking my breath away. I felt her back arch into mine as her own ripped through her. I couldn't stop pulsing. My God, my eyes rolled in my head. I collapsed half on her, kissing her.

Victoria

To feel him release in my hand was beautiful. I was in love with this man. No amount of time would ever change that. Every night, I would lay in this bed and think of this, think of the times we were together. The way his hands felt as he touched me, so gently, so lovingly. The way he smelled, the feel of his lips on mine, on my body.

His body started to relax, his kisses becoming less intense. Picking his head up to look into my eyes, he told me in his beautiful baritone voice, "I love you."

Releasing my leg, slowing moving his hand up my body to my back, he undid my bra, taking his time removing it. His eyes never looked away from mine as he gently cupped my breast, pinching my nipple. His eyes closed as he rolled it between his fingertips.

"A feeling I've missed," he whispered to me.

This man, this incredible man gave up everything for me, for us. I watched as his head moved toward my body. I felt like my skin was energized by his touch. When his tongue flicked out and swiped across my nipple, I could do nothing but close my eyes and feel him, let him love me like only he could.

As he drew it into his mouth, I lost it, my back arching into his chest. He pushed his thigh, his incredible sculpted thigh into my core, and it was over for me. I felt my body shake. He didn't break his movements; he never did, remaining so focused on me, on his worship of me. Never would I have this with another.

Moving down my body, he released my jeans, pulling them off but leaving my panties on. When I looked at him, he smiled. "Fucking beautiful," he whispered as he gently rolled me over. For so long, he devoured me. Ripping my panties from my body, he took his time on my ass, rolling me over and taking from me all that I could give him. Again and again, he took me. When he had had his fill, with my leg in the crook of his arm, he moved up my body.

Feeling him slowly push his incredible cock deep inside of me set me on a frenzy of orgasmic intensity that blew my mind.

Paul

Slowly, my mind became nothing but the incredible woman in my arms. She was a gift from God himself, put here just for me. What I felt as I moved inside her body was beyond my comprehension. Her back arched as her body pressed into mine. Her soft mews, barely audible, drove me to be everything she needed, wanted, and desired.

The feel of her body as she came undone was nothing I'd ever known. When I grew harder, her hands moved to my face, her own body tensing as my body prepared to release. We were that in tune with each other, so finely tuned that no words, no sounds were needed for us to know just how the other felt. Just as my body released, she pulled herself up to seal her lips against mine. I moved my arm around to hold her, to feel her shudder as she released with me.

I rolled over, pulling her on top of me still buried inside of her. Wrapping my arms around her, the tears slipped from my eyes. She was mine. For the rest of my life, she was mine and I was hers. We were one together, and all was right in our world. Our hearts beat as one. Complete.

More Books by Cin Medley

Justice
Within The Ashes
Broken
One Hundred Acres
Is this Life
Six Months
Winter Harbor
Lyssa's Journey
Secrets
Lines Crossed
Everything She Thought